HEARTS IN HARMONY

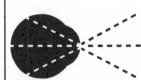

AN AMISH JOURNEY NOVEL

Hearts in Harmony

Beth Wiseman

THORNDIKE PRESS
A part of Gale, a Cengage Company

Fountaindale Public Library
Bolingbrook, IL
(630) 759-2102

GALE
A Cengage Company

Farmington Hills, Mich • San Francisco • New York • Waterville, Maine
Meriden, Conn • Mason, Ohio • Chicago

GALE
A Cengage Company

LIBRARY OF CONGRESS CIP DATA ON FILE.
CATALOGUING IN PUBLICATION FOR THIS BOOK
IS AVAILABLE FROM THE LIBRARY OF CONGRESS

ISBN-13: 978-1-4328-6242-8 (hardcover alk. paper)

Published in 2019 by arrangement with The Zondervan Corporation
LLC, a subsidiary of HarperCollins Christian Publishing, Inc.

Printed in Mexico
1 2 3 4 5 6 7 23 22 21 20 19

To Karen Desroches, for being my friend when I needed one and for gifting me with Renee, the best BFF a girl could ever have. RIP, sweet Karen.

GLOSSARY

ach: oh
Ausbund, the: songbook
boppli: baby
bruder: brother
daadi: grandfather
daadi haus: grandparents' house
daed: dad
danki: thank you
Englisch: those who are not Amish; the English language
fraa: wife
Gott: God
gut: good
haus: house
kapp: prayer covering worn by Amish women
kinner: children
Liedersammlung, the: songbook
maedel: girl
mamm: mom
mammi: grandmother

mei: my

mudder: mother

nee: no

Ordnung, the: the written and unwritten rules of the Amish; the understood behavior by which the Amish are expected to live, passed down from generation to generation. Most Amish know the rules by heart.

rumschpringe: "running around"; the period of time when Amish youth experience life in the Englisch world before making the decision to be baptized and commit to Amish life

schweschder: sister

sohn: son

Wie bischt?: Hello; how are you?

ya: yes

Prologue

Dear Diary,

I had never been to an *Englisch* funeral before today. I've only been to one funeral, when Uncle John died last year. But I'm only ten so maybe that's why.

This funeral was different from Uncle John's. There were a lot of flowers inside the church and people singing. I liked the singing even though I'm not supposed to. We don't sing the way the *Englisch* do. And nobody plays instruments, but a lady at the church played a big one with tall pipes. It looked a little like a piano, but *Mamm* said it was an organ.

The man's family left his coffin half open. I'm not sure why. When an Amish person dies, you can see the whole body. The man was old, but they tried to make him look young, and it didn't look right. His *fraa* cried a lot. Everyone followed in cars and buggies to the cemetery. There were almost as many buggies as cars. *Daed* said it's because the dead man was kind to our people and a man of the Lord. *Daed* had done work with him, I think. *Mamm* mostly says we are unequally yoked with the *Englisch.* That means we shouldn't be around them too much. But sometimes it's okay.

When we got to the *Englisch* cemetery, I saw big fancy headstones and even more flowers. A man like our bishop said prayers at the cemetery. He was the same man who talked at the church.

Then everyone went to the dead man's *haus* to eat. It looked like a farmhouse on the outside, but not on the inside. *Mamm* said it was old and had been restored, but I don't know much about *Englisch* houses. It was fancy inside with pretty furniture and pictures on the wall. People still cried, but not as much. Except for the dead man's *fraa.* She cried a lot. She's old too.

After everyone ate, the girls and ladies helped the old woman clean things up, then people started to leave. We were one of the last buggies still left there because not as many of the *Englisch* people stayed to help clean up. It was mostly our people from Montgomery, and there were some Amish families from a place I've never heard of. Orleans. *Mamm* said it is a small town forty miles away from Montgomery. I guess maybe that's why we've never been there. Even a strong horse can only pull a buggy twenty miles before it needs a good long rest.

Finally, it was time to go home, and I was glad. I prayed for the sad *fraa* and that her husband was in heaven. But I felt like my heart hurt through it all. I don't like to be sad, and I felt sad for everyone. Especially the dead man's wife. Her name was Adeline. I like that name.

Mei mamm, daed, and Lydia were in the buggy when I remembered how far it was home. *Daed* doesn't like to stop during trips, so I had to run back inside to go to the bathroom. I didn't want to see the sad lady — Adeline — so when I saw her on the porch talking to people, I hurried past her.

When I got in the *haus,* it was quiet, and I didn't see anyone. I walked down a hallway, and that's when I heard music. I could only hear it a little. I still hadn't found the bathroom, but maybe whoever

11

was making the music could help me find it. I slowed down when I could tell the music was coming from behind a closed door. I pressed my ear against the door to hear better. I liked the sound of it and wanted to listen longer. But I needed to find the bathroom so I opened the door. This room was even more fancy than the rest of the *haus,* and it had a pretty red couch and matching chair and shiny tables.

I think I might have made a noise like a gasp because the boy stopped playing the piano right away and stood up. He was taller than me, but I think he was my age. There are four boys my age at our school. He looked the same size.

I'd never seen one of our people play an instrument, and the boy had played the piano like he had been doing it his whole life. Maybe music is allowed where he's from. I knew he wasn't from Montgomery.

But when the boy asked if I was going to tell on him, then I knew music must not be allowed where he lived either. I told him I wouldn't tell. And I won't. He's the cutest boy I've ever seen. He has blond hair and pretty eyes.

He told me his name is Levi and that

he lived in Orleans. I told him my name is Mary and that I lived in Montgomery, and I asked if he wanted to be friends. He shrugged and said we lived too far away from each other. I asked if he wanted to write me a letter. My cheeks felt hot when I asked him that. He shrugged again, then said *ya.* I found a piece of paper on a table by the piano, and then I found a pen. I wrote down my address. It was the first time I'd given a boy my address.

He asked me again if I was going to tell on him. I shook my head. My stomach felt funny, all swirly. Then he waved and left. He was gone before I even asked him where the bathroom was. But I knew I would check my mailbox every day.

CHAPTER 1

Eight Years Later

"Is Adeline dying?" Mary Hershberger recalled her trip to the *Englisch* funeral when she was ten. She'd been to plenty of funerals since then — Amish and *Englisch* — but she dreaded every single one she attended. The *Englisch* focused more on the life the person led while on earth. Mary's people praised *Gott*'s goodness more than they reflected on the person who had passed. Both ceremonies always left her with a deep sense of sadness that she would hold on to for weeks. She'd been taught to accept all things as *Gott*'s will, even death, but she struggled with that part of her faith.

"I don't know." *Daed* flicked the reins a couple times, picking up speed in the buggy. "The fellow at the hardware store told me Adeline is having an estate sale. From the conversation, I sensed maybe she is in a bad way financially. So, I will try to find things we can use." He shrugged. "But I will buy things whether or not we need them. We can give to those less fortunate if need be."

Mary hadn't heard her father speak of Adeline or her deceased husband — Percy — in years. But Percy must have been a very *gut* man if her father was willing to go twenty miles to purchase things they might not even need just to help Adeline. Thankfully it was May, and the heat of the summer wasn't upon them yet. During the middle of the summer, they had to stop at least twice for such a long trip. Mary couldn't recall a trip to Shoals since Percy Collins's funeral eight years ago.

"Remember to call the woman Ms. Collins. The *Englisch* find it improper to call an adult by their first name, especially an elderly person."

Mary fought the urge to roll her eyes, a gesture that would surely irritate her father. "I know, *Daed.*"

His eyes wrinkled in the corners as he grinned. "Just a reminder."

Mary smiled. She was eighteen, old enough to get married, but her father still saw her as a little girl.

They passed a sign that said *Welcome to Shoals.* Not much looked familiar as they drove down Main Street, then wound through a neighborhood, before turning down a dirt lane. Rows of freshly tilled crops lined both sides of the road, corn seedlings sprouting from the dark soil. In the distance, Mary saw Adeline's house. *Ms. Collins,* she reminded herself. As they neared the white farmhouse, memories filled the forefront of Mary's mind. She recalled the brightness of the house, the pristine yard filled with flowers, and an old blue car in the driveway.

She glanced at her father's expression, the lines deepening on his forehead as he frowned. From the sight of things now, Adeline must have fallen upon hard times like her father mentioned. The formerly white house was grayer now, badly in need of fresh paint. The green grass needed mowing, and there wasn't a car in the driveway. Mary wondered if the inside of the house was the same.

"I should have checked on Adeline over the years." Her father winced as they neared the house.

Mary remembered the fancy furniture inside, and she wondered if Adeline would be selling all of her things or maybe just some furnishings. What Mary most remembered about that trip was the boy playing the piano. The cute Amish boy who never wrote to her like he said he would. But they were just children. She couldn't even remember his name, which seemed odd since she could recall so many other details from that day, along with the sadness that lingered in her heart for weeks after the funeral. She hadn't even known Percy Collins.

Levi Shetler had six brothers and three sisters, but he was always the one nominated to take his mother on errands. Today he was carting her twenty miles to an estate sale. They'd spent most of the journey from Orleans to Shoals in silence, his mother occasionally commenting about the weather and what a lovely day it was. Levi had nodded and continued on the trek, but he regretted that he'd had to change his plans for today. "Why are we going all this way to an estate sale?"

"Because Adeline is a fine woman. Until about a year ago I would see her at the Rural King in Bedford every week. She liked the store because of its hodgepodge of farm supplies, tools, clothes, and housewares. But mostly she liked the free popcorn." His mother chuckled. "She enjoyed eating it while she looked around."

His mother turned to him and sighed. "I

can tell you aren't happy about taking me to this estate sale, but that woman never left the store without buying something from me. And on really cold days when I was set up in the parking lot, she'd bring me a thermos of coffee, and I'd sit in her car to warm up for a while. I always enjoyed our chats."

Levi kept the horse's pace slow and steady to limit the bounce in the buggy. His mother had arthritis that gave her fits, and he knew this was a hard trip for her to make, even as a passenger. He drew in a long breath and reminded himself to be respectful, despite his disappointment.

"I just had other plans for today." Levi swallowed hard. His plans had included a trip to the river for some alone time, a hard thing to get with a family of twelve.

His mother cut her eyes his direction. "You never tell anyone what these *plans* are. Is it a girl?"

I wish. Levi barely had time to keep up with his chores. "*Nee,* it's not a girl." He cleared his throat, hoping to change the subject back to today's trip. "I remember that house was real fancy. Everything looked expensive." What he remembered most was the piano, the way the keys felt beneath his fingers, the music. The forbidden music. He shrugged. "Can we even afford to buy anything?"

His mother raised her chin, and Levi wished he hadn't mentioned money, or the lack thereof. The Shetler family was one of the few left in Orleans who relied mostly on income from the farm. His father had forbidden Levi and his siblings to work outside of their small community. If Levi was honest with himself, he knew why his mother chose him to make this trip with her. Out of all his brothers and sisters, Levi contributed the least at home, even if it was unintentional. Each of his siblings excelled at something, but Levi didn't have any special skills and often found himself with extra time on his hands.

Three of his brothers were craftsmen and made furniture, which was only for sale to the local Amish families. The oldest boys — Lloyd and Ben — shoed horses when time permitted, and Eli could do just about anything and helped out where needed. But the same rules applied: keep it local among their people. If ever a family practiced what they preached about being unequally yoked, it was Levi's. Left up to their father, none of them would spend any time at all around the *Englisch.* As it was, Levi rarely saw anyone outside of their small community.

He could still remember *Mamm* begging *Daed* to let her and the girls set up outside the Rural King one or two times a week to sell produce, jams, jellies, and cookbooks. *Daed* finally gave in after months of *Mamm*'s persistence. If the weather was nice, sometimes they'd add a third day of selling, but things at the house started falling apart if all the girls were gone too long, especially when it came to meals. *Daed* had balked about today's trip to Shoals, but *Mamm* pushed the issue and said the Lord would want her to help Adeline in some small way.

"I brought a lot of produce and handmade items for Adeline." She paused, glancing at Levi. "She is a kind soul. I am blessed to have found out about this sale, but I worry if maybe she is struggling financially."

Like us. Levi squinted against the sun's glare at the home up ahead. "*Ya,* it looks like maybe she is."

His mother shook her head. "*Ach,* look at the state of things." She turned to Levi. "I've never been able to return Adeline's kindnesses over the years. Not only did she buy from me every week, but she drove me to many doctor appointments. I want you to pretty up her *haus* and yard, Levi. It could be done over a few weeks, if you come once a week. That's all we could spare you.

It will be okay with your *daed* once I remind him about all Adeline did for me over the years."

Levi opened his mouth to argue, but then thought about the twenty-mile trek to Shoals and back. Alone. Quiet time all to himself. And hard work had never bothered him. It was the perfect time of year for painting and working outdoors. "*Ya*, okay," he said.

Mamm patted his knee. "That's my *gut* boy."

Levi smiled as he wondered if the piano was still there. Would he be able to play it during his breaks? Or would Adeline sell it along with her other fancy things?

He turned into the driveway and parked next to a buggy from Montgomery. He remembered coming here when he was younger, and he'd noticed then that buggies in Montgomery were a little different from theirs in Orleans. They were still black, but the wheels were a little smaller. It wasn't something the *Englisch* would notice, but since everything in a community was uniform, it was easy to spot someone from another district.

There were only five or six buggies besides theirs. Mostly it was cars parked in the driveway and on the grass. Levi doubted he would get a chance to play the piano. Too many people today. He'd gotten lucky the last time he was here. Even one song would fill his soul in a way he knew was sinful, but the instrument had called to him since the first time he saw a piano when he was six.

During a rare trip to an *Englisch* home with his mother, he'd seen the family's piano. He'd never seen such an instrument, but he instinctively sat on the bench when his mother and the *Englisch* lady went into the kitchen. He placed his fingers on the keys and made beautiful music. He didn't know how he was able to play, but he just could. Levi could still recall his mother's red face and the way she'd pinched her lips together as she yanked him off the bench and away from the piano. He also remembered how cold it was when she sent him to pick a switch when they got home, then whipped him behind the woodshed until his behind almost bled.

Levi hadn't touched a piano again until the funeral here when he was ten. He had found himself alone in the house after going to the bathroom, and on the way down the hall, he saw the huge black piano and felt it calling to him. He'd slipped into the room and gotten away with playing it for a few moments without getting caught. Except by some girl who walked in, but she promised not to tell on him. Just the thought of playing the instrument again sent his heart racing.

Adeline watched as strangers picked over the pieces of her life: furniture, jewelry, paintings. The antiques were selling quickly. She reminded herself they were just things, material possessions she no longer needed, and the money would help sustain her for a while.

Percy had provided a nice nest egg for them both, but her husband of fifty-two years couldn't have predicted the changes in the economy. Or that Adeline would outlive him by eight years, especially considering she was five years older than her husband. At twenty-three, she'd practically snatched his eighteen-year-old self from the crib. At least that's what her sister told her back then. The memory still brought forth a quiet giggle, which felt good in light of her current situation.

But with no family left alive and no children of her own, Adeline was going to run out of money if she didn't let go of some things. Medicare had recently stopped covering two of her medications, pills that now cost her almost $400 each month. She

24

was in the appeals process, but she had no idea if she would win. A large chunk of her savings had gone toward replacing her roof last year after a large branch fell on the house and caused several leaks. Adeline still thought that fellow overcharged her.

She no longer needed her pretty furniture and fancy trinkets, yet she cringed when a young woman ran her hand across the hutch by the front door, a gift from Percy when they'd first married. Part of her wanted to scream, to throw everyone out, and reclaim her property. She bit her bottom lip to keep from doing so. Maybe she was more attached to her belongings than she'd thought. Was this really a solution? Had she thought this through?

Her spirits brightened when she saw Helen Shetler come into the living room with a handsome young man by her side. The Plain folks weren't fond of public affection, but Adeline couldn't help but wrap her arms around the woman's neck. Adeline suspected Helen's family couldn't afford anything she had for sale, but she would find something to give them. Then she saw the bags Helen and the boy were toting, and Adeline wanted to cry. She couldn't remember the last time she had freshly grown produce, and she hoped tomatoes would be in the offering.

"Who is this strapping young lad?" Adeline eased out of the hug. Helen looked ten years older than the last time Adeline had seen her, even though it had only been a year. The lines feathering from her friend's eyes had deepened, along with those running across her forehead. Her skin was weathered from all the outdoor work the Amish were known for. Helen probably thought Adeline looked older than eighty-three, her own face a roadmap of lines, not to mention all the weight she'd lost.

"This is my *sohn,* Levi." Helen glowed as she said the boy's name. The Amish steered away from being prideful, but this was a cute kid any mother would be proud of. "And these are for you." Her friend held up the three bags, then nodded to three more her son was carrying.

Adeline winked. "I wonder if there is a tomato in there."

"*Ya,* lots. Levi can put all of this in the kitchen if you'll point him in the right direction."

Adeline did just that, and after he was gone, Helen touched her arm. "*Mei* friend, are you well?"

It was a question Adeline had expected. She'd aged a lot since she'd seen most of

26

these people. It was only normal for folks to think she was sick as well as broke.

"Yes, dear. I'm okay. It's just time to downsize." *Although selling almost everything is a bit more than downsizing.* "And I want you to choose something for yourself, a gift from me."

Helen brought a hand to her chest. "*Nee,* I couldn't possibly."

"Of course you can." Adeline winked at her, then waved her hand around the room. "I know you don't like fancy things, but I bet there is something here you can find useful. Maybe even a kitchen gadget." She pointed toward the kitchen again. "I've laid out some things on the counters that I no longer have use for."

Helen glanced around, then turned back to Adeline, chewing on her bottom lip.

"Honey, you don't have to take a thing if you don't want to. But if there is something you would like to have, you take it." She shrugged. "Maybe even just something to remember me by someday."

"You said you aren't sick." Helen pressed her lips together, frowning.

Adeline chuckled. "I'm not. But I'm eighty-three."

Helen nodded. "*Danki,* Adeline. I mean thank you. And there is something I would

27

like to give you as well."

Adeline lifted an eyebrow she'd carefully sculpted with a pencil for the occasion. Most days she didn't tend to her appearance much, but this might be the last time some of these folks saw her. It seemed fitting to look her best, even though her best wasn't all that good anymore. "You did give me something. Bags of goodies. I'll be happy for days, maybe weeks."

Helen shook her head. "*Nee*, something else. I would like for you to let Levi come here every Saturday to paint your house and tend to your yard. You have shown me many kindnesses over the years, and Levi would enjoy the work."

Adeline hung her head as an unwelcome blush crept into her cheeks. "Everything really does look a mess, doesn't it?" She lifted her eyes to Helen's. "I just haven't —"

"We all need a little help from time to time, so please accept our offer."

Adeline thought about how nice it would be to have company every Saturday. Her house was miles from anyone, and while well-intentioned friends stopped by occasionally, her life had become a lonely existence. Loneliness would kill a person quick as anything. Maybe she and Levi would have lunch together.

"I am going to accept the offer, but only if you let me pay the boy." Then she remembered that her house and yard were in this state because she had no money, but she wasn't sure how to take back the offer.

Helen shook her head. "*Nee,* you will not pay him, *mei* friend."

Adeline remembered to breathe. "You are good people."

Her friend smiled. "Now, I am going to go look around for a small something."

"Wonderful."

Adeline stood there for a while, watching. Her bottom lip trembled as two men carried her armoire from one of the spare bedrooms out the door. Also leaving today was a chunk of Adeline's heart, but she forced a smile.

The woman running the show — a young gal named Dixie — gave Adeline a thumbs-up. The more they sold, the more commission Dixie would go home with.

Amid the hustle of furniture being removed, and Dixie punching on her little calculator, Adeline thought she heard something. She closed her eyes for a moment, and sure enough, it was piano music. Sometimes she heard it in her sleep, as if Percy was in the next room playing for her. But today, someone would be playing the instrument so they could decide if they wanted to buy it.

Adeline didn't think she'd be able to watch a crew carry out Percy's precious piano. He had worked so hard to save money for it. She swallowed back the knot in her throat and decided to walk around what was left of her belongings. Estate sales usually happened after a person died. Adeline could see why. She felt like a ghost in her own home.

Mary stayed by her father's side as they walked from room to room in Adeline's house. She knew he was more interested in the tools and farm equipment outside, but he told her to pick out a few things she and her sister might like, along with something for her mother. Mary hadn't found anything yet, but her heart was so heavy, she hadn't looked very hard.

"This is so sad, *Daed.*" She nodded to Adeline. "She looks like she's about to cry." Mary ran a finger across the kitchen counter and pulled back a layer of dust, then she nodded at a roach making its way across the floor. "I was only ten the last time we were here, but I don't remember the house being like this."

"It wasn't." Her father cringed as he shook his head. "I suspect Adeline doesn't have the energy she used to."

"Or maybe she's just lonely and doesn't care."

Her father frowned, then stroked his long dark beard. "Why do you say that?"

"The *Englisch* families we know have lots of pictures framed and displayed all over their houses. The only pictures I've seen here are photos of Adeline with her husband. Doesn't she have family or *kinner*? Or friends?"

Her father pushed back the rim of his straw hat and scratched his forehead. "Her car isn't in the driveway. I wonder if she sold it, or maybe she is unable to drive. Being cooped up in this *haus* all the time would be hard."

"Especially because it's so dirty," Mary said in a whisper.

"Let's go see what we can find out." Her father motioned for Mary to follow him to where Adeline was standing.

"I imagine it's hard watching your possessions being sold," *Daed* said when they stopped in front of Adeline.

The older woman waved a dismissive hand. "Oh, they're just things, you know." But her eyes defied her words as tears pooled in the corners.

"I didn't see a car out front." *Daed* ran a hand through his beard again.

Adeline scrunched up her nose, then huffed a little. "The state took away my driver's license when I could no longer pass the eye test." She folded her hands in front of her and stood taller. "Although I think I drive just fine. The car is in the garage. I know you're not interested, but it's on the list of things to be sold. A bit of a clunker, but it's priced cheap."

She was a tiny lady. But Mary was tall for a woman, so she tended to think everyone was small. Mary had been reintroduced to Adeline by her father when they first arrived, but she didn't know the woman at all. She wanted to help in some way, but maybe she could do more than just find items to buy.

"Ms. Collins, isn't it hard for you to stay in the *haus* all the time? How do you get groceries?" Mary tipped her head to one side and waited.

Adeline's cheeks dimpled. "Honey, don't you worry about me. I have enough in my freezer to last for a year." Her smile faded. "But I do miss trips to the market, long drives in the country, and being somewhere farther away than my front yard."

"I love long rides in the country." Mary wondered if her father would approve of what she was about to say. "Maybe I could come for a visit Saturday. We could go for a drive or maybe even to the market." She glanced at her father who gave a nod of approval.

"Mary appreciates any excuse to go out for a long drive, and you could enjoy some fresh air."

Adeline brought her hands to her chest and smiled. "Now, aren't you the sweetest thing. But a beautiful girl like you doesn't need to be spending a Saturday carting an old woman around. It would be like *Driving Miss Daisy,* but in a buggy and not a car." She chuckled a little.

"Driving Miss who?" Mary had never heard that phrase.

"Never mind, dear. Don't worry about me."

Mary almost gave up, but there was the hint of a twinkle in Adeline's eyes when Mary first mentioned the visit. If a ride in the country went well, maybe Adeline would let Mary clean her house. Mary had always felt a fondness for older people. Her grandparents had all passed, but she used to love listening to them tell stories.

"If it's all right with you, Ms. Collins, I'd

really like to come for a visit next Saturday."

Mary saw the gleam in her eyes again.

"I'd like that very much, but I feel I would be putting you out."

"*Nee,* not at all." She smiled up at her father. "Like *Daed* said, it's an excuse for me to take a long drive, and the weather has been so nice." She pressed her palms together and waited as Ms. Collins tapped a finger to her chin.

"Hmm . . . you are making it hard for me to say no. It would give me something to look forward to."

"Then it's a date." Mary would look forward to Saturday too. "And we have lots of fresh produce from our garden that I can bring you."

"I appreciate that, dear girl, but another friend brought me several bags of produce today that will last a couple weeks." She glanced around the room. "I don't know if you know Helen. She's from Orleans."

Mary had heard of Orleans, but she'd never been there. Adeline's house was right in the middle of Orleans and Montgomery, where Mary's family lived. "*Nee,* I don't know anyone from Orleans."

"I didn't know if maybe you met Helen and her family at Percy's funeral. They were here, but there was a lot going on that day.

Helen and her son, Levi, are roaming around here somewhere, and they are the ones who brought me the produce."

That's his name! Levi. The boy who played piano. The boy who never wrote to her.

Mary excused herself to go to the bathroom, but instead she went to the room where she thought she remembered the piano was. She pressed her ear against the door but didn't hear anything.

When she pushed the door open, an older version of the piano boy was sitting on the bench, but he wasn't playing. His hands were in his lap. He turned to her, and Mary's eyes widened. Her cute ten-year-old crush had grown into a handsome man.

"It's you," she said as she lifted her chin a little and walked into the room. "The piano player who never wrote."

He stared at her, squinting a little, like maybe he was trying to recognize her. "*Ya,* it's me, I reckon."

"You don't remember me, do you?" She folded her arms across her chest and grinned. It shouldn't matter that a boy didn't write to her back then. Or remember her now. But irritation fell over her anyway.

"*Ya,* I remember you. You promised not to tell anyone I was playing the piano." He pulled his eyes away from her and stared at

35

the keys.

"Are you going to play now?"

"*Nee.* I haven't played since that day." He looked up at her and scowled a little. "It's not allowed."

"I know that. It wasn't allowed eight years ago either." She rolled her eyes a little, a bad habit she was trying to break. "And I know that you live in Orleans, and that Orleans and Montgomery are too far apart for us to be friends." She raised one shoulder and dropped it slowly.

"I guess you're wondering why I didn't write to you?" He stood up and walked toward her. He was taller than her by several inches. "We were ten. Does it really matter?"

Mary grunted a little. It wasn't very ladylike, but she'd never see Levi again. "*Nee,* it doesn't matter."

He walked closer. "Well, I'll tell you anyway why I didn't write."

"I told you. It doesn't matter. We were little."

Grinning, he edged even closer to her, enough so that she stepped back a little. "You wrote your address down for me. But you didn't write down your name."

"I told you my name before I wrote down my address." She gave a taut nod. "Okay, well, now I know." She spun around and headed toward the door that led out of the room.

She had her hand on the knob when Levi called out to her. "Hey, what is your name?"

Smirking, she said, "Does it really matter?"

She closed the door behind her.

CHAPTER 2

Mary was surprised to see a buggy parked outside Adeline's house on Saturday. As she tethered her horse, she noticed movement on the side of the house. After she poured a milk jug filled with water into a bucket for her horse, she made her way around the corner. A man, wearing a straw hat and suspenders, was on a ladder painting.

"Wie bischt?" She slowed a few feet from the ladder. When the man turned around, Mary recognized him right away. *The piano boy.*

"What are you doing here, *Levi?*" She put emphasis on his name as a reminder that he didn't know hers. It wasn't really fair since she'd forgotten his name until she heard someone say it last Saturday. But it was fun to toy with him.

"What does it look like I'm doing?" He grinned, stowed his paintbrush across the top of the paint can, and eased his way down the steps with it. "And why are you here?"

"I've come to take Adeline for a ride in the country since she doesn't drive anymore." She sighed. "And I'm hoping she'll let me do a little cleaning inside. It can't be healthy for her to live in such a mess."

"*Ach,* well, brace yourself. Almost everything is gone. The *Englisch* cleaned out her antiques. It's even more depressing inside than it was last Saturday when people were hauling off most of her things." He took off his hat and ran a hand across his sweaty forehead, then pushed up his cropped blond bangs until they stuck straight out. Levi had nearly perfect features, almost like he could be an *Englisch* movie star, except for one thing. A scar ran the length of one side of his nose. It wasn't unsightly, just noticeable, and it certainly didn't take away from his good looks.

"That's what she wanted, though." Mary raised a hand to her forehead to block the sun.

Levi lifted an eyebrow before he put his hat back on, flattening out his bangs again. "You and I both know it wasn't what she wanted. She looked like she was about to cry the whole time folks were carting away her furniture."

39

Mary pulled her black purse up on her shoulder. "*Ya,* I know. I best go inside to see if she's ready." She started toward the front of the house.

"Hey," he said.

She turned around.

"It's a nice thing you're doing." Levi locked eyes with her. "Taking her on a ride and wanting to clean her *haus.* It's real nice."

Mary looked around before directing her eyes up at the cloudless blue sky. "It's a beautiful day for a ride."

"Are you going to tell me your name now?" Levi looped his thumbs beneath his suspenders.

Mary tilted her head to one side and gave him a pondering look, even though her heart rate was elevated and she seemed to have developed a nervous twitch in one eye. "Does it matter?"

Levi walked toward her. "Are you going to be here every Saturday too?"

She hadn't planned on it until this very moment. "Uh, *ya.* I am."

"Then I guess it matters." His eyes crinkled as he grinned at her. "We can be friends."

She pressed her lips together to keep from smiling. "Maybe so." She pivoted to resume her walk toward the front of the house.

"What's your name?" he said again.

She turned around to face him, but kept walking backward. "It starts with an *M.*"

When she knocked on the door, Adeline answered right away wearing a pair of black slacks, a white blouse, and a black sweater. Her gray hair was up on her head and held in place with a black and white scarf tied underneath her chin.

"You are such a dear to do this." Adeline closed the door behind her.

"I'm happy to, but . . ." She bit her bottom lip for a few seconds. "Can I go to the bathroom before we leave? And afterward maybe we can just sit on the porch and chat for about thirty minutes so my horse can get plenty of water and have a short rest."

Mary's horse was young and strong, but even though she didn't plan to go far with Adeline, the animal needed a break.

Adeline turned around and opened the door, motioning for Mary to go in. "How rude of me. You've traveled so far. I'll wait out here and start enjoying this beautiful day. And we will give your horse as much time as you think he needs."

Mary nodded before she walked through the empty living room. Only a worn brown couch sat in the middle of the room that used to be filled with lovely antiques. Clouds of dust floated on sunbeams shining through dirty windows. Mary's mother would have a heart attack. Friends often told Mary's family that you could eat off the floor in their house. Mary's mother was a stickler for cleanliness, and she'd passed her desire for neatness on to her daughters.

After Mary found the bathroom, she walked back through the house and stepped onto the porch, closing the door behind her. Adeline was sitting on the porch step staring at Levi, who was walking from his buggy with a can of paint. He disappeared around the corner.

"That boy is a hard worker." She turned as Mary sat down beside her. "Can you believe he was here at seven o'clock this morning? He drove here in the dark. I hadn't even finished my coffee yet."

"Why is he the one painting the *haus*?" Mary wondered if he was getting paid.

Adeline beamed, her eyes twinkling. "The Lord has blessed me with two new young friends." She winked at Mary. "And God always has a plan."

Mary forced a smile, wondering if Adeline was trying to play matchmaker, but then reminded herself that coming here was her idea. Besides, Levi wasn't her type. He had blond hair and blue eyes that seemed to look right through her. Mary had always pictured herself with a brown-headed man with dark eyes. It was silly, but that was her vision of her future husband. And her type would be more reserved than Levi seemed to be, more serious, not so playful. Although she'd enjoyed his self-confidence mixed in with the teasing.

She recalled her mother asking her once, "What exactly *is* your type, Mary?" Lots of boys had come calling since Mary turned sixteen two years ago, and plenty of them had dark hair and eyes, but none of them made her heart flutter.

She and Adeline chatted about the weather, which route they'd take on their ride, and how long Adeline would like to be gone. Finally, Mary felt like they'd given her horse a good enough rest for their short trip.

As she walked alongside Adeline to the buggy, Levi rounded the corner. For a man who wasn't her type, he was the first one who caused her heart to flit about in an unfamiliar way.

Levi finished applying the primer, then lowered himself down the ladder, barely landing on his feet after losing his footing on a loose rung. He closed the paint can and rushed across the yard. Adeline said she wanted to be back by lunchtime, a couple of hours from now, so he wanted to make good use of the time he had, assuming the piano hadn't sold.

Relief flooded over him when he opened the door to the fancy room. The piano was still there, and so were the red couch, coffee table, and pictures on the walls. There was a framed photo of Adeline and her husband on a hutch in the corner. It seemed this room had gone untouched.

Levi sat at the piano for a long while and let his fingers rest atop the keys without pressing down on a single one of them. He wondered if he could still play the way he did when he was ten. He'd prayed often, asking God why He tempted him like this when playing an instrument wasn't allowed in his world. The Lord hadn't responded, or if He had, Levi had turned a deaf ear.

Finally, he took a deep breath, closed his eyes, and as his fingers found their way, relief washed over him. *I can still play.* He let the music fill his soul. It was exciting and terrifying, as if he was defying God but pleasing Him at the same time, which wasn't possible. Melodies came into his mind as if traveling down a road that never goes anywhere, but that fills all of space and time in a journey that never ends. He allowed himself thirty minutes, hoping it would be enough to satisfy the temptation that hung over him like a dark cloud.

When he returned to painting, he could hear the music in his head, but instead of calming his soul, the brief time he'd spent playing had only fueled his desire to play more. *Lord, help me shed this sinful longing.*

He tried to focus on something else. The girl. He wished he could remember her name. Adeline would call her by it soon, though, and then he'd know. Whoever she was, she had a snappy wit, in addition to being beautiful. She was tall and thin with deep-brown eyes and dark hair. She had a teasing, mischievous grin, and Levi was looking forward to spending time with her.

Hopefully he'd find out more about her at lunch since Adeline insisted on making a noon meal for him, and presumably her new friend too. He wondered if they would really become friends this time. At age ten the forty-mile distance seemed too great since neither of them were old enough to drive a buggy. But now it was only twenty miles for each of them to meet in the middle at Adeline's.

But even as he tried to keep his thoughts

focused on the girl, he could still hear the piano calling out to him. Why was God punishing him this way?

Adeline was still relishing the buggy ride as she prepared lunch for her young friends. Mary was a delight, and they'd chatted along the way, but they were also quiet part of the time. It hadn't been an awkward silence, just two people taking in the beautiful scenery.

Adeline jerked a hand to her chest, squeezed her eyes closed, and waited for the spasm in her esophagus to pass. Her medications had worked well for years, but it was probably time to visit the doctor and get her dosage increased again. Over the past few months, the painful tightness in her chest came almost daily. Most of the time it didn't last long, but it felt like what Adeline imagined a heart attack might feel like. Although it was over in less than a minute.

Luckily the spasm occurred in the kitchen, away from the young people. It was impossible to mask the pain when it came on, and seeing her grimace in such a way would surely frighten them. She was glad they were in the parlor.

It wasn't really a parlor, but she and Percy

had always called it that. It was more like a room in the middle of the house that they would have used as a nursery if they'd had children. Instead, it housed Percy's piano. It was their favorite room.

She put the chicken salad sandwiches she'd made on a platter, each with a side of potato chips. With trembling hands she picked up the tray as she recalled a time when she could have easily carried three full bowls of soup without spilling a drop. Today she was worried about keeping the sandwiches intact.

"It's nothing fancy," she said as she entered the parlor. "Chicken salad and chips." The Amish were wonderful cooks. Adeline suspected these kids were used to a hot meal at lunchtime.

"It looks very *gut.*" Mary accepted her plate, but waited to give thanks until Levi had his and Adeline sat down with hers. Then they all bowed in silent prayer. Adeline had grown up around the Amish, so she knew a lot about their ways. Today she thanked the Lord for these two kind young people.

"I'm sorry we're eating on our laps." Adeline shook her head. "I used to have some trays. Percy and I ate in this room a lot. These old red couches are out-of-date, but back in the day, we thought we were basking in luxury in this room."

"Did you decide not to sell anything in this room?" Mary took a bite of her sandwich. Levi was already finished with the first half of his in just a couple of bites.

"No, everything in this room was for sale." Adeline supposed everyone else thought her couches were unattractive and outdated.

"Even the piano?" Levi spoke with his mouth full. The boy had worked hard and seemed famished.

Adeline sighed. "Even the piano." She smiled as she picked up a chip. "I must admit that I'm glad I still have this room as it was. I wish I was a better hostess for you both, but a young couple from Mitchell bought my kitchen table and chairs."

"It's fine. I like this room. And this is very *gut* chicken salad." Mary had a sweet disposition about her, and the Plain folks raised their children with an overabundance of good manners. Adeline wondered if she would have done a good job as a parent. But the Lord hadn't seen fit to bless her and Percy with children.

"So, tell me all about yourselves. Levi, I know your mother, of course. And Mary, I know your father. But what about the rest of your families? If I met some or all of them at Percy's funeral, I apologize for not remembering."

Levi smiled. "*Mary,* why don't you go first?"

When Mary smiled back at him and said, "*Ya,* okay, *Levi,*" Adeline wondered if she was on the outside of an inside joke.

"As you both know, we live in Montgomery, and we always have." She glanced back and forth between Adeline and Levi. "I have a sister, Lydia. She recently turned sixteen so she's in the beginning of her *rumschpringe.*" Turning her attention to Adeline, she said, "That's our running-around period when some rules are overlooked prior to baptism."

Adeline nodded even though she was familiar with the word and its meaning. "And I know Henry, your father, has a large furniture company. I went with Percy once to see his warehouse. Very impressive."

Mary's cheeks turned red, and Adeline reminded herself that the Amish didn't want to appear fancy in any way. *Impressive* might not have been the best word.

"Some of *mei bruders* build furniture." Levi had finished everything on his plate. He shrugged. "But they are limited without power tools."

"We have power tools. Lots of them."

49

Mary nibbled on her sandwich, her pinky finger extended. The girl was tall, thin, and graceful, a true beauty. Adeline was surprised when Levi frowned.

"How do you *power* the power tools?" Levi's eyebrows narrowed inward.

"Solar power."

Levi scowled even more. "You mean those flat-looking panels that get energy from the sun?"

Mary chuckled. "*Ya,* those flat-looking panels that get energy from the sun — and batteries."

Levi didn't say anything for a few seconds, scratching his chin before he looked at Mary. "Do they cost a lot of money?"

"I don't think so. Maybe ten or fifteen thousand dollars." Mary set her plate on the coffee table, then leaned down to tie the laces on one of her shoes, so she likely didn't see Levi's bulging eyes.

Adeline considered ten or fifteen thousand dollars quite a lot of money, and apparently Levi did too. She cleared her throat. "Mary, tell us more about your family. Do you or your sister work outside the home?"

Mary nodded as she reached for her plate and placed it back in her lap. "*Ya,* Lydia and I work at a nearby bakery part time. And, of course, *Mamm* stays home and takes care of the household . . . and *Daed."*

Adeline smiled. It wasn't the way everyone thought, but for the Amish the man was the head of the household. "I always loved taking care of Percy."

"You must miss him very much." Mary's expression sobered.

"I do miss him very much, but I will see him again." What she wouldn't do for one more day with him, one more minute, a last goodbye. "Levi, tell us about your family."

Levi leaned back in the red high-back chair where Percy had sat so many nights, reading the newspaper or doing a crossword puzzle, usually after he'd dazzled Adeline with a round of Bach or Brahms on the piano. Closing her eyes, she envisioned her Percy in the chair, but she snapped back to the present when Levi cleared his throat and crossed an ankle over his knee. Adeline wondered if the boy knew the sole of his shoe was worn clear through to his black socks.

"I've got six *bruders* and three *schweschders.* I'm the second youngest of the boys, and all three of the girls are younger than me. We mostly work the farm, but Lloyd and Ben shoe horses sometimes, and *mei* other *bruders* build furniture." He shrugged. "Not much to tell."

Adeline had spent enough time with Levi's mother over the years to know the family didn't have much in the way of material possessions, but Adeline suspected they had an abundance of love that made up for it. Helen's eyes always shone when she spoke about her children, *kinner* as she called them.

"I do remember that you have a large family," Adeline said. "I think that's lovely." She became lost in her thoughts again as she remembered how badly she and Percy wanted a big family.

Mary was still eating long after Levi and Adeline had cleaned their plates. She'd always eaten slow and was always the last one in her family to finish a meal. But just in case Adeline had dessert planned, she rushed to finish her sandwich. She was chewing her last bite when Levi spoke up.

"Will you find a new husband soon?"

Mary stopped chewing and stared at him for a few seconds. Their people tried to remarry quickly after someone died, but it wasn't the *Englisch* way. Surely Levi knew that, and Mary worried he had spoken out of place. But Adeline laughed.

"Goodness, no. I'd never be able to replace my Percy." After giggling some more, she said, "I wouldn't even know how to date. And who'd want to go out with an old woman like me?"

"You're a pretty old woman." Levi's face turned red.

"Yes, dear. I'm certainly a pretty old woman." Adeline chuckled.

"*Nee*, uh . . ." Levi's face turned a darker shade of red. "That's not what I meant. I meant that *ya,* you are old, but you are pretty."

Mary stared at Levi for a few more seconds. She'd mistaken his statement, too, but what a lovely compliment he'd just given Adeline, who was clearly pleased, smiling and waving a dismissive hand at Levi.

"Oh my. You are a charmer. But the thought of a courtship of any kind would terrify me." She stood and collected their plates. "But, having said that, I might consider stepping out with a fellow if he knew how to play the piano. I miss the way Percy's music filled this house." She shook her head as she walked toward the kitchen.

Mary locked eyes with Levi. "Do you still play?" she asked in a whisper.

His expression was unreadable, and it took him a few seconds to answer. "You know it's not allowed."

"That's not what I asked." Mary raised an eyebrow. "I've spent the night with an *Englisch* friend a few times. Her father plays piano, but he doesn't play nearly as good as you did at ten years old. And he's been playing since he was a child."

Adeline returned, and the conversation ended. But Levi had looked at the piano repeatedly throughout lunch. If he could play it at ten, surely he could still play now. But, he was right. Listening to music and playing an instrument was forbidden.

As a preteen and even now, Mary had attended Sunday singings, but the songs were pre-approved by their parents. If Mary's family had any idea that she sang tunes like the *Englisch* when no one was around, they'd overlook it since she was in her *rumschpringe,* but they wouldn't like it.

Her favorites were songs on a Christian radio channel she listened to using earbuds at night. She'd traded an apple pie with an *Englisch* friend for the earbuds. Her parents would consider the songs inappropriate because of the upbeat tempo and some of the subject matter. Radios weren't permitted, but her parents overlooked that for now too. She liked the way the songs made her feel. Often, the music was about redemption, recovery, a lost love, a newfound love, or subjects that touched her heart in one way or another.

She'd never understood what was wrong with that type of music. Those songs were like a book with a happy ending. Mary had read plenty of books without a happily ever after, even ones that made her cry. Music made her sad sometimes, too, depending on the song. Books bring forth all kinds of emotions, just like music. *But books are allowed.* When Mary was younger, her mother screened the books she read, but once she turned sixteen she was free to choose what she wanted to read and often checked out books at the library.

"Do you play the piano at all?" Levi wrung his hands together as he directed the question to Adeline.

He was itching to play, Mary thought, as he snuck another look at the massive black instrument.

Adeline shook her head. "No. I would sit beside Percy and sing sometimes."

Now it was Mary feeling anxious as she pictured Levi playing the piano and herself sitting beside him singing. God was surely frowning down on her for having such thoughts, just like he most likely did when she was singing songs that weren't allowed.

Adeline sat taller and brought a hand to

her chest. "Oh my. I hope you kids don't think I would do anything to disrespect your way of life. I know that listening to the radio or playing an instrument isn't allowed for you, so even if I did know how to play, I certainly wouldn't." She held up a finger. "And I've so enjoyed your company today. If I've done anything to offend you in any way, I insist you let me know."

Mary shook her head. "Nothing at all." She glanced at Levi, then back at Adeline. "And we feel the same way. Please don't let us offend you either."

Adeline chuckled. "Well, I'm not easily offended. I'm just an old lady trying to do right by the Lord." She sighed. "I wish I had something to offer you for dessert, but these shaky hands make it difficult for me to bake these days." Her eyes took on a sparkle. "But back in the day, I was a fine cook."

"Next Saturday, I can bring some pastries from the bakery where I work, if you'd like. I don't work Saturdays, but I can pick up a few things Friday. Or *mei mudder* almost always bakes early on Saturday mornings." Mary smiled, but Adeline frowned a little and scratched her cheek with one finger.

"Sweet girl, I have enjoyed spending time with you more than you know. But I don't expect you to come take me for a ride every Saturday. I would never allow you to do that."

Mary's eyes drifted to Levi's. He was grinning, and heat rose up Mary's neck, surely turning her cheeks a rosy shade of pink. Levi would suspect she wanted to come back each Saturday to see him since Adeline had just made it clear that Mary's visits weren't scheduled to be weekly.

"I-I enjoyed our ride. I'm happy to come back next Saturday since we didn't get to the market today. I could even help you tidy up. Anytime furniture is moved, dust bunnies show themselves." She swallowed hard.

Adeline glanced at Levi, then back at Mary, the hint of a smile on her face. "I think that would be lovely, if you're sure."

"*Ach,* I am. I can clean inside while Levi paints."

Adeline yawned, then walked to the window. "Oh dear. Dark clouds are rolling in." She looked over her shoulder at Levi. "Is your paint dry enough to hold up to rain?"

Levi walked to the window and looked out. "Maybe it won't rain much, but it's only primer, so if I have to redo it next Saturday, I can."

Adeline hung her head. "That would be so much wasted work."

Mary joined the other two at the window and peered out at the fast-moving clouds.

Adeline put a hand on each of their arms. "This is my nap time. I'm afraid when my tummy gets full, it seems to signal the need for rest. But it's best if you kids wait and see what this weather does before you consider leaving. Help yourselves to anything you'd like in the kitchen. But, Mary, don't you dare start any cleaning today. I want to help you."

Mary smiled. "We'll see."

She gave them each a pat on the arm and left the room.

Mary sighed. "I guess I need to call *mei* parents to let them know I plan to wait out the storm." She took her cell phone from the pocket of her maroon dress.

"You have a portable phone?" Levi frowned. "That's allowed in your district?"

Mary nodded as she realized how close they were standing to each other. "*Ya,* most people in their *rumschpringe* have one. We just aren't allowed to have a smartphone." She paused. "Don't you have a cell phone?"

"*Nee.*"

"*Mei* parents each have one, but for emergencies and *mei daed*'s business calls. Most of the older people in our community still use shanties, and a lot of folks have a phone

58

in the barn. Which does your family have?"

Levi scratched his mostly clean-shaven chin, which told Mary he was single. The hint of a shadow had prickled to the surface as the day wore on, but an Amish man didn't grow a beard until after he was married. It appeared that Levi's beard would be dark someday, even though his hair was blond.

He tipped his head to one side. "We don't have a phone in our barn, and we don't have a shanty."

Mary scrunched up her nose and puckered her lips. "How do you communicate?"

"The same way generations before us did. We write letters."

Mary giggled. "Well, you don't always write letters the way you promise."

Levi's arm brushed against hers as he chuckled, then they both turned to look out the window as the first of the rain pelted against the tin roof.

"I need to call *mei daed.*" She walked to the couch, sat down, and made the call, which went to voice mail. "*Wie bischt, Daed.* I'm still at Adeline's, and there is a storm, so I am going to stay here until it looks safe to travel." She ended the call and turned to Levi, but he was gone from the window and standing by the piano. She went to him and sighed.

"You really want to play, don't you? I saw you looking at the piano all through lunch."

He kept his eyes on the ivory keys that must have been shiny white at one time but were now yellowed with age. "It's not allowed."

Mary sat on the bench. Levi sat beside her, their arms brushing against each other again. They were quiet for a long while before Levi turned to face her.

"Why would the Lord tempt me in this way?"

Mary was surprised at the intimacy of the question. She didn't tattle on him eight years ago, so maybe he assumed she wouldn't say anything now. Besides, they didn't even live in the same district.

"I don't know." She wanted to tell Levi how much she'd love to sing the songs she listened to on the radio right now. Maybe not as much as he longed to play the piano, but it was still a forbidden pleasure that she would eventually have to give up once she was baptized. But she chose not to say anything. Levi excelled at playing the piano. Mary enjoyed singing, but she wasn't sure she was very good at it.

"I don't understand why we can't play an

instrument or listen to certain kinds of music." His eyebrows drew into a frown again.

Mary thought about the *Ordnung,* and she couldn't recall anything about the reasoning behind the rule. "Me either."

Levi placed his hands on the keys but didn't press down on any of them.

"She'll wake up if you play." Mary swallowed hard, the wheels in her head churning.

"I know."

Levi sounded so sad. She knew something about him, a secret, but he knew nothing about her. If anyone would keep Mary's love of music a secret, Levi would. She worried again if he would think her voice was pretty, but she was going to chance it and hoped it would cheer him up.

In as soft a voice as possible, she began singing the song she most enjoyed listening to at night before she drifted off to sleep. It was a song an *Englisch* woman sang about turning away from God and her long journey back to Him. Mary closed her eyes and tried to hear the woman's voice in her mind. The song started out slow and soft, but by the end, a boisterous band joined the singer, and the woman's voice became loud and filled with redemption, telling of God's grace and love. Mary trailed off when she got to the louder part at the end.

She was afraid to open her eyes, to see Levi's reaction. But when she did, his jaw had dropped a little. Maybe she shouldn't have sang. Did Levi think badly of her? Was her voice awful? But as Mary tried to peg his reaction, she also wondered again why such lovely sounds were forbidden by God, especially when they told a story with a happy ending. *But they are forbidden.* She hung her head. Levi touched her arm, bringing her eyes to his.

"That was beautiful," he said softly, eying her with curiosity. "Did you make that up?"

Mary sighed. "*Nee.* I hear it on the radio a lot."

Levi scratched his forehead. "*Ach,* your district must be very different from ours. We don't have solar power or phones, and we surely don't have radios."

Mary twisted slightly on the bench until she was facing him. "We don't normally have radios either. That's just another privilege of my *rumschpringe.*" She smiled a little. "I go through a lot of batteries. I'm trying to figure out if I can get music on my phone, which is dead a lot. When I don't work at the bakery I don't have a chance to charge it. Like I said, we aren't allowed to have smartphones, and I know you can listen to music on them."

Levi chuckled. "Are there *dumb* phones?"

Mary laughed, but quickly stifled the sound by clamping a hand over her mouth so as not to wake Adeline. After a few seconds, she said in a whisper, "A smartphone can access the Internet and do other things in addition to making phone calls."

"I've heard of the Internet, but I don't really know what it is." He paused, thinking. "But I sure wish I had a way to listen to music."

They were quiet again, and something deep inside Mary stirred, emotions she couldn't explain, feelings the music always brought out in her. But there wasn't any music right now. And yet, the same fondness swirled around her. Was it left over from her singing? She didn't think so.

As she tried to understand why she was feeling so off-center, Levi's hand found hers, which only brought forth more of the same emotions.

He gazed into her eyes and smiled. "Maybe we really are going to be friends this time," he whispered, grinning.

Mary's insides swirled, her eyes fused with his as she smiled. "Maybe we are."

CHAPTER 3

Levi readied the buggy as his sisters hung clothes on the line. His father and brothers were rebuilding the back fence that had been damaged by the storm on Saturday. As he positioned the bit in the horse's mouth, he recalled his time with Mary.

Adeline had awoken not long after Levi and Mary got cozy on the piano bench, but during the short time they had to talk, Mary said maybe they were kindred spirits. Levi had no idea what that meant, and he'd been too embarrassed to ask her, but she smiled after she said it, so he took it to be a *gut* thing.

Today he was carting his mother to Widow Stutzman's *haus,* and as *Mamm* walked across their front yard and stepped over Abram's bike, she was limping more than usual. Levi wondered if there was a better route to the widow's place, a less traveled road without so many potholes. But he was pretty sure there was only one way to go.

As his mother climbed into the passenger side of the buggy, she flinched and grimaced. Levi worried there was more to her ailments than arthritis, but she had assured him there wasn't anything else wrong.

"Maybe you need to see a doctor, *Mamm,*" he said before he clicked his tongue and pulled on the reins, directing the horse to ease the buggy backward.

His mother folded her hands atop the black purse in her lap and lifted her chin. "I *have* been seeing a doctor."

Levi made the turn from their long driveway onto the street, then gave the reins a flick. "I mean a real doctor, an *Englisch* doctor." They always sought out natural remedies first, but the various herbs and spices Widow Stutzman was giving his mother didn't seem to bring her much relief.

Levi complained sometimes about taking his mother on long trips, but up until a month ago, it hadn't been an issue. *Mamm* had driven herself everywhere. Then she came home from the market one day, stormed into the *haus,* said she wasn't driving the buggy anymore, and slammed her bedroom door behind her. It was untypical behavior for their mother, and Levi could still recall the look on his father's face, a mixture of confusion and concern. His mother never gave a reason for why she chose to stop driving the buggy, and everyone seemed afraid to ask. Levi thought maybe she'd had a close call with a car and it scared her. The dent on the rear left side of the buggy seemed to indicate that might be the case.

"I want to give the natural medications a little longer to see if they work." She turned to Levi, squinting from the sun, but with a sparkle in her eyes. "What a beautiful day. The Lord blessed us with blue skies, and you'd hardly know a storm blew through two days ago."

It was clear his mother wanted to change the subject, so Levi decided not to push. "I'm going to have to redo some of the primer I painted on Adeline's *haus* since it started raining soon after I applied a coat."

Levi had been glad for the rain when Adeline suggested they all play a card game until the weather cleared. Mary wanted to clean house, but Adeline had insisted they all play cards. It was a blessing that the skies cleared in time for him and Mary to get on the road and make it home before dark. Levi didn't mind driving in the dark, but Mary said driving at night made her nervous.

"She's a lovely woman — Adeline. I'm glad you don't mind helping her out." She shook her head. "It's a shame she doesn't have any kin to help her. Did she sell a lot at the estate sale?"

"*Ya,* almost everything. And it's real dirty where all the furniture was."

"Maybe I need to go with you this Saturday and give the place a *gut* cleaning. I can take the girls with me." His mother shifted her weight in the seat, flinching again.

"She's got someone to clean for her."

His mother turned to face him. "*Ach,* that's *gut,* I reckon. Who is it?"

Levi shrugged and looked to his left, avoiding his mother's questioning gaze. "Just a girl she knows." He paused. "Well, I don't think Adeline really knows Mary, but Mary's father knew Percy real well. She came to take Adeline for a buggy ride since Adeline doesn't drive her car anymore. And she offered to clean the *haus.*"

His mother smiled a little when Levi looked her way. She was going to ask him about Mary, how old she was, and so on, but Levi had an equally uncomfortable conversation he wanted to have with his mother about another topic. There was no easy way to break into it, and it would avoid her questioning him about Mary.

67

"There's this one room in Adeline's *haus* with a real fancy red couch and chair. Nothing in that room sold." He swallowed hard. "Not even the piano."

His mother scowled. "Levi Shetler, you're not playing that piano, are you? I still shudder when I think about you playing that one time when you were a young boy."

Levi was quiet. There was nothing he disliked more than lying, but the temptation to tell her he hadn't played the piano was strong.

"You *did* play it, didn't you?" His mother hissed, clicking her tongue. "What would the bishop think?" Her eyes widened. "And even worse, what would your *daed* have to say about it?" She shook her head, clicking her tongue even more. "Not to mention the Lord."

Levi had managed to pull off the time he played Percy's piano when he was ten without his mother knowing, but he couldn't bring himself to lie. "*Ya,* I played it. But no one was around. Mary had taken Adeline on a ride. But I don't understand why we're not allowed to play instruments or sing." He looked at his mother. "There are a lot of Bible verses about music."

Mamm faced forward again and lifted her chin. "You *are* allowed to sing. You've been

68

to plenty of Sunday singings to know that." She turned toward him frowning. "And we sing in church."

Levi wasn't sure the slow drawn-out notes of the church songs could really be called singing.

His mother folded her hands in her lap and sat taller. "That's just the way it's always been. We don't sing except at worship service and the singings."

"But why?" Levi had already prepared for this part of the conversation. " 'O come, let us sing unto the Lord: let us make a joyful noise to the rock of our salvation.' Or, what about 'Let the word of Christ dwell in you richly in all wisdom; teaching and admonishing one another in psalms and hymns and spiritual songs, singing with grace in your hearts to the Lord.' And —"

"That's enough, Levi. I know there are many references to song in the Bible, and we do sing the songs allowed in the *Liedersammlung,* and in other districts, they use the *Ausbund.*"

"*Mamm,* you know what I mean. I don't normally question the *Ordnung.* I know it's important to stay detached from the outside world, so I can understand why we don't use electricity and things like that. But . . . music is beautiful." He turned to her, knowing his eyes and his voice were pleading with her to bend the rules. But permission to play the piano wasn't hers to give. It was a long-established rule that had been in place for generations.

"Levi." She turned her head to face him. "I'm not arguing that fact. Music *is* beautiful, and as I said, it *is* allowed. But songs must be appropriate." Pausing, she rubbed her forehead for a few seconds. "Do you understand why we have as little contact with the *Englisch* as possible? There are exceptions, of course, like Adeline and Percy, God rest his soul." She took in a breath. "It's because we are unequally yoked. There are a lot of *gut Englisch* folks out there who are Christians and who love the Lord, but we have no way of discerning which ones do and don't adhere to the laws of Christ. If we were to turn everyone loose to listen to any kind of music they wanted to, what messages would our *kinner* get from some of those songs?"

Levi wasn't sure he'd ever heard his mother use words like *discerning* and *adhere*, which made him wonder if she'd given this speech before. Had one of his siblings asked this question?

"But playing the piano doesn't involve any words, so there aren't any messages." He turned on the street where Widow Stutzman lived. "I'm not playing music that sounds evil or wild. It's just pretty. I don't understand how we can have a rule that has no meaning behind it. And for some unknown reason, I know how to play the piano."

She leaned her head back, closed her eyes, and exhaled. Lifting her eyes to Levi, she shook her head. "I thought I just explained the reasoning behind the rule." She pressed her lips together and pointed a finger at him. "Levi, you promise me that you won't play that instrument when you are at Adeline's. We can debate about singing all you want to, but playing an instrument is strictly forbidden. You are there to work, not to do things that go against our ways."

Levi stared long and hard at his mother. "I can't promise that, *Mamm.* It feels like that piano is calling me to play." He pulled into the widow's driveway, then shook his head. "I know it's wrong, but how can something that is in the Bible be so forbidden, something that brings out all kinds of emotions?"

His mother pressed her lips together and pointed a finger at him again. "And *there* is your answer. Music invokes unnecessary emotions." She sighed heavily as she lowered her hand and pulled her purse over her arm.

"And it's prideful to show off by doing something that others can't. What if one person could play piano, and another one played a guitar, or maybe a violin? Everything in the *Ordnung* makes it clear that we are to do things the same way, not to stand out among each other. Our buggies are the same color, our clothing is the same, and we follow the Lord's teachings in the same manner."

Levi brought the buggy to a stop as he thought about his mother's reasoning. "I'll wait here."

His mother sat still a few seconds, then slowly eased off the seat, but turned to face Levi once she was standing. "*Sohn,* there are a lot of voices that call to us. And sometimes it is difficult to discern whose voice it is. But I guarantee you, if you think that piano is calling to you, that isn't the voice of our Lord. It's the *other* voice. Keep that in mind as temptation calls to you."

Levi was quiet. He'd put up a good argument with his mother, but maybe she was right. There was nothing good to come from playing the piano. The wonderful feelings that rushed over him as he played were nothing but trickery from the devil. It had to be.

And he'd keep telling himself that until

his temptation to play the piano went away forever.

Mary waited behind her friend Katie to clock out at the bakery. "Do you know anyone from Orleans, or have you ever been there?"

Katie pulled her timecard from the slot and stepped aside so Mary could stamp hers. "*Ya,* I went there a few years ago for a cousin's wedding. Why do you ask?"

"I was just wondering. I met someone from Orleans, and I was surprised to learn they don't use any kind of phones, not even cell phones. No solar panels either." Mary paused, pressing her lips together for a few seconds. "I can't imagine *mei daed* not having a way to power his tools."

Katie opened the closet in the back room of the bakery and pulled out her purse, draping it across her arm, then she handed Mary hers. "That's not all they do without. They don't use propane for stoves, ovens, or refrigerators. They still cook in wood stoves, and anything that has to be kept cold is stored in freezers with big ice blocks."

Mary walked in step with her friend as they left the bakery and made their way to their buggies. "Why?"

Katie shrugged. "I don't know. I asked *mei*

73

mamm about that after the wedding, and she said that's the way it's always been in Orleans. Not every family lives that way, but a lot of them do." Her eyes widened as she turned to Mary. "Some families still use an outhouse and don't have any indoor plumbing."

Mary untethered her horse. "How can that be? They are only forty miles from us."

Katie chuckled. "I guess that's why. They are forty miles from us. That's nothing in a car, but it would be a long trip by buggy." Katie gave her horse a scratch on the nose. "Why do you ask?"

Mary wasn't ready to tell Katie about Levi. "I'm visiting a woman on Saturdays. Her husband has passed, and she can't drive anymore. I took her on a buggy ride last Saturday, and this Saturday I will help her clean her house. *Mei daed* was friends with her husband, and right now, she just needs a little help and company."

Katie nodded, then scowled. "That's too far to push your horse, forty miles. How are you getting there? Are you hiring a driver?"

"Nee, nee." Mary shook her head as she ran a hand over her own horse's mane. "She doesn't live in Orleans. She lives in Shoals." Swallowing hard, she could read the confusion in Katie's expression. "There's a

painter that works for the *Englisch* woman, too, and he's from Orleans. Their way of life sounds different from ours, stricter."

"*Ya,* that's what I've heard." Katie walked around the buggy but quickly trekked back, grinning. "Is this about the painter?"

Mary felt a blush starting up her neck, and as she avoided Katie's eyes, she couldn't stop the smile from spreading across her face.

"It *is.* Tell me." Katie bounced up on her toes a little. "Is he courting you?"

Mary bit her bottom lip. She'd been friends with Katie since they were little, but Katie spread gossip faster than a herd of cattle heading toward a feed trough. Mary shook her head. "*Nee,* we're just friends."

Katie chuckled, then gave Mary an all-knowing wink. "Sure you are."

Mary rolled her eyes, then silently chastised herself for it. "We are just friends," she repeated before she climbed into her buggy. Katie blew out a breath of frustration before she got into her own buggy and waved goodbye.

After establishing a steady trot on a back road to her house, Mary dug a pair of earbuds out of her purse. Earlier Katie had shown her how to listen to music on her phone, and her friend had an extra set of earbuds since Mary kept hers in her night-stand drawer.

She found the song she sang for Levi and listened and sang along. But she had trouble focusing on the words. Levi's face kept flashing into her mind. The way he looked at her when he held her hand. She'd even told him maybe they were kindred spirits. She regretted saying that. Mostly, they just had a love of music in common. That didn't make them kindred spirits, a term she'd learned from an *Englisch* friend who worked at the bakery.

She tried to shake loose her thoughts about Levi. Eventually the house would be painted, and he wouldn't have a reason to keep coming on Saturdays. Since he lived so far from her, she needed to be prepared for the friendship to end.

Mary would continue taking Adeline for buggy rides or to the market as often as she'd like. She enjoyed time with the older woman, and she loved hearing her stories about Percy, their special times together, and how she couldn't wait to see him in heaven. Adeline told Mary she was in good health for a woman her age, but Mary had noticed that her hands trembled a lot, and she wasn't always steady on her feet. She'd also seen Adeline in the hallway holding her chest and gritting her teeth as she made her way to the bathroom.

She wondered if there was more going on with Adeline than just normal aging.

Adeline carried her tomato-and-cheese sandwich into the parlor, stared at the piano, and again recalled how they'd saved and saved for the instrument. She remembered how she would haul a kitchen chair into the room to watch her husband play before they had any other furniture. Percy was a large man, and his hands needed the freedom to run the entire length of the keys. They'd purchased the red couch and Percy's chair at an estate sale a few months later, items they never could have afforded new back then.

It was a miracle that Percy had stumbled upon a piano — a grand piano — that they could afford. But the man selling it didn't have long to live, and Adeline always thought the fellow could feel Percy's passion about music. When Percy told him how much he had to spend, the man said that sounded fine. They saved for another month to hire professional piano movers.

Adeline sat down on the couch and took a bite of her sandwich, thinking how much better it would be if it was grilled. The last time she attempted to cook with her shaky hands, she'd dropped the skillet and broken a toe.

Closing her eyes, she envisioned Percy at the piano, seemingly healthy as a horse. He had a heart attack after taking a shower one evening, and he died before the ambulance arrived. Adeline had just enough time to tell him how much she loved him before he slipped out of this world and into the next. Some days, she wished she'd have a heart attack too.

She savored the flavor of the cheese and tomatoes and forced such morbid thoughts away. Instead she thought about her two new friends, wondering if they saw the spark igniting between them. Adeline caught them sneaking looks at each other during their visit, a thought that brought her right back to Percy.

She remembered clearly the first time she met him. She'd gone with her father to a cattle auction, as she almost always did. Adeline couldn't remember a time when she didn't love animals. She'd even wanted to be a veterinarian someday.

Percy owned the prize cow that everyone wanted. Her father had paid top dollar for the animal. And Adeline had fallen in love with Percy Collins that day when she was twenty-one years old. It had been a brief encounter in front of her father, but Adeline could still recall the way Percy took off his hat, smiled at her, and told her father what a pretty daughter he had.

Looking back, it seemed a bold thing to say to her father, but Adeline's cheeks still warmed when she thought about the way Percy had looked at her, the warmth in his eyes, the way he squared his shoulders with confidence. He was handsome, and younger than her, but she was drawn to him right away for reasons she couldn't identify at the time. Now, all these years later, she knew that love wasn't always logical. What draws one person to another, besides physical attraction, is often a mystery that perhaps only the Lord is privy to. It was another two years before he came calling to ask her on a date. And three months later, she became Mrs. Percy Collins.

Smiling, she took another bite of the sandwich, but she jumped when there was a knock at the door. She wasn't expecting anyone until Saturday when Mary and Levi arrived. She stood up, set her plate on the chair, and shuffled to the door as she smoothed the wrinkles from her blue blouse and knocked off a few crumbs in the process.

"Can I help you?" She smiled at the young woman on the other side of the screen door, the dry air outside colliding with the air-conditioning inside.

"Ms. Collins, it's me, Natalie. Do you remember me?"

The small woman with long blond hair and big blue eyes looked familiar, but Adeline couldn't place her.

"I'm Cecelia's daughter."

Adeline smiled as she brought a hand to her chest. "Of course." She motioned for Natalie to step back so she could open the screen door. "Come in, come in." She studied the young woman as she stepped across the threshold. She looked to be about Mary's age, maybe eighteen or nineteen. "It must have been at Percy's funeral, the last time I saw you."

Natalie nodded. "I think so."

Adeline pulled her into a hug, then held on to her shoulders as she eyed her up and down. "What a lovely young woman you've become. How is Cecelia?" Adeline had never been close to Percy's side of the family. Percy hadn't kept in touch with his kin either. There hadn't ever been any ill will about it. Sometimes distance causes folks to lose touch, and from what Adeline could remember, Percy's cousins lived on the other side of Indianapolis, at least a two-hour drive.

Several times, the family had asked Percy and Adeline to join them for a holiday meal, but Percy never wanted to go. If Adeline's memory served her well, Cecelia and her husband had two children. But Cecelia's mother and aunts and uncles also attended the holiday events. In hindsight, maybe that was the reason she and Percy hadn't stayed close with them. It was the big family she and Percy had always wanted. She couldn't even remember Cecelia's mother's name, the cousin who would have been about Percy's age. But she did remember Natalie from the funeral, even though most of that day was a blur. Adeline didn't have any family. She often forgot that Percy did, even though there wasn't any relationship there.

"Mom's fine." Natalie hung her head for a few seconds, then looked back at Adeline and sighed. "Her and Dad got a divorce not long ago, so things were a mess for a while."

"Oh dear. I'm so sorry to hear that." Adeline glanced around her almost-empty living room at the squares and circles on the floor where furniture had been for nearly fifty years. "Forgive the appearance of the place. I had an estate sale recently." She felt a shudder of renewed humiliation and didn't want word of her financial status getting back to Percy's family. "It was time for those old antiques to go." She felt another tear in her heart as she spoke. "But, please, follow me into the parlor where we can chat. I still have some furniture in there."

Adeline scooted past the brown couch, not wanting to subject her guest to the loose springs protruding randomly on the piece of furniture.

"Wow, this is a cool room." Natalie's eyes lit up as she took in the space Adeline so loved.

"Percy and I spent a lot of time in this room." Adeline looked around, then remembered her sandwich on the chair. She hurried to scoop it up. "Let me just put this in the kitchen. Are you hungry? I can make you something to eat."

Natalie shook her head, her lovely blond hair swaying past her shoulders. "No. Thank you, though. I was just in the area and decided to stop by. Don't let me interrupt your lunch."

"I've had plenty. Be back in a moment." Adeline put the dish on the counter and hurried back to her guest, her heart filling a tiny bit as she wondered if Percy would welcome the child into his heart if he were alive. After turning it over in her mind, she decided he would. It was the large crowds that congregated on holidays that he wasn't fond of.

When she returned, Natalie was sitting in the red chair where Levi sat on Saturday, where Percy sat for decades.

"This really is a super cool room." Natalie set her purse on the floor beside her and crossed one leg over the other as she leaned into the chair. "And I love this furniture."

That was nice to hear. Adeline thought she was the only one who appreciated it these days. She wondered if she should offer to patch the tear in Natalie's jean, a fringy slit right above her knee. It didn't look right with her crisp white blouse and high-heeled white sandals. But she didn't want to hurt the girl's feelings. And kids dressed a bit differently these days. "So, tell me, what brings you to Shoals?"

Natalie rolled her eyes, something Adeline had caught Mary doing a few times. Adeline remembered being reprimanded by her father for the gesture when she was about Natalie and Mary's age. Just when you think everything in the world has changed, you find something familiar to cling to. *Teenagers will always be teenagers.*

"Job training," Natalie said. "I work for

Rural King. I mean, not as a checker or anything. I'm in management." She huffed. "I'm not sure why the training is way out here instead of where I normally work." Another eye roll, followed by a smile. Adeline used to frequent the Rural King in Bedford. The store carried a hodgepodge of items, everything from farming supplies to clothing, along with tools, home goods, and hunting gear. "So, I thought I'd stop by. Mom told me the address, and I just put it in my GPS."

Adeline knew what a GPS was, even if she'd never known what GPS stood for. *Generalized property search?* "Well, I don't get many visitors, so I'm happy to have you."

Natalie looked around again, her gaze heading toward the window, the red curtains tied back with gold strands of decorative rope. "You don't have any neighbors. Just a lot of fields. It must get lonely out here."

Adeline smiled. "Those fields fed us for many years, until Percy became too old to tend the land anymore." She suppressed a sigh as she recalled shelling peas on the porch while Percy was out on the tractor. "It wasn't lonely when Percy was alive. But sometimes it is now." Could it be that the Lord was gifting her with yet another young person to fill the emptiness?

"I'm going to be coming to Shoals every Wednesday for a while, for the training I mentioned. Maybe I could come and visit you?"

Thank you, Lord. Adeline brought a hand to her chest. "I'd like that very much." She might be running out of money, but her circle of friends was growing, and that felt more important. She thanked God again, then listened as Natalie told her about her parents, how her brother — Sean — had joined the Army, and then she finally mentioned her grandmother, the one closest in age to Percy.

"My grandma died last year." The girl looked away for a few seconds, her eyes traveling back to the window as she blinked a few times.

Adeline still couldn't remember the woman's name, but it was clear that Natalie was still grieving. "Honey, I'm so sorry to hear that."

Natalie tucked her hair behind her ears before she slowly found Adeline's eyes. "I loved her very much. In a lot of ways, I was closer to her than my mother." Pausing, a smile filled her face. "Mimi Jean drove a racecar for a while in the sixties. She even won a trophy. She was kinda wild like that. But she was the kindest person I've ever

85

known. And no one could bake bread the way she could."

The girl's eyes glowed as she spoke about her grandmother. *Jean.* Adeline remembered her, and the few times she'd been around the woman, she'd always laughed a lot. Adeline remembered her daughter, Cecelia, being not quite as friendly. Not rude, just not as outspoken and cheerful as her mother. The qualities must skip a generation, Adeline thought, as she watched the animated way Natalie talked about her grandmother. There was no doubt she'd loved the woman very much.

Adeline wondered if anyone would speak of her with such fondness after she was gone. Maybe this was her chance to leave a bit of legacy with Percy's family. Perhaps this young woman would like to know more about the third cousin she'd never really known.

But the visit was cut short when Natalie's phone rang from her purse. She reached for it, studied it, then stood. "I'm going to have to go."

Adeline slowly lifted herself from the couch, disappointed that their visit was coming to an end. But when Natalie crossed the room and hugged Adeline, she felt sure the girl would be back next week, and in addition to Mary and Levi on Saturdays, she'd have Natalie's visits to look forward to. Eventually, Levi would finish painting, and Mary would tire of carting Adeline around. But Natalie was Percy's family, so she was Adeline's kin by extension.

And sure enough, at the front door Natalie said, "See you next Wednesday."

Adeline smiled and waved as Natalie headed to her car. "I'm looking forward to it."

CHAPTER 4

Natalie waited until she pulled into the training center before she returned her mother's call. It was only a short drive, but as her mother breathed an exaggerated sigh into the phone, Natalie could almost feel it slap at her face.

"Well, how did it go?" Cecelia Collins always got right to the point.

"It went fine, but I'll have to tell you about it later." Natalie sighed, rolling her eyes.

"You can take five minutes to talk to me. Was the house about the same as eight years ago?"

Natalie held her phone away from her face and looked at the time. "Mom, I have two minutes, and then I'm hanging up. My training class will be starting. No, the house doesn't look the same. The paint is peeling off outside, the yard is a wreck, and there's hardly any furniture left."

"What do you mean, no furniture left?"

Natalie could tell her mother was gritting her teeth as she spoke. "There were some very expensive antiques in that house. Some of those could have been family heirlooms."

Natalie grunted. "Well, if they were, they're gone now. Adeline said she had an estate sale."

"I wonder why. Is she planning to sell the house?"

"She didn't say she was, so I don't know." Natalie glanced at her phone. "One minute left."

"How did she look? I mean, she must be in her eighties by now."

Natalie smiled. "She looked fit as a fiddle." It was something Mimi Jean used to say, and almost everything about Mimi Jean irritated Natalie's mother.

"Did you make plans to keep going over there? We are the last living relatives that woman has."

"Actually, Adeline is *Dad's* cousin, not yours." Natalie spat the words at her mother and waited for the predictable comeback. "But, yeah, I'll visit her on Wednesdays."

"Your father is off living his life with that tramp he chose to be with. He doesn't care a hoot about that old woman."

"But now that she's old, you suddenly care about her. Is that correct, Mother?"

"Watch your mouth, Natalie. What did you two talk about?"

Natalie pulled back for the punch, grinning. "Mimi Jean."

Her mother growled on the other end. "I'm sure the entire conversation didn't revolve around your grandmother."

"Yep, pretty much." Natalie got out of the car and started walking toward the store. "I gotta go."

"Wait, wait. Was the piano still there?"

"Yeah, it was still there, along with a bunch of old red furniture in the same room. It's a cool room."

"I remember that hideous furniture from the funeral. I'm not surprised no one bought it at the estate sale. But thank God that piano is still there. Your father told me once that Percy paid a lot of money for it."

Natalie rolled her eyes again as she picked up her pace. "I don't know, Mom. The keys were kinda yellow. It might not be worth much."

"Next Wednesday, look at the brand name. See if it's a Steinway."

"I never should have agreed to this," Natalie mumbled.

"You'll be thanking me if Adeline leaves us that house and piano. They would pay for the college education I can't give you now, after what your father has done."

Natalie was sure she'd never see any of the money, even if such an arrangement came to pass. "Well, Adeline looks healthy as a horse, so if you're waiting for her to kick the bucket, you might have to wait another decade. Or longer."

She pushed End on the phone before her mother could respond. Some days she just wanted to pretend she was adopted. Today was one of those days.

Mary finished sweeping the kitchen floor Wednesday evening, then checked the cookies in the oven. It was the third batch she'd baked so far, and she was wondering if that would be enough when her mother walked into the room.

"*Mamm,* do you think three dozen cookies is enough for today?" It was their turn to host Sister's Day tomorrow, but there was never a way to know how many ladies would show up. Most of the older women didn't have phones, or if they did, they were for emergencies only.

"I think that's plenty since we have so many other offerings." Mary's mother wiped down the kitchen counter for the third time today, and it was still early. Naomi Hershberger wouldn't be caught with an inkling of dust anywhere in her house. Especially not today. And that made Mary think of Adeline.

"*Mamm,* I'm planning to go back to Adeline's — Ms. Collins's — *haus* Saturday, if you don't need me for anything." She held her breath and hoped her mother didn't have something planned. "Ms. Collins sold most of her things at her estate sale, and the *haus* needs cleaning badly, especially in places where furniture had been for a long time. I'd like to clean things up for her, and then take her to the market if she needs groceries, or maybe just for another buggy ride."

"*Ach, ya.*" Her mother looked up and smiled. "That's very nice of you."

Mary felt a tinge of guilt creep over her. She enjoyed Adeline and wanted to help, but part of her motivation stemmed from wanting to see Levi again.

Her mother sat down at the kitchen table and brushed away a strand of hair that had fallen from her *kapp.* "I think we're ready."

"Everything looks great." Mary glanced around the room. "Where's Lydia? I haven't seen her this morning."

"She's helping your father in the shop. I think they are sanding the kitchen table for the Watkins family." *Mamm* chuckled. "I guess she's the boy your father never had."

Mary cleared her throat, deciding this was as good a time as any to question her mother about the thing heaviest on her heart. *"Mamm . . ."*

Her mother frowned a little. "What is it, *mei maedel?* You look so serious."

"I was just wondering . . . why can't we play musical instruments?" Mary bit her bottom lip and waited.

"That's just the way it's always been." *Mamm* shrugged. "It's just not allowed."

Mary squirmed in her chair. *"Ya,* I know. But *why?"*

Following a heavy sigh, her mother tapped a finger to her chin. "I honestly don't know. It's just always been our way."

"I understand the rules of the *Ordnung,* but I can't recall any reasons for why we can't play instruments or sing songs that aren't included in our hymnal."

Mamm rubbed the back of her neck with one hand as she squinted her eyes at Mary. "Where is this coming from?"

Mary twirled the string on her *kapp.* "There is a piano at Adeline's — Ms. Collins's *haus.* It just made me think about the reasoning behind the rule."

Her mother sat taller and locked eyes with Mary. "She isn't trying to teach you the piano, is she?" She held up a hand when Mary opened her mouth to speak. "Let me finish. I know you are in your *rumschpringe,* but I've seen what can happen when a child ventures into an area that isn't allowed. It's one thing for you to go to a movie or wear lip gloss, but learning a skill that you eventually have to give up isn't healthy. And music has even lured young people away from our community in the past."

"*Nee, nee.* She doesn't even know how to play it. The piano was Percy's — Mr. Collins's. I was just curious."

They were quiet for a few moments, then her mother chuckled, which was nice to hear after the serious tone her mother had just used. "Your Uncle John bought a guitar when we were young. He was probably twelve, which would have made me about nine. He used to play it in the barn when your *daadi* was gone." She paused, grinning. "But *Daed* came back from town early one day, and he tanned your Uncle John's hide when he heard him playing that thing. Then he used the guitar for kindling."

Mary had never heard this story, and as she envisioned her mother's brother in the barn with a guitar, she laughed. "I didn't think Uncle John had ever broken a rule in his life."

"Not many," her mother said before she laughed too.

"Did *Mammi* know?"

"*Ya,* I think so. If I could hear it sometimes, I'm sure *mei mudder* could too. But she never said anything."

"I just feel like a rule needs a reason to back it up." Mary nodded to the window. "The first of our guests is pulling into the driveway."

She stood and started toward the front door. It would be a wonderful day of quilting, eating, and laughing. Hopefully the activities would keep her mind off Levi. He'd crept into her dreams the past few nights. And now he was invading her thoughts during the days. But in a good way.

Levi was the last person to take a seat at supper. There was plenty of daylight left, and he hoped to sneak away after the meal, maybe take a walk as the sun made its final descent or just find a quiet place to sit for a while. He wanted to talk to God without all the noise.

As everyone bowed their heads in prayer, Levi savored one of the few quiet times observed in his house. Abram was the youngest — six — and a chatterbox. There was no telling what would come out of his mouth at any given time. Lloyd would likely brag about how much work he'd gotten done today. Levi reminded himself that he was supposed to be thanking the Lord for the food and blessings of the day.

When Levi's father cleared his throat, everyone raised their heads, and the rush for the food began. Isaac Shetler was a patient man and always waited until the chaos quieted before he filled his plate. As usual, Levi's mother reminded them not to pile more on their plates than they could eat. Most of the time there was enough to feed everyone until they were full, but not always.

His mother busily filled Abram's plate before her own with a small slice of ham, a spoonful of green beans, and a heaping portion of mashed potatoes. Levi's youngest brother would eat anything if it was mixed with mashed potatoes.

His sisters quietly giggled at the other end of the table. Probably about a boy. At fifteen, sixteen, and seventeen, Sarah, Hannah, and Miriam were consumed with finding the perfect husband. Miriam was the only one who had a real boyfriend, though. And Sarah wasn't even in her *rumschpringe* yet.

Levi filled his plate — with mashed potatoes more than anything else. They always had potatoes, and their mother always made plenty. He went easy on the ham even though he was starving.

"*Daed,* I refinished that old table that's been in the shop for a decade, but it ain't up to our standards." Jacob talked with his mouth full. They'd all stopped scolding him about it years ago. He was a year older than Levi, nineteen, and the sloppiest of them all, but he was probably the best craftsman, aside from their father. "I don't feel like we can sell it. I'm sure it would be fine for some folks, but it doesn't really represent the quality of our work."

Levi stopped chewing and thought for a moment. "Are there chairs that go with it?"

Jacob nodded. "*Ya,* they're in better shape than the table, but . . ." His brother shrugged. "There's only four. Ain't nobody around here got a family of just four that I know of."

Levi scratched his chin. He couldn't think of anyone in their district with only two *kinner* either. "I know someone who could use it. *Mamm*'s friend, Adeline, sold her kitchen table and chairs, so she eats on a plate in her lap." He turned to his mother. "I think you were right when you said she'd come upon hard times, so I don't know how much she can afford."

"She's a dear woman." *Mamm* smiled as she peered across the food to the other end of the table.

His father finished chewing a bite of ham, then wiped his mouth with his napkin. "Take the table and chairs to her Saturday when you go to paint. You'll have to haul the trailer behind your buggy."

His father ran a hand the length of his beard. Levi glanced at his mother, who always frowned when *Daed* did that at the table. But it meant he was thinking. *Mamm* was busy with Abram again, wiping his mouth. "And tell her it's a gift. If she argues and wants to pay, tell her we consider it damaged furniture that isn't for sale."

Levi's family didn't have much, but he'd seen both of his parents do for others his entire life. His father could be too strict at times, but Levi hoped to always be as generous as his folks, and to have their integrity. The best gifts were those you really couldn't afford to give.

"*Ya,* it's a beautiful table and chairs." *Mamm* looked up, and Levi was reminded of his mother's ability to appear tuned out of a conversation, but she didn't miss anything. "That would be *gut* if Adeline can use it."

"It would fetch several hundred dollars," Jacob said as he crinkled his nose. "But it just don't represent our best work."

"Agreed." *Daed* pushed back his chair. He was always the first to finish eating, and it was an unspoken rule that once Abram finished his meal, the rest was fair game. Levi glanced around at his other five brothers who resembled a pack of wolves ready to pounce. Even his sisters were watching Abram. Levi would be glad when his siblings started getting married and moved out. He loved them all, but there was always chaos. None of the girls were even close to taking a spouse, except maybe Miriam.

Abram lay his napkin across his plate, and hands flew, reaching for spoons, chunks of ham, and anything else that was left. Levi was right in there with them, snagging the last slice of buttered bread.

After the girls cleaned the kitchen, there would be devotions in the den. Levi glanced at the clock on the wall, hoping he'd still get the chance to take a walk, to talk to God. He wondered what he'd done to have such temptation put in his path. He trembled every time he saw Adeline's piano, and his attraction to music felt as abnormal as it was forbidden. But he couldn't shed the desire deep within to fill his soul with the sounds he heard in his head, for reasons he couldn't explain. He looked forward to Saturday. He enjoyed the work, and he enjoyed Adeline's company. He liked being around Mary. Mostly, he wanted to play that piano again.

As everyone gathered in the living room on worn couches and recliners, Levi looked around at his family. By *Englisch* standards, they would probably be considered poor. It shouldn't matter, but he wondered what life was like at Mary's house. They had all sorts of fancy gadgets, and Mary was graceful. *Proper* was the word that came into Levi's mind.

All the families in his district tried to keep things uniform. Everyone had the same style black buggies. The blinds on the windows were white. They practiced traditions that had been handed down from generation to generation — Sunday singings, Sisters' Day, attending school through eighth grade and worship service every other Sunday, but every family was still unique in its own way. Nobody wanted to appear fancy, or so they said. But Levi couldn't help but notice how some houses were much bigger than his, some buggies were newer, yards tidier, gardens more plentiful, and clothes not all hand-me-downs.

Levi would be content with only two or three children someday, even though it was unlikely. The average household in his community had ten children. He'd heard that the *Englisch* used methods of birth control, which seemed odd since children were a gift from God. Levi could secretly long for a small family, but he'd be happy with the Lord's choices for him.

He glanced at his mother. It was no wonder she was tired all the time and looked older than she was. Tending to ten children and running a household would be a lot for anyone, even with everyone chipping in to help. He looked around at his siblings. Everyone was quietly in devotion to God. If it could only be this quiet all the time.

After supper, Mary and her sister cleaned the kitchen, and following devotions, Mary bathed and went to bed early. As she brushed her hair, she stared at her cell phone on the nightstand. The battery was almost dead, but she could charge it at the bakery tomorrow.

She stowed her brush in the drawer of the bedside table, lowered the flame on her lantern, and fluffed her pillows. Picking up the phone, she looked at it again. Levi didn't have a phone. If he did, would she be brave enough to call him? She tried to corral her thoughts about Levi, and she wondered what it was that she found so attractive about him. He was nice looking, for sure, but lots of handsome young men had vied for Mary's affections over the last couple years. None had caused her stomach to flip or her heart to race. She put the phone on the nightstand and picked up a book she'd been reading. Maybe she could escape thoughts of Levi by distracting herself with the cozy mystery she'd chosen at the library recently.

She read for almost two hours, but finally set the book aside when she could barely keep her eyes open. After snubbing out the lantern, she yawned, fluffed her pillows again, and lay down. She was almost asleep when she thought she heard the front door open and gently close. She was awake later than normal, so who else was up? Sometimes her mother had trouble sleeping, but she usually just curled up on the couch and knit or read a book.

Mary looked out her bedroom window, which she'd left cracked a few inches to enjoy the last of the cool breezes before summer came. Squinting, she watched as the person walked near the propane lamp in the yard, and she recognized Lydia. Her sister was still fully dressed, had on her *kapp,* and was carrying something under one arm. *What in the world?*

After Lydia walked out of the area that was illuminated by the lamp, she became a dark figure, but as Mary peered out the window, someone joined her sister. A very tall person. A man wearing slacks.

Mary felt the urge to run down the stairs to protect Lydia, but thought better of it. Lydia was obviously in the yard of her own free will. But when Mary saw her sister set down whatever she was holding, wrap her arms around the man, then lean up and kiss him, Mary's chest tightened.

Lydia is only sixteen. Mary had kissed one boy in her life, and it occurred almost by accident over a year ago, not long after her seventeenth birthday. Her friend Luke was all torn up about a breakup with his girlfriend, and Mary had kissed him, but it was more of a friendly kiss. Lydia hadn't separated from this boy since their lips met, silhouettes against an almost-full moon.

Mary's mouth hung open as she watched her sister making out with a boy in their front yard. *Rumschpringe* didn't start until a teenager was sixteen, and Lydia had just become of age last month. Mary shivered as she thought about what their father would do if Lydia got caught. Mary was torn. If she ran out in the yard, the additional ruckus might wake up her parents. She'd embarrass Lydia and the boy if she did that.

She folded her arms across her chest and sighed, deciding she would just have to talk to Lydia in the morning. But until then, she was going to keep an eye on her sister to make sure they didn't try to go any farther than the front yard.

After another minute or so of kissing, Lydia and her beau finally separated, and Mary breathed a sigh of relief. But her respite didn't last long as she got a better look at the person. Mary's jaw dropped when she recognized the man.

CHAPTER 5

Saturday morning, Adeline finished eating the eggs she scrambled for herself, which she considered a big accomplishment. As she put the plate in the sink, she was about to prepare a hot lunch for her young friends, but another esophageal spasm cut off her air supply as her chest tightened. It was the second one that morning. After each episode, she recalled it feeling like something was around her heart, squeezing so tight it might explode.

The spasms were coming more often. Maybe she would call the doctor to see about doubling up on her medication. As soon as she got her phone turned back on. She cancelled the service when money got tight, and now she didn't have a phone to make the call to get it turned back on. She said a quick prayer that she'd be spared any more of the spasms today.

She opened the refrigerator and stared at

the chicken she'd taken out to thaw the night before, then at the pan she'd set out to cook it in. When both of her hands began to tremble, she thought better of baking it today. Chopping onion and celery for the chicken salad last Saturday had been tedious enough. She was lucky she still had all her fingers — and toes — after dropping the knife twice. But getting the bird in and out of the oven without losing her grip on the pan felt like too much of a challenge this morning.

Sighing, she searched her pantry for something the children might enjoy, but that wouldn't end up in a pile on the kitchen floor. Like the lasagna she'd tried to make last night. She had lovely visions of serving Mary and Levi her specialty.

She shook her head and pulled out two large cans of beef stew. Her friends would know it came out of a can, but it would be a hot meal. She used her electric can opener, then poured the contents into a pot for warming later, and she carefully placed it in the refrigerator. When she closed the door, she heard a buggy pulling into the driveway and smiled.

By the time she put on her shoes and got out the door, Levi was carrying a chair across the front lawn, and there was more furniture atop a small trailer behind his buggy.

"What have you got there?" She held a hand to her forehead to block the sun as it rose in the distance, the dewy grass twinkling beneath Levi's steps.

Smiling, he came up the steps and set the chair down on the porch. "*Daed* said we can't sell this stuff, and he wondered if you would like to have it."

Adeline regretted selling her kitchen table and chairs, more so now that she was having visitors. But it fetched $600, and that would pay three months on her electric bill. She ran a hand along the top of the oak chair. The Amish made beautiful furniture, and Adeline recognized charity when she saw it, even if she'd never been on the receiving end until now. "I-I can't accept this, Levi."

He picked up the chair, smiled, and scooted past her. "Sure you can," he said over his shoulder.

Adeline followed him inside, folding her arms across her chest when she got to the area where there had once been a table and four chairs. A thought hit her. "Do you kids not like eating in the parlor?"

Levi chuckled. "I love that room. I think Mary does too." He pointed out the window.

"But you said you're an early riser, and now you'll have a place to sit and drink coffee where you can watch the sun come up, since this window faces east." He paused, tipping back the rim of his straw hat. "I should probably eat in here because I'm messy. I probably left crumbs in that pretty room."

Adeline waved a dismissive hand at him, although she had picked up quite a few crumbs after they left last Saturday. A small thing to her these days. She thought about the jigsaw puzzle she'd had for a couple years. She bought it at a yard sale, thinking it would fill her days after Percy died, but she'd never even taken the five hundred pieces out of the bag. She didn't even know what the picture would be once it was put together. The pieces were in a plastic bag, and she'd only paid a quarter. Maybe if she dumped them out on the table, Mary and Levi would be tempted to help her put it together. And Natalie, too, on Wednesdays.

But it wouldn't be right to accept such a luxurious gift. Mary and Levi were already doing way too much for her.

"That is much too nice." She shook her head, knowing she should offer to pay for it. But it didn't take a brain surgeon to figure out that Adeline sold most of her possessions because she needed money to live.

"We can't sell it," Levi said as he left the room.

A minute later he came back with two more chairs. After he set them down, he said, "Unless you don't like it. I can haul it all back, but the table will likely stay in the barn and end up as a workbench. The chairs will probably end up as firewood."

Adeline gasped. "That would be tragic." She suspected the table was made from the same oak and with the fine craftsmanship the Amish were known for. "Why in the world doesn't your father want to sell it? I-I . . ." A flush filled her face as she thought about having to tell her young friend she couldn't afford the furniture.

"Look." Levi pointed to a small nick on the side of one of the chairs. "This is faulty wood, and Jacob couldn't get this sanded out to make it look right."

Adeline slammed her hands to her hips. "Levi Shetler, not a person in the world would notice that tiny imperfection." She shook her head, but could already see her puzzle spread atop the table. Maybe she would drink coffee there in the mornings as Levi suggested. The parlor didn't get much morning light. She hadn't used her old dining table much since Percy died. A kitchen could be a lonely place when you take most of your meals alone. At least in the parlor she could envision Percy doing what he'd loved best, playing the piano.

"*Ya,* well . . . *mei bruder* and *daed* are perfectionists, so they ain't gonna sell this."

Adeline resisted the urge to correct Levi's grammar. She was once an English teacher, but she knew the Amish only had an eighth-grade education. Although, Adeline had noticed Mary's vocabulary and grammar sounded more advanced than Levi's. But it clearly didn't matter to Mary. That girl had a crush on Levi. And Adeline suspected it ran both ways. Or maybe they had just clicked and would be nothing more than friends. Adeline smiled and hoped they'd fall in love. Young love in bloom. It made her think of her early years with Percy.

"Here's the last chair. I'll need Mary to help me carry in the table."

Adeline started looking around for the puzzle while Levi inspected the chairs again. She pulled out the bottom drawer of her cabinet, the large one where she often stashed odds and ends, but she didn't see it. She looked in the pantry, but she didn't think she would have stashed it with the food. She'd have to find it later.

Adeline eyed her new furniture. "You tell your father I will make good use of this.

110

You're right. I'll have my morning coffee in here. And there's a jigsaw puzzle I've been wanting to work on." It's funny the things a person thinks of when most of her possessions are being hauled away. Adeline had thought about the puzzle just as the couple who bought her old table and chairs passed by her carrying it out the door. She was going to make a point to put the puzzle together, with or without help from her friends.

Levi went back outside to check on his horse.

Mary knocked on the door a few minutes later. The girl's eyes were swollen and red. "*Gut* morning." She smiled, but it looked forced, and Adeline had never been one to beat around the bush.

"Dear girl, what's the matter?" Adeline touched the sleeve of her green dress and matching apron. "You've been crying."

Mary eased away and headed toward the kitchen carrying a bakery box. "I'm fine," she said as she walked. "And I have pastries."

Adeline wasn't going to push her. She didn't know her very well, and Mary would open up to her if she wanted to. Adeline followed her to the kitchen and breathed in the aroma of freshly baked goods. "Oh my.

111

Those smell wonderful."

Mary lifted the lid. "I chose a variety for us."

Adeline wondered if Mary had to buy the pastries or if it was a perk of working at the bakery. She eyed the whoopee pies, fried apple pies, three slices of shoofly pie, and various cakes and cookies. *Maybe we won't need lunch.*

"I'm going to go help Levi carry in a table." She smiled a little. "He was worried I couldn't handle it, but he was wrong."

"Girl power." Adeline shook a fist at Mary. She'd heard that phrase on a television show before her TV went out the door. She didn't watch it much anyway.

Levi asked Mary again, "Are you sure this won't be too heavy for you?" He'd managed to manhandle the table off the trailer, but he couldn't carry it by himself.

"*Ya,* I'm stronger than I look." She positioned her hands under the lip of one side.

He nodded as he lifted the other side, but something was wrong with Mary. She'd been crying. "You okay?" he said as they started moving, Levi walking backward.

"*Ya.* No problems. It's not as heavy as it looked anyway."

That wasn't what Levi meant, but he

didn't say anything else. The aroma of the baked goods filled his senses when they made it to the kitchen. Adeline was already enjoying a whoopee pie.

Levi was happy to see that there were a lot of pastries. He pushed the four chairs in place around the table before he walked to the box. He chose a fried apple pie, then nodded at the table. "It looks *gut* there."

Adeline turned to Mary. "Can you believe Levi's father is refusing to sell this lovely dining room set because of a few nicks in the wood here and there?"

Mary turned to the table. "It's a lovely set, but *mei daed* is the same way. If it's not perfect, he won't sell it. He has a lot of furniture in the back of his warehouse, pieces he just felt weren't up to his standards."

Levi chuckled. "Sounds like your *daed* and mine would get along real well."

Mary smiled, but it wasn't the full-faced smile she'd had the previous Saturday, and the mischievous twinkle was missing from her eyes.

Levi picked up a whoopee pie. He wanted to take three more pastries. But he resisted and decided to wait until Adeline and Mary had their fill. "I'm off to paint. The sun is out, and there's no chance of rain today."

He hesitated for a moment, sneaking another look at the dark circles below Mary's swollen eyes. Maybe she'd tell them what was wrong at lunch.

"What would you like to do today, Ms. Collins?" Mary folded her hands in front of her and tried to smile. She was still rocked about Lydia, and she wasn't sure what to do. "It's a lovely day for a buggy ride, or I can take you to the market. But either way, I'm going to do some cleaning today."

These things might help take her mind off the situation with her sister. She'd been tempted to talk to her parents, but Lydia had provided plenty of reasons why she shouldn't. Mary prayed all morning, but she wasn't getting any answers.

"Honey, I'd hate for you to clean my house." Adeline hung her head a little. "And maybe you can just call me Adeline. Isn't it common among your people to use first names?" She shrugged. " 'Ms. Collins' makes me feel old." Grinning, she brought a hand to her chest, then laughed. "Oh, wait. I *am* old." She motioned for Mary to follow her to the new breakfast area.

They both sat at the table and were quiet for a few moments.

"Adeline . . ."

The older woman looked at Mary, her expression soft but concerned.

Mary started again. "Adeline, it's okay to accept help sometimes. Having a clean house will be healthier for you. There's nothing to be ashamed of because all that furniture was in the same place, I'm guessing, for a very long time." She paused, looked past Adeline out the window. "And cleaning keeps my mind from wandering aimlessly. I don't mind it at all. I really don't. But it's a beautiful day, so we can also go for a ride in my buggy if you'd like."

Adeline stared at her long and hard, squinting her eyes a little. "I'll make a deal with you, honey." She pointed a finger at Mary. "You and I will clean this house together. We can skip the buggy ride, open all the windows, get this place aired out and cleaned up a bit, but . . ." She still had her finger pointed at Mary, only now she was wiggling it and grinning. "Then we do something fun to help with whatever is ailing you."

Mary smiled. She wasn't sure if she could tell Adeline her troubles. She barely knew the woman. But a day of cleaning would be good for her, so she just nodded.

Adeline pulled out a bucket of cleaning supplies from underneath the sink, and

Mary picked up various bottles and looked them over.

"You know, a lot of the chemicals in these commercial cleaning formulas are harmful to your health. I'll bring you some of *Mamm*'s natural solutions that she makes for us to use." She paused, worried she'd overstepped. "I mean, if that's okay."

Adeline leaned against the kitchen counter, set the bucket on the floor, then folded her arms across her chest and lifted her chin. "Exactly how long are you planning to come visit me weekly?"

Mary lowered her gaze, a bottle of glass cleaner in her hand. "Oh dear. I guess I am kind of forcing myself on you." She pressed her lips together and waited to see if she was going to be dismissed after today.

Adeline laughed. "Honey, I would never tire of your visits. But you don't need excuses to come see me. We'll get the house clean. I won't need trips to the market or buggy rides every weekend. But I will always welcome your company, so don't think you're forcing yourself on me. I know your father was friends with Percy, and you're partly here because of that. I also won't hold it against you if you never show up again."

Mary tipped her head to one side and studied Adeline. "You're very easy to be around and to talk to, and I like being here." She paused, twisting her mouth from side to side. "But also . . ."

Adeline chuckled. "I'm old, honey, not blind. You and that boy are sweet on each other."

Mary's heart fluttered. "Did he say something?"

"No. But he's as smitten with you as you are with him. It's plain to see. He's always looking at you, and I catch you sneaking peeks at him too."

Mary could feel herself blushing. "There's something about him," she said softly.

When Adeline sat down at the kitchen table, Mary did also. Adeline reached across the table and placed her hand on Mary's. "It's kindness. And kindness attracts kindness."

Mary smiled, relieved that she didn't have to hide her growing feelings for Levi.

"But you'll probably have to make the first move. Men are shy creatures."

Mary thought about the way Levi held her hand on the piano bench, but didn't say anything.

"I know it isn't your way. Amish women tend to let the men take the lead. But Levi might need a push." She took her hand back and straightened in the chair. "Now, let's get to cleaning, and if we're lucky, I'll find my jigsaw puzzle."

Mary found a cleaning solution that would work on Adeline's floors, so she decided to start there since that's where most of the dirt and dust had collected. And she kept trying to force worries about Lydia out of her mind, while knowing she couldn't keep her sister's situation from bombarding her thoughts. She wished she had someone to talk to about it.

Levi stepped off the last rung of the rickety ladder, then took a few long strides backward so he could inspect his work. He'd sanded and applied the last of the primer. It hadn't taken as long as he thought, and after a few more Saturdays, the outside of the house would be painted. He'd probably be able to knock out the trim around the windows by then too. Then he would tackle the yard and repair the fence.

He might have a couple more months of Saturdays before he had to say goodbye to Mary and Ms. Collins — or Adeline, as she'd asked him to call her. He was needed at the farm, and this was a goodwill project that couldn't go on forever.

When he walked into the house, he smelled something cooking, and right away he could tell the women had been busy cleaning. A lemony scent hung in the air, and the wood floors shone as if they'd been waxed. Most likely mopped with a special cleaner, he decided. He could no longer see the areas where furniture had once been, except for one spot in the corner of the living room, a big square, where something large and heavy must have been for a long time. He found the women in the kitchen.

"It looks nice in here. And it smells *gut.*" He went to the sink, squirted some soap into his palms, then scrubbed until he had most of the paint off his hands.

Adeline was glowing, and Mary's eyes weren't swollen and red anymore. Hard work had a way of straightening a person out. At least, that's what his *mamm* always said, and it seemed true today.

"Well, we have Mary to thank for cleaning this place up and for this fine meal. She's prepared a chicken she found in my refrigerator." Adeline pressed her palms together. "It's seasoned and stuffed and only has thirty more minutes to cook. What a treat."

"Ach, it's just an easy recipe I learned from *mei mamm.*" Mary kept her head down as she sliced tomatoes. "And Adeline helped me clean."

Levi walked to the kitchen table and eyed

119

what looked like hundreds of pieces of a puzzle. He picked up a couple. "I've seen these before in the store." When he looked up, Adeline and Mary had stopped what they were doing and stared at him.

"Young man, don't tell me you've never put together a jigsaw puzzle?" Adeline was tearing lettuce and putting it in a bowl.

Levi shook his head. "*Nee,* I've never played this game." He'd played cards with his siblings, and when he was younger they had a croquet set and a volleyball net. But he'd never played the puzzle game. "How does it work? Do you draw pieces like you draw cards?"

Adeline and Mary looked at each other, grinning, then Mary set her knife down and walked to the table where Levi was standing. "*Nee,* silly. You connect all the pieces and it makes a big picture." She smiled, and despite being embarrassed, Levi was happy she was better this afternoon.

"What's the picture gonna be?" Levi flipped a few pieces so the colored sides faced up. "There's a lot of brown and tan."

"And that's the million-dollar question," Adeline said before she chuckled. "I bought that thing at a yard sale. The woman promised me all the pieces were there. I hope she's right. There wasn't a box, and I didn't think at the time to ask what the picture was. I'll go mad if we get to the end and pieces are missing." She added the tomatoes Mary had cut to the bowl of lettuce. Levi's mouth watered as his stomach growled.

Mary batted her eyes at him. At least, that's what he thought he saw. Maybe he just wanted to believe she was flirting with him as her thick dark lashes opened and closed over high cheekbones.

"Adeline and I thought it would be fun to make a list of what the picture might be," Mary said. "Maybe each of us can write down five things and see who gets the closest."

She smelled a little like lemons, or maybe it was the whole house. Either way, she was glowing and had color in her cheeks, nothing like she looked earlier in the day. And the bird cooking in the oven, mixed with the lemon scent, somehow emitted the perfect aroma. Odd, but welcoming.

"That would be fun." He continued flipping pieces over. Since the table was covered with puzzle pieces, they'd probably sit in the parlor for lunch. He'd missed his only opportunity to play the piano since Mary and Adeline didn't go out for a ride today. Which was probably for the best. The temptation would have been there, and Levi wasn't sure he was strong enough to walk away from it.

"Lots of blue pieces too."

"I think that's water." Mary had rejoined Adeline at the kitchen counter. "Or maybe sky."

"After we eat, I say we start building the sides of the puzzle, finding all the pieces with a straight edge. Mary worked so hard today. I'd never have gotten this house so clean." Adeline patted Mary on the arm.

Levi could think of nothing better than sitting down with Mary and Adeline and working out the puzzle, but it wouldn't be right. "I've got work to do."

"It's not exactly like I'm paying you, Levi. So unless you just can't wait to get back up on that ladder, you can stay and spend a little time with us." Adeline leaned against the kitchen counter as a spoon slipped through her fingers and bounced across the tiled floor. She squeezed her eyes closed, pinched her lips together, and pressed both hands to her chest.

Levi froze for a couple seconds, then rushed to Adeline and wrapped an arm around her waist. "Adeline?"

She didn't open her eyes, but she groaned slightly.

Mary didn't waste any time reaching in

the pocket of her apron for her phone. "She's having a heart attack!" Mary's bottom lip trembled. Her hands shook as she pushed numbers on her phone.

CHAPTER 6

Adeline caught her breath, felt Levi's arm around her waist. Mary had her phone to her ear, her eyes wide, her lip trembling. "Don't call 9–1–1. I'm fine. I'm not having a heart attack." Levi kept his arm around her as she straightened.

Mary hesitated, but stowed her phone back in her apron pocket.

Levi eased his arm away from Adeline. "It looked like a heart attack. My great aunt had one during worship service a few years ago."

Adeline frowned. "I miss church." Right away, she wished she hadn't voiced the thought. One of these young people might offer to take her, and they were already doing too much as it was. "But I have my own weekly worship service right here at home, and I give thanks to the Lord daily."

"If it wasn't a heart attack, then what happened?" Mary blinked a few times. "It scared me."

Adeline scratched her forehead. "I was hoping I wouldn't have one of those episodes while you kids were visiting. They are esophageal spasms. I've suffered them for years." She shrugged. "They never last more than a few seconds usually, but the pain became unbearable a few years ago when they started to last longer and come on more frequently. My doctor put me on medication, but I've been having them more often lately. I just need to call my doctor and have the dosage increased."

Mary's forlorn expression hadn't lifted, and her bottom lip still trembled. "I should cart you to the doctor right now."

"Absolutely not." Adeline looked at the timer on her oven. "I've been dealing with those spasms for years. That bird is going to be ready soon, and I'm not missing out. I'll just call the doctor." She cringed, determined to ask God for forgiveness for the lie later. She briefly considered asking Mary to borrow her phone, but cell phones only had a certain number of minutes, and Adeline didn't want to burn up the girl's time.

"Are you sure?" Mary bit her bottom lip.

Adeline patted her on the arm as she moved toward her new kitchen table. "I say we find a few border pieces of this puzzle while we wait on the chicken." She waited until Mary and Levi were seated, then focused on the boy. "And, before I forget, Percy's closet is full of clothes and shoes, Levi. I know you wouldn't have use for some of the clothes, but his shoes might fit you, and there are several coats." She paused to take a deep cleansing breath. "I just haven't made myself clean out his belongings, but it's way past time."

Levi nodded. "That would be *gut,* Ms. Col— I mean, Adeline. If you're sure. But you don't owe us anything for the table and chairs."

"And you don't owe me for looking through Percy's clothes for items you might could use. And whatever you don't keep can go to one of the local charities for others who might benefit." Sighing, she said, "I should have done that a long time ago." Visions of her husband danced in her head. "Percy was a sharp dresser."

"*Ya,* sure." Levi was searching for puzzle pieces with a straight edge. Mary too. After lunch, Adeline would go lie down and give the two young people some time alone.

"I have another new young friend. Actually, she is a distant cousin of Percy's. She showed up on Wednesday, and we had a nice visit. She was near here for training for her job, and she'll be coming every Wednesday for a while." She paused, recalling her time with Natalie as she also began examining puzzle pieces. "Such a lovely girl. The Lord has blessed me with special new friends. Her name is Natalie, and she's about your age."

Adeline shared with Mary and Levi the little bit she knew about Natalie before the timer on the oven dinged. Mary was out of her seat right away, pulling out the bird and setting it on top of the stove.

Adeline breathed in the aroma of thyme and sage that had filled the house the past few hours, like a home with family in it. She would enjoy today with Mary and Levi, and then Natalie would be back on Wednesday. She silently thanked the Lord again for bringing these young people into her life and keeping the loneliness at bay.

Natalie knocked on her mother's front door and waited.

The door swung open after a few moments. "Why do you do that? You lived here your entire life until recently. You don't need to knock."

Natalie eyed the top of her mother's head, the dark layers spreading through the blond strands that curled inward right below her shoulders. "You need to get your roots done." She scooted past her mother toward her old bedroom. "I left something here that I need to get."

"If I could afford it, I would. Your father isn't paying child support since you turned eighteen and moved out, and since Indiana isn't an alimony state, I'm out of luck." Her mother stayed on Natalie's heels all the way to her upstairs bedroom.

"Mom, just buy the kind of dye that comes in a box. I could even do it for you." Natalie opened the drawer of what used to be her nightstand. She'd opted not to take any of her furniture when she moved out two weeks ago. She didn't want any reminders of the life she'd lived for the past two years. Prior to the divorce, her parents fought daily. She wanted a fresh start with new everything when she could afford it. Right now, sleeping on an air mattress suited her just fine. And she'd also moved out because her mother needed to learn how to function on her own.

"I'm not dying my hair out of a *box*."

Natalie shrugged. "Suit yourself." She pulled a wad of folded papers from her desk drawer. "Found it."

"Found what?" Her mother tightened the sash around her robe, then took a sip from the glass she had yet to set down. Natalie hoped it was just orange juice her mother was sipping on, but she doubted it.

"My SAT scores. I'll need them when I start applying for scholarships and grants to colleges." She should have already done that before she graduated, but the divorce had consumed all of their lives.

"I told you I don't have the money to send you to college. And you know we can't count on your father for anything." Her mother took a long drink of the orange liquid.

"That's why I'll apply for scholarships and grants. And I'll save my money."

"I don't know why you moved out, or why you left all this furniture in your room. You could have taken it. We paid a lot of money for it. It was handcrafted by the local Amish."

Natalie tucked the papers in her purse. "I'm getting a promotion at work after the training classes, so I'll just buy some new furniture. If you decide to sell the house like you mentioned, it will show better with my room full of furniture." It was a partial version of the truth, but her mother didn't argue about it anymore as she followed Natalie back to the living room. The bedroom set had been a surprise gift from her parents on her sixteenth birthday. It wasn't her style anyway. She preferred more of a shabby chic–eclectic look, as opposed to her mother's more traditional furnishings.

"I gotta go." Natalie found her keys in her purse as she walked to the door.

"I made that chicken casserole you like. You could stay and eat, at least."

She stared at the woman her mother had turned into. Bitter, unhappy all the time, and apparently going broke. "Mom, I can't stay. It's Sunday, and I have work tomorrow, and I want to review my stuff for the class before Wednesday gets here." She paused, took a deep breath, and said, "Mom. I love you. But maybe if you got a job you would be happier."

Her mother's jaw dropped. "I'm not sure what I'm qualified to do besides run a household and tend to a man."

Natalie didn't have a lot of argument for that. Her mother had never worked. She'd been totally dependent on Natalie's father, who had pretty much ditched them both when he hooked up with a younger woman he met at the gym.

"Mom, I'm upset with Dad too. But it's over and done with. The divorce is final, and you need to get on with your life." Eighteen seemed too young for role reversal, but Natalie had slipped into the position without even realizing it until now.

Her mother hugged her and kissed her on the cheek. "Good luck with the class. And let me know how it goes with Adeline."

"She's a nice lady," Natalie said just before she closed the door behind her. She'd thought the visits might be a chore, calling on an elderly woman she didn't even know. She regretted letting her mother push her into the visit, but at the time, it seemed easier than fighting with her.

But she was kind of looking forward to visiting with Adeline again, and it didn't have anything to do with money. Natalie would find her own way to get to college. Adeline reminded her of her Mimi Jean. Not a day went by that Natalie didn't miss her grandmother.

Mary had a hard time focusing on the worship service, and every time she looked at Samuel Bontrager, her stomach roiled. He was only a year older than Lydia, but he had dated a lot of girls, most of them right after they started their *rumschpringe.* The courtships never lasted very long. Mary didn't want Lydia to get her heart broken. But her sister had put up some good arguments when Mary confronted her about what she'd seen. There was a lot at stake if Mary told anyone about the relationship. The conflict was churning her insides into twisted knots.

By the time they returned home after worship, Mary found Lydia in her bedroom and entered, closing the door.

"I'm not going to talk about Samuel, if that's what you're here for," Lydia said.

Yelling at Lydia the way she had early Saturday morning hadn't worked and only fueled Lydia's determination to be with Samuel. Mary had to take another approach.

"It must be a wonderful feeling to think you are falling in love," Mary said as her thoughts spiraled to Levi, but she refocused. "But you must realize that Samuel has dated a lot of girls in our community, and he never dates them for long. I just don't want you to get hurt."

"We were just kissing. And besides, he's different with me."

Mary hoped so, for Lydia's sake.

Her sister sat on her bed, and Mary sat beside her. Lydia turned to face Mary. "If you tell *Daed,* he might fire him. Samuel provides sole support for his parents, ever since his mother took ill in the fall. You know that."

"*Ya,* I do know that. I don't want *Daed* to fire him either. But sneaking around isn't *gut.* Samuel should ask *Daed* if he can date you properly."

Lydia sighed. "Lots of couples in their *rumschpringe* sneak around."

Mary never had, but it was true. "*Ya,* I know. But *Daed* specifically told us both, when we entered into our *rumschpringe,* to be honest with him and *Mamm,* not to sneak around. They are willing to give us both some liberties, but if you get caught with Samuel, it won't go over well with our parents. You need to just tell them." Mary wasn't sure her father wouldn't fire Samuel anyway, just because of his reputation when it came to girls.

Lydia ran a brush through her long dark hair. There would never be any denying they were siblings. People had mistaken them for twins when they were younger. Lydia had Mary's dark hair and dark eyes, as well as similar facial features. But that was before Mary shot up in height and now stood at least three inches taller than her younger sister.

Lydia knotted and tucked her hair beneath her prayer covering as she huffed. "It's my life. Just don't tell anyone, at least for now."

Mary swallowed back a lump forming in

her throat as she recalled the way Samuel and Lydia had carried on in the yard. "I don't know if I can promise that."

Lydia stormed out of the room and left Mary sitting on the bed. She couldn't talk to their mother about this because *Mamm* would tell their father. Samuel was a hard worker and generally a good man. But if he took liberties with his boss's daughter, acted in a way the Lord wouldn't approve of, their father would fire him for sure.

This might explain why Lydia had been in the shop working with their father so much. Mary scanned her memory, trying to remember how much time Lydia might have been in the shop with Samuel when their father wasn't with them. She shivered to think that more could be going on between them than just kissing. She wanted to talk to Samuel, no matter how mad Lydia got. He was playing with fire and putting his family's welfare at stake.

She finally stood and went to her own room. Sunday was supposed to be a day of rest, but all Mary felt was worry, and there was nothing restful about that.

Levi dumped the clothes he'd taken from Percy's closet on the couch in the living room as his brothers hovered around like vultures. He couldn't blame them. Levi was equally anxious to go through the clothes and coats. He'd already chosen a pair of shoes and put them in his room underneath his bed. Lloyd and Ben wore the same size as Levi, and they would have taken the shoes. Levi needed them more than his brothers did.

"I don't know about wearing a dead man's clothes," Jacob said. "It might be bad luck."

Levi sighed. His people were prone to superstition, but not enough that it kept Jacob from pulling a heavy coat from the pile and trying it on.

Their mother walked into the room, frowning as she moved toward them. "Be very careful what you choose. Black slacks, blue shirts, and black shoes only." She looked at Jacob. "And you're not keeping that coat. It's much too fancy."

Levi thought his mother should bend the rules a little since there was a shortage of coats in the winter, but he stayed quiet, knowing his father would back her up.

"Adeline said to take whatever was left to a charity place." Levi managed to pull a pair of black slacks from the pile. He was taller than some of his brothers, and as he held the pants up, he thought they would be the right length. Percy had obviously been bigger around in the middle, but his sisters could take in the waist area, and they all had suspenders.

"We can drop the rest of the clothes at a place I know of on Saturday when you cart me to Widow Stutzman's *haus*." His mother limped toward her room, and Levi followed her.

"I can't, *Mamm*. I go to Adeline's on Saturday. We always visit Widow Stutzman during the week."

"You'll just have to skip this Saturday at Adeline's. Annie is out of town all week visiting relatives near Bloomington."

"Why can't someone else take you?" Levi heard the snappiness in his voice, and his mother apparently did too. She turned to face him, and thrust her hands on her hips. "Everyone will be working that day."

"I have work plans that day too. Why can't one of the girls drive you? Or you could drive yourself." He winced, regretting that last part.

His mother's eyes narrowed into slits, her nostrils flaring. "The girls will be helping their friend Rachel with her wedding preparations. It's been planned for two weeks. And I don't drive the buggy anymore. You know that."

The room behind them had gone quiet.

No one ever mentioned their mother's decision not to drive the buggy anymore. Levi had noticed that one of his brothers — or his father — had pounded out the dent, which was now barely visible.

"If this is about that girl you see at Adeline's, then maybe you should invite her here. Maybe for Sunday supper since we don't have worship service."

His brothers snickered, and Levi huffed before he left the room. He didn't answer his mother. He wasn't proud of his behavior, but there was no way he was going to invite Mary to his house. He suspected her home life was perfectly organized. What would she think about the reign of chaos at Levi's house?

He would have to mail Adeline a note explaining why he wouldn't be there. Hopefully it would arrive before Saturday. He hadn't realized how much he looked forward to the visits until now. He recalled the fine meal they'd had, working on the puzzle, and the feeling of accomplishment he felt after finishing a large part of the painting later in the day. And before Levi had gone back to work, Adeline laid down for a nap, which left him a little time with Mary by himself.

Levi had been pleasantly surprised at all the things they had in common in addition to their love of music. They both had a fondness for cats, which wasn't something Levi mentioned to many people since it didn't seem very manly. They had read some of the same Christian books. They both despised beets, fried eggs, and liver with onions.

But it was more than their common interests that kept Mary at the forefront of his thoughts. She was beautiful, but something about her made his heart rate speed up every time he was around her.

Adeline had managed to connect one side of the puzzle border while drinking her coffee Wednesday morning. She'd been up and dressed about an hour when Natalie pulled in her driveway. The girl had a blue SUV about the same color as the car Adeline had before the estate sale. A woman had purchased it for her teenage daughter.

"I'm so glad you came back," Adeline said when she opened the front door. "Although I'm not sure if I'm good company for someone your age." She chuckled.

Natalie stepped across the threshold and smiled. "Wow. It smells good in here, like lemons." She glanced around the house. "You've been busy cleaning."

Adeline sighed. "I wish I could take credit,

but I have two young Amish friends who come to see me every Saturday. Levi is painting the outside of the house, and Mary did almost all the cleaning inside. This coming Saturday I think we're going to the market. They are wonderful friends. I haven't known them long, but Percy knew their parents."

"I noticed the fresh paint on the outside of the house. It looks nice."

"They're getting the place spiffed up, that's for sure." Adeline motioned for Natalie to follow her into the kitchen. "They brought me a kitchen table and chairs."

Natalie moved closer to the table and hung her purse over the back of one of the chairs. "I'm a whiz at puzzles. Mom says I had a natural knack for it." She smiled. "I haven't worked on one in forever."

"You're here earlier than last time. Would you like to work on it with me? I'm still trying to get the border finished."

Natalie pulled out a chair. "Sure, I've actually got a couple hours until my class starts." She began searching for border pieces and setting them aside.

"How is your mother doing? We didn't talk much about her during your last visit, just that your parents had divorced not long ago."

"She's okay, I guess. Dad left her for another woman, someone a lot younger, and Mom is super bitter about everything." She glanced up for a moment. "I don't really see my dad. He sends me a text every now and then." She hooked two border pieces together as she shrugged.

Adeline shook her head. "That's a shame. I suppose divorce is like death in some ways."

Natalie clicked a few more pieces of the border together. "Maybe this is wrong of me to say, but they probably should have gotten a divorce a long time ago. They fought all the time. I finally moved out a couple weeks ago. My mother needs to learn how to function on her own, and I just needed a fresh start."

"Where do you live?"

"On the outskirts of Montgomery. You might remember us living on the other side of Indianapolis, but we moved about four years ago so Dad could be closer to his job. I didn't get a place too far from Mom because I worry about her, but it's a little closer to work. But I just couldn't live under the same roof with her anymore. I rented an apartment. It's super small. I'm saving my money to get the things I need."

Adeline thought for a few moments as she

pulled the tan puzzle pieces into a pile. "I have a lot of room in this big old house. I sold most of my belongings. You know, simplifying things. But I do have a spare bedroom that didn't get stripped like most of the house. A few pieces sold, but there is still a twin bed and a small dresser in there. You'd be welcome to stay with me if you'd like to save on rent. Montgomery isn't that far by car."

Natalie stopped lining up puzzle pieces to see if they'd fit and locked eyes with Adeline. "Really? You'd let me live here?"

"Of course. You're family." Adeline had enjoyed her time with Mary and Levi, but it was only on Saturdays. If Natalie lived with her it would feel almost like having a granddaughter living with her.

"Ms. Collins, that's so nice of you to offer." She smiled. "But I want to try to make it on my own. I'm terrified of ending up like my mother. She has no skills other than being a housewife. I want to get a good education so I can always be independent, no matter what life throws my way."

Adeline's vision of a granddaughter faded, but it didn't disappear. She had three new young people in her life, and she was grateful for that.

"Well, I'm proud of you. And maybe you

can just call me Adeline. Mary and Levi do."

They worked on the puzzle quietly for a while, then Natalie cleared her throat. "I-I do have a favor to ask, though. And if it's too much trouble, please tell me. I just really don't want to ask my mother because every time I talk to her it turns into a conversation about the divorce and how awful my dad is."

Adeline hoped the favor didn't have anything to do with money. She'd help Natalie with anything she needed, but by the time she'd gotten caught up on bills with money from the estate sale, she had barely enough left to live on. She was trying to save her small social security checks to rebuild her savings, in case of anything unexpected. "What's the favor, dear?"

Natalie took her purse from the back of the chair. "I'm applying for college scholarships and grants, and I had to write an essay for them about the person who has most influenced my life. Would you be interested in reading it?" Her cheeks turned a bit pink.

Relief washed over Adeline as she pressed her palms together and smiled. "I would love to. I actually used to be an English teacher."

Natalie nibbled on a fingernail for a few seconds. "Uh-oh. Grammar isn't my strong suit. You'll probably pick up on that."

"Well it's a good thing you asked me to help you. If the emotion is there, we can fix the grammar."

Natalie handed Adeline her essay. No way she wanted her mother to read it. She'd only skim through it and pretend to be interested, then want to talk about the divorce.

"Thank you so much for agreeing to read it." Natalie excused herself to go to the bathroom. She crossed through the parlor — as Adeline referred to it — since her mother would surely ask her about the piano. She leaned close to look at the inscription, and sure enough, it was a Steinway.

Natalie didn't know anything about pianos or their value, but her mother had specifically mentioned that brand. She wasn't sure if she should tell her mother the piano was a Steinway. She left the room and walked down the hallway.

Adeline had referred to her home as a big old house. It really wasn't that big, although it had several rooms. As she made her way down the hallway, she passed by an empty bedroom with nothing but a few boxes stacked against the wall, then she slowed her stride when she passed by a room with a twin bed and a small dresser. She tiptoed inside and tried to envision it being her bedroom. Her room at home had been twice the size, but this one was about the same size bedroom she had at her apartment. It was cozy with light-tan walls and two windows. There were square smudges where pictures had hung, and a few nails still in the wall.

She walked out and saw another room, the door just barely cracked. She pushed it all the way open. There was an air mattress, about the size of the one Natalie was sleeping on. It was covered with a bedspread and two pillows in shams, like a regular bed. There wasn't any other furniture in the large room.

Natalie found the bathroom, and when she was back in the kitchen, she stood by the kitchen table. Her cousin looked up.

"Adeline, why are you sleeping on an air mattress?" She hung her head for a few seconds. "Sorry, I just wanted to see the rest of your house, and the door was cracked."

"Honey, you're welcome in any room in this house. As for the air mattress, I'm fine with that. I really am." Adeline refocused on the puzzle.

Natalie sat down, but she wasn't interested

in the puzzle anymore. "Why don't you sleep in the room across the hall with the twin bed in it?"

There was a hint of a smile on Adeline's face as she locked eyes with Natalie. "I spent my entire married life in my bedroom with Percy. After all my furniture sold, I couldn't bear not to lay my head down and picture him next to me."

"But we could move the twin bed into your room." Natalie couldn't stand the thought of someone Adeline's age sleeping on an air mattress. She thought of her Mimi Jean, who would have been around the same age.

"It would seem strange for me to sleep in that small bed." She lowered her gaze. "It's silly, I know, but all these years later, I still sometimes reach over looking for Percy. I'm perfectly fine sleeping on that air mattress."

Natalie's wheels were turning. "But if you had a queen-size bed, would you sleep in it?"

"I reckon I would, but I'm in no hurry to purchase one." Adeline avoided Natalie's eyes as a blush filled her cheeks.

Natalie suspected the estate sale had been a way for Adeline to get money. She let the subject go so as not to embarrass her further.

They worked on the puzzle for a while longer, losing track of time. When Natalie glanced at the time on her cell phone, she stood up abruptly and lifted her purse from the chair. "I have to go. I didn't realize I'd been here this long, but I enjoyed our visit. Thank you for saying you'd read my essay. It definitely needs proofing before I send it in."

Adeline stood and hugged her. "I'm happy you asked me to read it. And will I see you next Wednesday?"

"I'll be here." Natalie stared at the puzzle, at the groups of colors that had been separated. "There's a lot of tan and blue in this puzzle. Where's the box? What's it a picture of?"

Adeline chuckled. "I have no idea. I bought it at a yard sale. The pieces were in a plastic bag."

Natalie looked at the blue and white pieces, likely sky. There was another shade of blue bunched off to one side that looked like maybe the ocean. And there was some red. "It's hard to tell without the border done and only a few inside pieces fitting together so far, but it looks like a beach scene."

"I used to love the beach when I was young. I hope it's a beach scene."

146

Natalie continued staring at the pieces. Adeline was right. It was too soon to tell.

"My young Amish friend, Mary, suggested that she, Levi, and I should each write down five ideas about what the puzzle might be. You should do the same."

"I'll do that next Wednesday when there's more of it put together." Natalie studied the colored groupings. "It could be anything, I guess, but I think my vote would be that it's something red on the beach. All that tan has to be sand."

She told Adeline goodbye and hugged her again. After she was in her car, she thought about what to tell her mother. Should she tell her about the Steinway? If she told her Adeline had offered for Natalie to move in with her, Mom would have a fit that Natalie declined the offer, since that might have solidified Adeline leaving the house to them.

But as she called her mother, another subject was on her mind. And it would require telling her a big fat lie.

Chapter 7

Mary was surprised that she beat Levi to Adeline's. He'd gotten there before her the last two weekends. She carried a box of pastries across the front yard, pausing to look around the corner in case Levi was there without a buggy for some reason. But no ladder or painting supplies were in sight.

"Oh, more goodies." Adeline opened the door for Mary. "Levi will be disappointed he won't be here to enjoy them."

Mary's heart sank as she followed Adeline to the kitchen and placed the box on the counter. "*Ach,* is Levi ill?"

Adeline lifted the lid of the box and chose a fried apple pie. "These make my mouth water." She took a bite. Mary waited.

"Oh. Levi. I received a letter from him yesterday saying he was needed at home, but he would see us next Saturday."

Mary took a chocolate donut from the box, keeping her eyes down as she tried to hide her disappointment.

"I'm afraid you're stuck with just me today." Adeline finished chewing a bite of the pie. "And it's dreary weather for a buggy ride or a trip to the market. Honey, you didn't have to come in this weather, and you don't have to stay."

"I look forward to it." Mary put the donut on a napkin. "And not just because Levi is here."

Adeline chuckled. "Well, I suppose it is good that you came." Smiling, she lifted an envelope from the counter near the box of pastries. "Because Levi also sent a letter for you. I suppose he didn't know your address."

Mary's adrenaline spiked as she took the letter and hurriedly ran her finger under the seam. She had stalked the mailman waiting for a letter from Levi eight years ago. Smiling, she unfolded a piece of white paper, and in squiggly handwriting, she read,

Dear Mary,

I have to take *Mamm* somewhere on Saturday. She doesn't drive the buggy anymore. I'll miss seeing you and Adeline. Do you want to meet me at the pizza place not far from Adeline's on Tuesday for supper? We could meet at four so you can get home before dark. There's not time for you to write me back. I'll be there at four. I like the food there, even if you can't make it. But I'll be hoping you're there.

Your friend,
Levi

Mary smiled, reread the letter, and looked up at Adeline. "He wants me to meet him at the pizza place not far from here for supper on Tuesday night." She paused, biting her bottom lip. "Do you think that's like a date?"

Adeline giggled. "Yes, dear. I think that's exactly what it is." She pointed a finger at Mary. "I told you that fellow was sweet on you."

Mary smiled. "I like him too."

Adeline winked at her. "I know."

Mary walked over to the kitchen table and eyed the puzzle. "You got a lot done on the puzzle."

Adeline joined her. "I've had a few sleepless nights I worked on it, but Natalie — the cousin of Percy's I told you about — she worked on it with me for a while on Wednesday."

"We can work on it today if you like. I brought you some of *Mamm*'s natural cleaning supplies. They're in my buggy."

Adeline pulled out a kitchen chair. "Levi was right. This room gets so much light, and I've enjoyed having my coffee here in the mornings. I don't know why I never did that before when I had a dining table here." Pausing, she picked up a puzzle piece. "But, honey, this house is cleaner than it's been in years. I say we play hooky on chores and just work on the puzzle. Or if you have other errands to do, don't let me keep you."

Mary sat down across from Adeline. "I don't have anything else to do, and working on the puzzle will take my mind off things."

They were quiet for a few minutes as they fitted pieces.

"Mary, it was obvious last Saturday that you were upset. I don't want to pry, but I'm a good listener if you need someone to talk to."

Mary twisted her mouth back and forth, considering the idea as she fit two pieces together. But what would Adeline think? Mary's mother said it was never good to air family problems with others, especially *Englisch* outsiders. But Adeline might be the only person Mary could talk to about Lydia and Samuel. Adeline didn't have any ties to their community, and as far as Mary knew, she didn't have many visitors.

After thinking it over for a few minutes, she told Adeline about seeing Lydia and Samuel together and about the complications that could arise if Mary told their parents.

"Samuel is a *gut* man. But he has dated so many girls and then broken up with them." Mary paused, avoiding Adeline's eyes. "I'm worried about Lydia getting hurt, and I hope there hasn't been anything more than kissing going on."

She finally looked up at her friend, and Adeline was frowning. Mary feared she'd made a mistake by telling her, that the woman would judge her family.

"Honey, I can see the pickle you're in. You don't want a good young man to lose his only source of income, but you also don't want your sister to get hurt." Adeline tapped a finger to her chin. "You said you hope there hasn't been more than kissing going on. Do you think there has been?"

Mary thought for a few moments. "I'd like to believe Lydia wouldn't let that happen."

Adeline shook her head. "I'm sure even Amish boys have desires that could tempt a young girl like Lydia to venture in a direction she's too young to travel."

Mary closed her eyes and let out a heavy breath. "That worries me a little, but I'm more concerned she'll get hurt. But I don't want Samuel to lose his job, and *mei daed* wouldn't be happy that they were sneaky about their relationship. But he'd be even more upset if Samuel hurt Lydia."

Adeline stared at Mary for a few seconds, her lips pressed together, her eyebrows drawn into a frown. "If your father were to fire him, that is a consequence of his actions and nothing you should feel bad about. There are other jobs out there, I'm sure." She clicked her tongue. "Dating the boss's daughter is risky business if things go badly."

"Lydia will hate me if I tell *mei* parents." Mary hung her head when she thought about that possibility. "But if Samuel holds true to his past relationships, this whole thing with him and Lydia won't last long. It's probably best to just stay quiet and see what happens. I just hope they don't get caught."

A knock at the door interrupted their conversation.

"Maybe Levi made it after all." Mary's worries about Lydia didn't vanish, but they diminished at the thought of seeing Levi.

"Could be." Adeline stood up. "I'm not expecting anyone."

Mary followed Adeline to the front door,

her stomach doing the now familiar flips when she thought about Levi. But it wasn't Levi standing on the other side of the screen when Adeline opened the door. It was two *Englisch* men. They were young. Teenagers.

"Are you Adeline Collins?" the heavier of the two boys asked.

"Yes." Adeline and Mary peered around the men at a small U-Haul truck. "Why?"

"We have a delivery for you. Just tell us where you want it."

Adeline's mouth was open, her eyes wide. "I didn't order anything."

"It's a bed, a dresser, two nightstands, and a desk and chair." The smaller boy tucked his hands in the pockets of his jeans.

Adeline didn't say anything, but her jaw was dropped. "You must have the wrong address."

"Nope. It's the right address. And it's some cool furniture." The smaller guy smiled as he glanced at Mary. "It's all handcrafted by the Amish, I was told. Can we bring it in?"

"Who is it from?" Adeline peered around the boys to have another look at the truck.

"Can't say." The heavier boy raised an eyebrow, waiting.

"Yes, I suppose so. Although I can't imagine who would do such a thing."

Mary gasped after the boys were off the porch and crossing the yard toward the truck. "It's from Levi. It must be."

Adeline's eyes widened even more. "How much non-perfect furniture does that boy's family have holed up?" She twisted her mouth back and forth. "I suppose my bedroom is where it should go."

Mary had never seen Adeline's bedroom. The door had always been closed when she walked down the hallway.

"What about the furniture in your bedroom now? Will they move that to the empty bedroom? I saw it on my way to the bathroom."

Adeline sighed. "I think we can ready the room before they return with the first item."

Mary followed Adeline through the parlor, down the hallway, and into her room. An air mattress was the only thing in the room, the covers on it pulled back, and two pillows pushed to one side.

"Is this where you've been sleeping?" Mary brought a hand to her chest.

"Honey, don't look so upset. I don't need much."

Mary stifled tears as she thought about Adeline sleeping on the floor. What else was this woman doing without? Why hadn't she mentioned she didn't have a bed? Why wasn't she sleeping in the room with the twin bed?

Adeline and Mary stood off to one side as the boys carried in the box springs, mattress, dresser, nightstands, and a small desk and chair. Adeline didn't hesitate about where to put things as she latched onto Mary's hand.

"I don't think Levi's people have much money," she said, her voice cracking. "And their generosity overwhelms me." She swiped at her eyes with her other hand. "There doesn't look to be anything wrong with this furniture."

"Do you have sheets to fit a bed this size?" Mary squeezed Adeline's hand.

The older woman's face lit up. "I do. They're in the closet at the end of the hallway."

"I'll help you make it up."

Mary couldn't get over Levi's generosity either. She couldn't wait to see him on Tuesday.

She was also wondering what furniture her father might have stashed in his workshop. *Maybe something for Adeline's living room?* Mary sat on that brown couch only once, and right away she understood why Adeline preferred the parlor and why no one had purchased the old piece of furniture. There were springs poking out of the worn fabric.

Thinking about her father's workshop brought her thoughts back to Lydia and Samuel. She prayed God would keep her sister safe.

Adeline settled into her new bed Saturday evening. It was a solid oak four-poster bed with a matching dresser and two night-stands. In the corner where she'd once had her mother's rocking chair, there was now a desk and chair. She'd spent all afternoon moving clothes she'd been storing in plastic bins in her closet. She filled the drawers, sang while she worked, and repeatedly thanked the Lord for His blessings. And Adeline's back thanked her. It hadn't been as easy as she'd thought sleeping on an air mattress. Her bed sold for very little, and she'd wished more than once she had kept it.

She fluffed her pillows behind her, rubbed some lotion on her hands, and reached for Natalie's essay on the nightstand. She hadn't critiqued a project since she taught high school English decades ago.

Adeline wasn't far into Natalie's essay when she brought her hand to her chest, the emotional impact of the girl's words touching her deeply. Natalie had chosen to write about her Mimi Jean and how the woman had influenced her. She also wrote about her hopes and dreams for the future, but it was the last paragraph that gripped Adeline's heart.

> It is not the events in my life that will define who I am, but how I interpret them and choose to move forward. Being intentional and practicing due diligence is how I will become the person I want to be. The path won't always be sturdy beneath my feet, but laying the foundation stone by stone will strengthen and guide my journey.

Adeline smiled, believing a bright future was in store for young Natalie.

Natalie flipped through TV channels from her perch on the air mattress, wondering only a little what her friends were doing on a Saturday night while she was curled up with a bowl of microwave popcorn and already in her pajamas at seven o'clock.
A peaceful feeling swept over her. It was quiet. No yelling and screaming between her parents, on the phone or otherwise. And she didn't have to have the same daily conversations with her mother about what a

horrible man her father was.

She felt good about giving Adeline her furniture. And she'd stumbled upon an employee at work who was selling a 20-inch television for thirty dollars. Bingo. It had been a good day. Her apartment came with cable, so all she had to do was hook it up.

Jeremy and Paul had whined at first about delivering the furniture to Adeline, but Natalie quickly reminded them that they owed her. The brothers had been her neighbors before she'd moved, and Natalie had repeatedly seen them sneaking out of their window, and she'd never blabbed. She'd also helped Paul patch up things with his girlfriend more than once.

Her cell phone rang, interrupting her perfect Saturday night. She figured she couldn't ignore her mother's calls anymore.

"I have been calling you since Wednesday night. Did you run out of minutes or something?" Her mother huffed before she went on. "I want to know how it went with Adeline and how you're enjoying having your own furniture in your apartment. It must feel good to sleep in your own bed. Although, I miss you terribly, and it's only been a couple weeks."

Natalie squeezed her eyes closed and took a deep breath. "Everything at Adeline's went fine. But . . ." She braced for the yelling and screaming that was about to pierce her eardrums. "I didn't keep the furniture, Mom. And before you start yelling, let me tell you why. Adeline was sleeping on an air mattress on the floor, and yes . . . I am, too, but she's old, Mom. I had it delivered to her house."

Silence.

"Mom? Please don't be mad. I'll buy furniture when I've saved more money, and it won't be long. I found a place that does rent-to-own, so I'll have my own furniture soon. You said the bedroom set was mine. So I figured I was free to give it away. I know you always loved it, but it really wasn't my style, and I think Adeline needed it more than me."

More silence.

"Mom? Say something."

"I think that was a *brilliant* move. You are ingratiating yourself into that woman's life. So kind and giving of you. She'll see that. She'll leave you her house, and then we can sell it and put you through college."

Natalie had a college fund prior to the divorce, and it had remained untouched at her father's insistence, until one day her mother cleaned it out. And Natalie didn't see her replenishing it. Even if she did, they

160

didn't deserve Adeline's house. Surely the woman had others she was close to. But for now, Natalie didn't feel the need to tell her mother she'd given Adeline the furniture anonymously.

"What about the piano? Did you notice if it was a Steinway?"

Natalie squeezed her eyes closed and cringed. So far, she'd been able to stray from lying. She told her mother she was sending Jeremy and Paul to pick up her bedroom furniture, and her mother had assumed it was for Natalie's apartment. But this was a direct question.

"It's a Steinway." Natalie cringed. "But it looks really old, and the ivory keys are even a little yellow." She reached for a handful of popcorn.

"Fantastic! That's wonderful." She paused. "Is that a TV I hear in the background? I'm surprised you're not out on a Saturday night, and where did you get a TV? I offered you the one in the study, but you didn't want it."

"You stay in there and watch TV sometimes. I didn't want to take that one. A guy at work sold me a small one for thirty bucks. It's all I need right now."

"Well, hopefully Adeline will leave us the house, but if she doesn't, hopefully we'll at least get the Steinway because that's bound to be worth something, maybe a few thousand dollars. That would get you started in college."

Natalie didn't want any part of her mother's plan, but she didn't want to stop seeing Adeline either. Adeline was the closest person she had who reminded her of Mimi Jean, and there was a feeling of safety in Adeline's house. Natalie hadn't felt safe in her own house for years. It wasn't a lack of safety in the literal sense. Her parents hadn't ever been violent or anything like that. But here at her apartment and at Adeline's, she felt emotionally safe, and that had become as important to her as physical safety — maybe more so.

Sunday morning Mary overslept, something she rarely did. But sleep hadn't come easily the night before. She'd tried to catch Samuel by himself Saturday afternoon and into the evening to see if she could feel out his intentions with Lydia. He wasn't required to work on Saturdays, but he had lately, and now Mary knew why.

It occurred to her that her father did very little work on Saturdays, which left more opportunities for Lydia and Samuel to be alone. Despite Mary's efforts, she hadn't been able to talk to him. After dark she'd paced back and forth between the bed and the window, deciding that if she caught the two together again, she was going to confront them and tell them that if she could see them together, so could their parents. Maybe that would scare Samuel into being forthright about his relationship with Lydia. But all was quiet into the evening, and even now the house was eerily quiet.

She looked at the clock on her nightstand, but the battery had gone dead. It was daybreak, so she was sure it wasn't three in the morning. She sat up rubbing her eyes, guessing it must be around seven based on the height of the sun. But why wasn't bacon cooking? It wasn't a church day, so whoever got up first usually started breakfast, unless it was their father. He'd sip coffee on the porch until the meal was ready.

Mary dressed quickly, but didn't even run a brush through her hair. In her gut, something didn't feel right. She rushed down the stairs, and when she shuffled into the kitchen barefoot, only her mother sat at the table, which wasn't set. No coffee percolated on top of the stove, and no eggs or pans sat on the counter.

Mary wrapped her arms across her stomach. Her mother didn't even look up when she entered the room, but held her forehead in her hands, her elbows resting on the table. The last time Mary felt this sobering mood was when her grandfather died.

"*Mamm,* what's wrong?" Mary's heart pounded, making her feel a little light-headed. Her mother finally looked up with red, swollen eyes. Scowling, she stood and faced Mary.

"You *knew*! You knew about Lydia and Samuel." Her mother's fists were clenched at her sides, and Mary instinctively backed up. Her mother had never lashed out at her physically. Mary and Lydia used to giggle after they got spankings from their mother because it was barely a light swat. But the accusing look in her mother's eyes, the clenched fists, and the way she was trembling from head to toe caused Mary to take another step back. "How could you not have told us?"

A tear rolled down Mary's cheek. "I just found out a few days ago."

Her mother covered her face with her hands and cried. Mary was speechless for a few seconds, surprised that her mother was reacting this strongly. Then Mary recalled the way she had yelled at Lydia, much the same as her mother was yelling at her now. She wanted to tell her mother it was only kissing, but Mary had a strong reaction when she saw Lydia and Samuel being intimate. *Mamm*'s maternal instincts likely overpowered Mary's sisterly concerns. Or did their mother or father catch Lydia doing something more than kissing with Samuel?

"*Mamm,* I'm sorry," Mary said through her tears. "I didn't know what to do. I was afraid *Daed* would fire Samuel, and how would he support his family? I tried to talk to Lydia about it, about Samuel's relationships with girls . . ." She locked eyes with her mother. "I'm sorry."

When her mother finally uncovered her face, she took a tissue from her apron pocket and dabbed at her eyes. Then she pulled Mary into a hug.

"I'm sorry, *mei maedel.* I'm just so upset and angry." She eased back, pushed Mary's hair away from her face, then kissed her on the cheek.

Still sniffling, Mary said, "I saw them kissing outside this past week, and I talked to Lydia about it the next morning and tried again another time. But she wouldn't listen. I knew you and *Daed* would be upset that she was sneaking around, but I was hoping it would just end on its own, the way Samuel's other relationships have."

"Samuel and Lydia have shamed both of our families." Her mother shook her head, starting to cry harder. "Your *daed* and Lydia are on their way to Samuel's house now to discuss the situation with his family. I just couldn't bring myself to go."

"Mamm, I know it's not ideal. But Lydia *is* in her *rumschpringe."* Mary's mother had worked hard to have a perfect house, to raise proper children, and to maintain a high level of esteem in a community that didn't demand it. But Lydia hadn't officially gone against the *Ordnung,* no matter how much this upset her parents. *Shame* seemed a strong word. "No one knows since apparently their escapades have only been here."

Her mother locked eyes with Mary, her chin jutting out, eyes wild like a feral cat. "The entire community will know when the *boppli* arrives in seven months."

Mary's jaw dropped as she latched on to the back of the kitchen chair to steady herself.

CHAPTER 8

Levi checked the clock on the wall of the pizzeria. It was four fifteen. Maybe Mary was just running late, but he feared she wasn't coming. Could his invitation for supper have been too forward? He wasn't sure he would have had the nerve to ask her out in person, so he'd taken advantage of the opportunity to write her a letter.

He reached into his pocket and counted his money again, hoping she didn't want a salad or breadsticks with the pizza. He had already planned to order water, so if she ordered a soda, he would still have enough for the meal.

Levi had talked to his father about taking on some extra painting jobs after Adeline's house was done, maybe even some outside of their district. Surprisingly, his father said it might be all right. His brothers all had side jobs, but only in their district since that's all their father would allow. They all

167

had more pocket money than Levi. The little bit of money he had saved was from breaking two horses for a neighbor a few weeks ago. In the end it hadn't felt like a victory because he'd cracked a rib in the process.

He was lost in thought and didn't see Mary until she slid into the booth seat across from him. "Sorry I'm late."

He opened his mouth to say something but froze. Just like almost every other woman he was around, Mary didn't have on any makeup. Her dark hair was tucked beneath her *kapp.* He'd seen her this exact same way before. Had missing one Saturday caused him to forget how beautiful she was?

"Wie bischt?" he finally said, hoping the shakiness in his voice wasn't as obvious as it sounded to him. He'd been a little nervous around her at Adeline's some of the time, but not like this. He'd have to carry the conversation if she didn't. Adeline was cheerful and always talking, so there hadn't been any awkward moments. Levi could feel one building if he didn't think of something else to say. "I'm glad you could make it."

The waitress took their order. One pepperoni pizza with extra cheese. Two waters. No breadsticks or salad. Levi hoped it wouldn't always be like this. Adeline would give him a good reference, so once he started some painting jobs that paid, hopefully he could save more. And eventually get his own house.

When the waitress turned the corner and was out of sight, Mary reached across the table and took one of his hands in both of hers and held tightly. Levi looked around to see if anyone was watching. Public affection was frowned upon in his district.

"What you did for Adeline . . ." She sighed, smiling. "It was a wonderful thing to do."

Levi felt as much like a deer in the headlights as he probably looked. "Huh?"

Mary chuckled. "The furniture. All that beautiful bedroom furniture you had delivered." She shook her head, still clutching his hand. "Although neither Adeline nor I could find more than a few little nicks here and there. And we had to really look hard. I couldn't believe it when I saw that she's been sleeping on a blow-up mattress in her room. How did you know?"

Levi's jaw dropped farther. He forced his mouth closed and remembered he had his hat on, so he eased his hand out from under hers, took off his hat, and lay it on the seat next to him. Then he scratched his chin. "I'm sorry, but I don't know what you're talking about."

Mary chuckled again, and it made her dimples show. She found his hand again when he put it on the table. He liked that she wasn't afraid to show affection in public, even if it was just hand-holding. But it was new to him.

"You don't have to pretend with me. It was a wonderful thing to do. I'm even going to ask my father if maybe he has some spare furniture in his shop that we could give to Adeline. She needs a couch, at the least. Have you ever sat on the one she has in the front room?" She frowned as she shook her head. "It has springs poking out everywhere."

Levi was having trouble forming thoughts with her hands on his, and he still had no idea what she was talking about. "Um . . ."

"I'm sure Adeline sold her belongings because she didn't have enough money to sustain her. It's wonderful the way you are helping her refurnish her house. She's such a dear woman, don't you think? And not to mention, you are doing all that work outside, painting and all."

Levi eased his hand from hers, probably quicker than he should have because she stopped smiling. "Mary, I didn't send any bedroom furniture to Adeline's house. I have no notion as to what you're talking about."

She sat taller, pressed her lips together for a few seconds. Then she slumped against the bench. "If it wasn't you, maybe someone else in your family? The furniture is beautiful, and one of the delivery boys said it was handcrafted by the Amish."

Levi shook his head. "*Nee,* I would know. I don't know of any bedroom furniture that *mei daed* would be giving away." He paused as the server brought two waters and a pepperoni pizza. After Mary thanked her, Levi said, "It had to be another friend of hers."

"I don't think she has any friends. I mean, I think she used to see people before she wasn't able to drive anymore. But she looks forward to our visits so much, I think she gets lonely."

"*Ach,* well, somehow a *gut* Samaritan must have gotten word that Adeline needed a bed."

"It's more than a bed." Mary picked up a piece of pizza. "It's a bed, two nightstands, a dresser, and a small writing desk and chair." She was about to take a bite of the pizza but held it away as she locked eyes with Levi. "Adeline was so happy, she cried."

Levi's heart was full. This was a good day.

He loved hearing the good news for Adeline, and he was spending time with Mary. He said a silent prayer of thanks as he chose a slice of pizza. Levi was sure he could eat the entire thing, so he would try to eat slowly to make sure Mary had enough.

"What about that cousin Adeline said was coming over on Wednesdays? Maybe she sent the furniture." Levi couldn't keep his eyes from drifting to Mary's lips. He'd wanted to kiss her since the day he saw her at Adeline's as a grown woman. At ten, he'd only been afraid she'd tell someone he played Percy's piano.

"Maybe. But that would seem like a huge coincidence that the cousin's family was in the furniture business too. Don't you think?"

Levi forced himself to finish chewing and then swallow, something he wouldn't have done at home. But Mary was proper, so Levi was determined to do better about his manners.

"My family isn't really in the furniture business. We mostly farm. Jacob just builds some furniture on the side. But *Daed* is real picky about it. He doesn't want anything going out that isn't perfect."

"Well, whoever sent it did a *gut* thing." She took a sip of water.

He smiled, trying to work up the courage to ask her what he'd been thinking about since he wrote and mailed her letter. Her eyes homed in on his face.

She tapped a finger to the left side of her nose. "How did you get that scar?"

He instinctively reached up and touched it.

"It doesn't look bad or anything. I was just wondering about it."

Levi had been reprimanded by his bishop only once in his life, and the scar was his constant reminder. "I got in a fight at school when I was twelve." He could still remember the terror he felt when the bishop arrived to talk to him and the other boy, who moved away about a year later.

Mary grinned. "So you were a fighter, *ya*?"

Levi shook his head. "*Nee.* It was a one-time thing."

They were quiet for a few moments as Levi thought about that day on the playground. He'd gone against their ways and promised the Lord that he'd never fight again. With six brothers, he'd had plenty of temptations.

"Will you be at Adeline's Saturday?" Mary asked. She was still working on her first piece of pizza.

"Um, *ya.* I'll be there." Levi had downed

three slices, and his focus kept shifting from Mary's lips to the uneaten pizza still on the pan.

"Gut." She smiled at him.

His courage was building. She'd shown up, held his hand, and now she wanted to make sure he would be at Adeline's Saturday.

"I want to ask you something." He'd gone out with a few girls in his district, but not enough to feel confident about putting his heart on the table. "I'd like to, um . . . take you on a date. I mean, a real date." He raised an eyebrow and waited for her reaction.

She playfully batted her eyes at him. "I thought this was a *real* date."

"Well, *ya.* It is." Levi could feel his face turning red. "But *mei daed* is a stickler about manners. I'd like to pick you up and take you somewhere, and he said I need to meet your family."

Her expression fell flat. Not even the hint of a dimple remained. Levi should have expected this. Her family was obviously well-off, and they were real modern. Levi's family lived the way generations before him lived. Those differences shouldn't matter, but maybe they mattered to Mary.

The server returned with the check and

placed it on the table by Levi. He picked it up and knew right away he didn't have enough money. Extra cheese was two dollars, and he surely didn't have money for a tip. He reached into his pocket, pulled out some bills, and began fumbling with the few coins he had, counting them out on the table.

Mary came to his aid. "I'd like to leave the tip, if that's okay."

He couldn't even look at her as she reached into her purse and placed a five-dollar bill on the table. Levi opened his mouth to tell her he didn't need it, but the server came back right then. Levi put the money on the tray, including Mary's five-dollar bill.

"Thanks," he mumbled.

She's embarrassed to introduce me to her family. Can't say that I blame her.

Mary's heart beat like a bass drum. Levi was blushing, clearly embarrassed that he was short on cash, but Mary couldn't care less about that. She didn't want to lie to Levi, but there was no way she could introduce him to her family right now. It was horrible at her house, and twice she'd heard her father yelling — once at Lydia and once at *Mamm.* There had been lots of crying, and Lydia wasn't speaking to Mary, even though she knew Mary hadn't spilled the beans about Samuel.

Lydia and Samuel had been caught kissing in the barn by their father, and her pregnancy came out amid her tears. She wasn't allowed to see Samuel now, although their mother was working hard to get the two married as quickly as possible.

They were all nervous about an upcoming meeting with the bishop. If Levi walked into all of that, he'd never want to see her again. Lydia's actions were attached to the word *shame* now.

Their father didn't fire Samuel, but he sent him home the moment he found out Lydia was pregnant. Maybe he would come to accept the circumstances and let Samuel continue working for him. It was too soon to know.

"It's too far for you to travel by buggy to meet my family." She took a deep breath. "Besides, don't people in your district who are dating keep it a secret? In our community, no one knows a person is dating until it's serious. And even then, most folks don't know until an engagement is published." She put a hand to her mouth as a timid gasp escaped. "I-I don't mean that I'm thinking that far ahead. I just, uh . . ."

Be quiet, stop talking. She bit her lip so hard, she was afraid it would bleed.

Levi shrugged and didn't seem bothered by her words. "I could give the horse a *gut* long rest, the same way we do when we go at Adeline's. By late afternoon, the animals have had plenty of rest to get us home. Or I bet Adeline would let me stay in her extra bedroom in the twin bed, then I could make the rest of the trip the next day to meet your family."

It was a good argument, and she wanted to see Levi more than just on Saturdays, but she just couldn't expose him to her family right now.

"It's not necessary to meet *mei* family. And *mei* parents know you're doing work for Adeline. I'm sure they've already decided that you are a *gut* man."

"Okay. We can just keep seeing each other at Adeline's on Saturdays." Levi wouldn't look at her, and she wondered if his feelings were hurt.

"Since it's important to your family that you meet my family, they probably want to meet me too. That same arrangement, staying at Adeline's, could work for me, and I could come meet your family."

Levi opened his mouth to say something but then didn't.

"Should we do that?" Mary finally asked.

"Nee, that's not necessary either. As the man, they just felt that I should introduce myself to your *daed."*

She felt the sting she had delivered to Levi bounce back at her. He didn't want her to meet his family either. Gossip, although forbidden, was known to travel quickly, but Mary didn't see how Levi could have gotten word about Lydia yet. Eventually, someone from Montgomery would talk to someone in Orleans or Shoals, and everyone would know that Mary's sixteen-year-old sister was unwed and pregnant. Mary understood the shame her parents must feel.

"Maybe we can just enjoy today and talk about it another time."

"Ya, sure." Levi nodded at the last piece of pizza. Mary hadn't even finished her first slice. "Are you going to eat that?"

Mary shook her head. The atmosphere had grown cold, and she needed to say something to bring their conversation back to a good place. But Levi wasn't looking at her as much as he had when she arrived. And he wasn't saying anything.

"I'll see you Saturday, *ya?"* Mary twisted the string on her prayer covering as she chewed on her bottom lip.

"*Ya.* I'll be there. I've still got a lot of work to do."

Mary wanted to confide in him, to tell him that she'd love for him to meet her family. Normally, her mother would put out a perfect spread of food and they would present themselves as the truly happy family that they were. Until now. It was wrong for anyone to judge another person. Only God could do that. But they were all human, and all it would take was one outburst from Lydia to get everyone screaming and yelling again.

She couldn't put Levi in that situation.

After an awkward silence, Levi walked Mary to her buggy. "You should be able to make it home before dark."

She smiled. "If you had a cell phone, I could call you to let you know I made it safely home."

That was never going to happen. His parents wouldn't allow it, and Levi didn't have the money for it. Mary's world was so different from his. Maybe it was best not to let his feelings for her grow. Maybe they needed to stay friends and keep their time together limited to Adeline's house.

But when Mary reached for his hand and smiled, thoughts of friendship jumped out of his mind and scurried across the asphalt parking lot.

"*Danki* for the pizza and for inviting me." She smiled as she moved a little closer to him. She leaned up and kissed him on the cheek. If Levi didn't know he'd still see her on Saturdays, this might have felt like goodbye. But as her lips hovered near his, so close he could feel her breath, he decided it was now or never.

He was going to find out if Mary was interested in more than friendship. After glancing around the parking lot to make sure there was no one around, he cupped her cheeks in his hands and pulled her lips to his. And he kissed her the way he'd been dreaming of. And it wasn't the way you kiss your friend. When she returned the kiss, Levi was sure they were going to be more than friends, no matter how different their upbringings.

Adeline woke up Wednesday morning after another good night's sleep. Since her new furniture arrived on Saturday, she'd slept better than she had since she sold her bed. *Which was a dumb thing to do.* She couldn't wait to thank Levi on Saturday.

But today she had Natalie's visit to look forward to. She learned a little more about

Percy's cousin every time she popped in. Most telling, however, was the essay she'd asked Adeline to read. It was beautifully written. The girl was right to admit she had some issues with grammar, but the emotion that spilled out on the pages touched Adeline deeply.

Adeline's chest tightened, and she got ready for a spasm. It was longer this time, and a moan actually slipped out as she waited for the pain to pass. She regretted that Mary and Levi had witnessed one. Maybe Saturday she would ask to borrow Mary's phone. The doctor's office wouldn't be open, but she could leave a message and ask them to increase her dosage. Then the following Saturday, she'd ask Mary to cart her to the pharmacy to pick it up. She said a quick prayer and asked God to temper the spasms, or at least help her bear the pain. Adeline didn't want to make a big fuss in front of Natalie, so she bargained with herself, saying she'd ask to borrow the girl's phone if the pain continued during their time together.

Natalie arrived a few minutes later, and Adeline greeted her with a hug. They got settled at the kitchen table, and Natalie was already fitting puzzle pieces together when

Adeline mentioned that she'd read the essay.

"I'm sure you found plenty of mistakes." Natalie sighed.

"Dear girl, it was a lovely essay. I'm sure your Mimi Jean is smiling from heaven. Yes, there were some grammatical errors, but it would have been easy to overlook them if I didn't have trained schoolteacher eyes." She pointed to the counter. "I left it over there, marked up with my handy red pen that I hadn't used in a long time."

Natalie looked up and smiled. "Thank you so much."

"I have a confession. I made a copy. Is that all right?" Percy's ancient photocopier hadn't sold at the estate sale. There'd barely been enough ink to make copies of the three pages.

Natalie slipped a piece of the puzzle into place. "Sure, that's fine." She looked up. "But why?"

"It's filled with such hope, and it reminds me of myself at your age. I'd like to be able to pull it out and reread it from time to time."

Natalie's eyes shone with deserving pride. "That makes me feel good." She refocused on the puzzle and grouped together more of the tan pieces. "You and your friends got a lot done this past Saturday." She clicked more pieces into place.

"Your mother was right." Adeline chuckled. "You are a whiz at this. But actually, only Mary was here Saturday. Levi wasn't able to come. But I've worked on it in the evenings." She brought a hand to her chest and smiled. "Levi and Mary should both be here this coming Saturday. At least I hope they are. I can't wait to thank Levi for a most generous gesture." She pushed back her chair and stood up. "Follow me. I want to show you something."

When they got to Adeline's bedroom, she pushed the door open. "All of this was delivered to me on Saturday. Levi's family is the one who gave me the kitchen table and chairs, and now they've given me this beautiful bedroom set." She frowned a little. "I don't think that boy's family has much, and I'm floored that they would do this. But I am grateful beyond words."

"It looks really pretty in here." Natalie smiled a little. "I'm glad you don't have to sleep on the floor now."

Adeline lifted one shoulder and dropped it slowly. "I wasn't actually sleeping on the floor." She laughed. "But my back is thanking me every morning. It didn't care much for that air mattress."

Natalie pulled her long hair into a knot and tied it on top of her head.

"I'm sorry it's so warm in here. I think my air conditioner is going out. I haven't needed to turn it on until yesterday, but it doesn't seem to be blowing cool air." It would be a hot summer with no AC, if it was in need of repair.

"It's okay."

They walked back to the kitchen table. Adeline sat, but Natalie stayed standing, folded her arms across her chest, and eyed the puzzle. "I used to think this was a beach scene, with all the shades of blue and tan." She leaned in closer. "But I don't think that's sand, Adeline."

Adeline rose from her chair and stood beside Natalie, seeing if she could get some perspective. "Well, that looks like sky." She pointed to the top of the puzzle where shades of blue blended with white, like clouds.

Natalie tapped her finger several times on the tan places that were starting to come together toward the bottom of the puzzle. Then she looked up at Adeline grinning. "That doesn't look like a beach. And I don't know about the red, but the tan isn't sand."

Adeline studied it. "Well, I don't know what it is, but I think you're right. It's not sand." She pressed her palms together and smiled. "This is half the fun, wondering what the picture is. Oh! We forgot to make lists of what we think it might be." She turned to Natalie, who had an odd look on her face.

"Adeline, that looks like *skin*. And that looks like it could be, uh . . ."

Adeline gasped as she finally saw what Natalie saw. "Oh dear. Oh dear. Oh dear."

"Are you sure you want to finish this puzzle?"

Adeline eyed the picture that was forming and shook her head. "Maybe not."

CHAPTER 9

Saturday morning, Natalie was on her way to Adeline's house, hoping to end the phone conversation with her mother soon.

"All I want you to do is to check out the Amish kids who visit her and are doing all this work on her house. I doubt Adeline is paying them, so it sounds like they're trying to get in good with her — gold diggers trying get in her will."

Natalie huffed. "Mom, don't you think that's the pot calling the kettle black?" Natalie didn't want Adeline's house, and she didn't think her mother deserved it, but she also didn't want anyone taking advantage of Adeline. "I'll let you know about Mary and Levi. That's what Adeline said their names are. I gotta go though."

Natalie had already told her mother that maybe she should be the one to go see Adeline if she was so determined to be in the woman's will, but her mother said that wasn't possible, that she lived with daily migraines. Natalie wasn't sure about that. It seemed more likely that she lived with hangovers.

As she ended the call and turned her Ford SUV into Adeline's driveway, she saw a man halfway up a ladder. He started down the rungs when Natalie got out of her car. Her SUV was one of the few things she owned these days, a gift from her parents before the divorce. It was a used vehicle and nothing fancy, but it got her around — most of the time. Her promotion was only a couple weeks away now, and maybe she could trade up for something a little more reliable.

She still planned to visit Adeline after her classes were over. Adeline had no idea how much her kind words about the essay meant to Natalie, and she enjoyed the older woman's company.

The guy was walking toward her now. He was tall with cropped blond hair beneath a straw hat. He wore the traditional Amish garb — black pants, blue shirt, and suspenders. He was cute, in an Amish sort of way.

"Adeline's not here right now. Can I help you with something?" He took off his hat and ran a hand across his sweaty forehead, then put his hat back on.

"Oh. Well, she wasn't expecting me." She

extended her hand to the man she presumed was Levi. "I'm her cousin, Natalie."

He shook her hand and smiled. "I've heard a lot about you from Adeline."

"Good stuff, I hope." Natalie was disappointed she'd missed Adeline.

"All good." Levi scratched his clean-shaven chin. Natalie knew enough about the Amish to know that Levi was single. "I was wondering, though . . . did you happen to give Adeline some bedroom furniture?"

Natalie swallowed. "How did you know?"

Levi shrugged. "Besides her visits from me and her friend Mary, you're the only other person I've heard her talk about."

"Please don't tell her it was me." Natalie didn't want Adeline thinking she was trying to work her way into her good graces with an extravagant gift. She wanted in Adeline's good graces because the woman reminded her of her Mimi Jean, and she hadn't felt a whole lot of love coming from her parents the last couple years. They'd been too busy with their midlife crises and bitter divorce to throw any positive vibes Natalie's way.

"Why don't you want her to know?" Levi narrowed his dark bushy eyebrows into a frown.

"It's complicated. But Adeline needed bedroom furniture, and I had some to give.

But she doesn't need to know it was from me."

Levi scratched his chin again, then looped his thumbs beneath his suspenders. "I already told her this morning that it wasn't from me. She threw her arms around my neck and thanked me repeatedly, until I was finally able to tell her I didn't send it. I already knew Mary didn't and suspected maybe you did. But I don't understand why you don't want her to know. It made her really happy. Mary was with her when it arrived, and she said Adeline cried happy tears."

She couldn't tell Levi that despite her mother's encouragement to do otherwise, she didn't want to do anything that might present her motives in the wrong light. Natalie wanted Adeline's friendship, nothing else. "Just please don't tell her. The best gifts are the ones we don't get credit for."

Levi smiled a little. "That's true."

"So you won't tell her?"

"*Nee.* I mean no. I won't tell her."

Levi brought a hand to his forehead and looked up for a couple seconds before he lowered his gaze. "It's close to noon. Adeline and Mary should be back soon. Adeline called her doctor's office this morning, and the nurse called back even though they're officially closed on Saturday. They called in some medicine Adeline needed, so Mary took her to pick it up."

Natalie grinned. "Did you just figure out what time it is by looking at the placement of the sun?"

Levi smiled, which made him even cuter. *"Ya."*

"Well, that's cool. You're like a walking sundial." Natalie peered past him at the work he'd been doing. "The house looks so much better with fresh paint."

"I've still got another coat."

Natalie tossed her thoughts around for a few seconds. "I thought Adeline sold her belongings because maybe she was running out of money. But maybe I was wrong if she's able to hire you to paint."

Adeline had never said whether or not she was paying Levi and Mary. The Amish people were known to be honest and upstanding, but just like the rest of the world, there were still bad seeds, and Natalie didn't want anyone taking advantage of Adeline by overcharging her for a job.

"She's not paying us. *Mei mudder* has known Adeline for a long time, and when we saw the condition of her house, we wanted to help. Mary's father knew Adeline's husband — Percy — so her family wanted to help too."

Natalie nodded. "That's really nice of both of you."

"She's a nice lady that just fell on hard times, although she's never come out and said that."

Natalie had been to an Amish barn raising when she was younger. Her father took her to show her how a community comes together to help one of their own. She supposed the Amish stepped out of their circle when outsiders needed a hand too. Natalie's wheels were spinning in her mind as she wondered if she might be able to do something to make Adeline's life easier.

"Maybe I'll wait since you said Adeline and Mary will be back soon."

Levi nodded toward the house. "*Ya,* she'll be happy to see you. She said she's enjoying getting to know one of Percy's relatives." He paused, smiling. "She's young at heart, so I think she enjoys being around younger people. But it's hot in the house. The air conditioner isn't working. It doesn't matter much to Mary and me, since we're used to not having electricity, but I think the heat is getting to Adeline, and you'll probably be hot too."

"That's okay. I need to use the bathroom,

and then if it's too hot, I can sit on the porch."

Natalie waved as she walked off.

Levi sighed and headed back to the ladder. He'd lost track of time and hadn't played the piano like he'd planned. A lost opportunity now. Maybe God was trying to tell him something.

He'd only seen Mary for a few minutes earlier. She brought pastries again, which was nice, and they shared several all-knowing looks when Adeline wasn't watching them. He'd been thinking of ways to share another kiss with her. And wondering how they were going to spend more time together.

It was clear that she didn't want him to meet her family any more than he wanted her to meet his. Hopefully his *daed* wouldn't ask if he'd made it a point to meet Mary's *daed*. And now *Mamm* was pushing to meet Mary. Levi argued that they'd only been on one date and that didn't qualify as being in a relationship. His mother had winked at him and said he and Mary had spent lots of time together at Adeline's. Then she frowned and told him to behave himself, and that it wouldn't be proper to spend time alone with Mary if Adeline wasn't home. Levi was quick to tell his mother that

Adeline never went anywhere unless it was with Mary.

His heart fluttered a little when he heard the clip-clop of hooves, but he dipped his paintbrush, determined to take advantage of the clear day. No rain was in the forecast according to the newspaper, so he wanted to get as much painting done as he could. But after Mary tethered her horse, she hollered at him that they needed help with something. As he drew closer, he saw two big boxes in the back seat, and he'd already noticed the one strapped to the top of the buggy.

"I begged Mary not to buy all these things." Adeline lowered her head. "But she insisted."

Mary reached for a box in the back seat, and Levi quickly took it from her even though it wasn't very heavy. She had bought battery-operated fans.

"Why batteries? She has electricity," he whispered to her.

"You didn't notice this morning when you were stuffing yourself with pastries that the power is off?"

Levi's eyes widened. "*Nee,* I didn't. I guess I'm so used to it, I didn't realize. I just thought the AC wasn't working."

"Adeline said the air-conditioning stopped

193

working before the power went off. It's tolerable right now, but soon it will be too hot for her. The house has good ventilation, but these are what we use at home during the summer. The one on the roof has a water mister that she can use when she's sitting on the porch."

Levi began unstrapping the large box on top of the buggy. He shared a room with three other people, and they constantly fought over which direction the fan would blow, sometimes flipping a coin to see who would feel the breeze that night. His family didn't have this many fans in their entire house, and there were twelve of them. These kinds of fans were also expensive and not something Levi's family could afford. Mary had enough money of her own to purchase three of them. It was yet another reminder that they were worlds apart.

"You kids are too good to me." Adeline folded her hands in front of her. "But, Mary, you are going to let me repay you for these."

Mary shook her head as she picked up one of the boxes to carry to the house. "Adeline, this didn't cost much, and you need to learn how to accept a gift."

Levi knew otherwise, but he stayed quiet

about the money. "She's right, Adeline. It's a gift."

Adeline lifted her arms above her head in a dramatic way. "I am being gifted in more ways than I could have dreamed of." She dropped her arms and glanced back and forth between Levi and Mary. "But my greatest gift has been the gift of friendship that you two have given me."

They both smiled, and Mary said, "I feel the same way, and I know Levi does too. I'm going to carry this in now." She readjusted the box on her hip.

"Mary, leave it. I'll carry it in." Levi lifted the large box from the roof, then caught Mary looking over her shoulder, grinning.

"I'm stronger than you think." She winked at him, and his insides got that weird feeling again.

"*Ach,* wait. I forgot to mention . . ." He glanced at Adeline but then spoke loud enough that Mary could hear too. "Adeline's cousin, Natalie, is inside."

Adeline's eyes brightened. "Oh, how wonderful. I've been hoping my three favorite people could meet."

Mary slowed her stride but didn't turn around.

Jealousy was a sin, but when Mary saw Natalie, the emotion bubbled to the surface like an allergic reaction. Adeline's cousin was beautiful and had long blond hair and big blue eyes. She was dressed in jeans that were rolled up a few times and a fitted yellow blouse. Her toenails were painted bright pink and housed in a pair of white sandals. Her fingernails were painted the same color. Natalie's eyelashes were long, dark, and lush, her cheeks rosy, and her lips glistening with a shiny pink gloss.

What does Levi think of her?

After introductions were made, Mary began to open one of the fan boxes. She'd only had enough money to either try to get Adeline's power on — depending on how much she owed — or to buy the fans. Even if the electricity was restored, the air conditioner wasn't working, so the fans seemed to make more sense.

Adeline and Natalie sat on the edge of the worn-out couch in the living room as Mary pulled out a fan and began to assemble it. They were small but efficient.

Natalie got up and went to where Mary was sitting on the wood floor and sat down beside her. "Here, I can help."

Mary smiled as Natalie began to open the other box.

"This is awful, just awful." Adeline shook

her head as she spoke in a wobbly voice. "My new friends are sitting on the floor in my hot house putting together fans. That's just not right. I don't understand why my electricity is off. I paid the bill. I'm sure of it."

"Did you call the electric company?" Natalie pulled the second fan out of its box. "Maybe it doesn't have anything to do with not paying the bill. It could be a problem on their end."

Mary didn't have any experience dealing with an electric company, so she stayed quiet, even though she didn't like seeing Adeline so upset. Adeline had made a call to her doctor's office that morning before they left, using Mary's phone, after admitting that hers didn't work.

"My phone doesn't work either," Adeline said to Natalie.

At almost the same time, Mary and Natalie reached into their purses and pulled out cell phones. Natalie's wasn't anything like the one Mary had that flipped open.

"I didn't know you could have a cell phone." Natalie handed Adeline her phone, but she was speaking to and looking at Mary.

"Some of us do. We just can't have smartphones. Levi doesn't have one at all." Mary forced a smile. *In case you were thinking of calling him.* Where was this horrible jealousy coming from? Mary hadn't even seen the two of them together. Her feelings for Levi were stronger than she realized, but that didn't excuse the nasty thoughts she was having.

Mary put her phone back in her purse.

"Honey, I don't know how to use this." Adeline stared at the phone, scowling.

Natalie eased it out of her hand and pushed a few buttons, then gave it back. "There, you can dial the number from here. Or if you don't know the number, we can Google it."

Mary recognized the odd name but had never used it herself.

"I have a list of important phone numbers in my bedroom. I'll just go get them." Adeline slowly lifted herself from the couch and left the room.

In a few minutes, she returned and sat down again.

Natalie was on the floor screwing the back of the fan in place. She was handier than Mary would have thought.

"Adeline, did you get your list of numbers?" Natalie tightened one of the screws.

"What list?" Adeline smiled. "This is so nice of you girls to do this."

198

Mary shot a quick look at Natalie, who also glanced at Mary before she turned back to Adeline. "You know. Your list of phone numbers."

Adeline blinked her eyes a couple times, her expression blank. "Who should I call?"

Mary wasn't sure what was happening. "Adeline, you were going to call the electric company to see why your electricity is off."

"Yes. I was." She lifted herself off the couch again and walked toward the back of the house.

"I've never seen that happen before," Mary whispered.

"The few times I've been here, she's been fine." Natalie looked at the fan. "Ha! Not bad for a girl." She chuckled. "I even put together a crib recently for a girl I work with. She's single and pregnant." She lifted an eyebrow. "But not too handy with tools."

Mary thought about Lydia. She was still trying to wrap her mind around the fact that she was going to be an aunt. Their people occasionally married young, some even at sixteen or seventeen, but typically a couple was in their early twenties. At least in Mary's district. Lydia was going to be a mother at sixteen.

Levi pulled the screen door open and joined them in the living room. Mary kept her eyes on him, but he never even looked at Natalie. He just smiled at Mary.

"Do you ladies know what you're doing?" Levi crossed his arms in front of him.

"What does it look like?" Mary stood and pointed to the two fans they'd assembled, which really only required tightening a few screws. "I'm guessing you're hungry?" She glanced at Natalie. "He's hungry all the time."

"I think all guys are." Natalie laughed as she sat on the couch, then shifted her weight from side to side.

"That couch is awful. We usually sit in the parlor, so we should probably put one of the fans in there. Then we can put the other one in her bedroom."

Levi nodded as Mary gathered the packing material from the floor and stuffed it back inside the boxes.

"So, about that food?" Levi grinned as he nudged Mary's shoulder when she stood up. She bumped his shoulder right back, smiling.

"You two are like a cute married couple, but I know enough about the Amish to know that a man has a beard if he's married." Natalie smiled. "So, how long have you two been dating?"

Mary held her breath, glanced at Levi, and

then back at Natalie. "Um . . ."

"We've only gone out once." Levi tipped back the rim of his hat and grinned. "But I'm hopeful for more dates."

Mary could feel the heat in her face, but she couldn't hold back from smiling.

"Well, you're cute together. And I'm so glad I got to meet you. Adeline thinks the world of both of you." Natalie eased off the couch. "Ouch. Too many springs poking out in that old thing."

"Like I said, she spends most of her time in the parlor or at the kitchen table." Mary picked up the empty boxes and put them by the front door. Shame was a sin, too, but she was feeling it for allowing jealousy to momentarily latch on to her for no reason.

"Where is Adeline anyway?" Levi asked.

Mary glanced at Natalie, then back at Levi. "She was going to get a list of phone numbers, but that was several minutes ago."

All at once the three of them rushed down the hallway, nearly stumbling over each other to get to Adeline.

CHAPTER 10

Adeline jumped when her three young friends came rushing into her bedroom, but she went back to the business at hand.

"Are you okay?" Mary asked as Adeline dug through her nightstand drawer.

"Here it is." She pushed her reading glasses up on her head and held up a piece of white paper. "I had stashed important papers in a plastic container in my closet, but after I received this beautiful furniture, I cleaned out my closet. I thought I put this list in the desk, but here it is in my nightstand." She scowled. "I sure wish I knew who to thank for this special gift."

She was still holding Natalie's phone. "I'm going to call the electric company now."

"Check the bars. I get sketchy service inside this house."

Adeline pulled her glasses back down. "What bars am I looking for? I've used a cell phone before, but these gadgets sure have changed a lot."

Natalie gently eased the phone from Adeline's hand and pointed to the left corner. "There aren't any bars showing right now, so you probably need to go outside to call. You'll have better service out there."

Adeline grunted. "All this new technology is overwhelming."

Natalie showed her again how to place the call so she'd know when she got outside. The trio followed her back through the parlor, and Adeline turned to face them. "Why don't you kids visit in here? I made us some ham sandwiches for lunch. I'll get them after I phone the electric company."

Adeline stepped out onto the porch. The fan that sprayed water was still in its box. She wished Mary hadn't bought them. These young people were doing way too much for her, but she continued to thank God daily for their friendship.

She looked at the phone, knowing she was supposed to call someone. She had her list in her hand, so she scanned the names and numbers until she saw the electric company's phone number. *That's what old age will do to a gal.*

After being on hold for several minutes, a live person finally answered and Adeline inquired about the status of her electric bill.

"Ms. Collins, you're almost two months behind on your bill, so your power was scheduled to be terminated yesterday. Would you like to pay your bill now so we can get your service restored?"

Adeline's heart raced faster than it should. "How much do I owe?"

"Three hundred and seventeen dollars."

That isn't too bad. "I don't know how I forgot to pay the bill." She rubbed her forehead with one hand. "I'm very sorry."

"Would you like to pay right now by credit card, and we can get your service back on tomorrow?"

"Yes, I would. But I will have to call you back after I get my credit card."

"That will be fine, ma'am."

Adeline studied the phone until she saw a red button that said End, so she pushed it, hoping that disconnected the call.

When she walked back into the house, she joined the children in the parlor. They were laughing, something about a rooster that got loose in Levi's house one time.

Adeline handed Natalie the phone.

"Did you get everything handled?" Natalie crossed one leg over the other where she sat in Percy's chair. To Adeline, it would always be Percy's chair.

"Yes, I did." Adeline smiled. "Who is

ready for lunch?"

"Well, we know Levi is." Mary grinned, rolling her eyes. The girl had already told Adeline about her pizza date while they were on the way to town earlier. Love was in the air, and Adeline enjoyed watching their romance unfold.

"Actually, I better not stay for lunch." Natalie stood. "When you handed me my phone back, I saw that my dad sent me a text. He wants to meet for lunch." She shook her head, frowning. "He never does that, so I hope nothing is wrong." She glanced around the room at each of them. "Believe me, I'd much rather hang out with you three." She gave a little wave to Mary and Levi, then she hugged Adeline.

"I hate that you can't stay." Adeline gave her an extra squeeze before she eased away. "Your parents are both welcome here anytime too."

"No way." Natalie cringed. "I come here to hang out with you. If I wanted to be around them, I'd go to their houses. See you Wednesday."

Adeline, Mary, and Levi ate lunch in the parlor. All the windows were open, and the fan generated a nice breeze. "Are you kids hot?"

She saw Mary and Levi exchange a grin,

and Levi spoke up. "*Nee,* we're used to it. Remember?"

"This is an old house, you know. At least a hundred years old." Adeline searched back decades in her mind as she smiled. "Percy and I bought it, and it needed so much restoration. It was truly a labor of love. Even though the rooms are small, it's built in such a way that there's a nice cross breeze if all of the doors and windows are open."

She closed her eyes, picturing Percy at the piano playing "Moon River" or another one of their favorites. "Sometimes I think I see Percy playing the piano. He loved it so. And I loved listening to him play. These days, I see him everywhere. In the kitchen and the bedroom, but mostly seated at the piano. Oh, what I wouldn't do to hear him play. Just one song. Just one more time. He used to love 'Amazing Grace.' " Adeline leaned her head back against the couch, sighed, and closed her eyes, lost in her memories.

Levi's fingers twitched, his heart pounded. He was a human magnet drawn to something forbidden, and he had to resist. He glanced at Mary.

"Play for her," Mary mouthed to him without making any sound. "Just do it."

Levi shook his head, but Mary nodded.

Levi was having a hard enough time resisting the temptation. He wanted to make Adeline happy as much as Mary wanted him to, but at what cost? God would be disappointed in him, and what if it upset Adeline instead of comforted her? "Adeline?"

She eased her head toward him, smiling. "Yes, dear. I might have drifted off."

"Do you like people playing Percy's piano, or does it upset you?"

Adeline folded her hands in her lap. "I didn't like strangers pounding on the keys during the estate sale. Most of them didn't know how to play, although a few did, but not very well." Adeline smiled. "Percy was a wonderful pianist, and I felt that some of those people were doing a disservice to his memory. I have no idea what that old piano is worth, but I think the woman running the sale — Dixie something or other — priced it much too high, and that's why it didn't sell. The people at the sale probably didn't know much about pianos, and five thousand dollars is a lot, don't you think? We saved for a long time to buy that instrument, but that was back in the day, and I couldn't even tell you what we paid for it." She locked eyes with Levi. "But I'd give anything to hear someone play with the grace and talent Percy had."

"Levi . . ." Mary spoke aloud now. "Just do it."

Adeline glanced back and forth between them. "Just do what, hon?"

Levi closed his eyes, recalling his mother's words about discerning which voice he was hearing when it came to temptation. He'd asked God for guidance, but he hadn't received an answer.

Adeline chuckled. "I feel left out on a secret."

"Nee, nee." Mary turned to face Adeline from her spot next to her on the couch. "*Ach,* maybe we do have a little bit of a secret."

"Oh my. Sometimes I love a good secret." She winked at Mary, then glanced at Levi before she brought a hand to her chest and gasped. "Is this about the two of you? Are you officially dating?"

Levi's eyes traveled to Mary, and her cheeks were as red as his felt. He stood and slowly walked to the piano without responding. He would play for Adeline, then resist the temptation from now on, even if Adeline and Mary were away from the house.

He sat on the bench and lowered his hands to the keys, breathing in the smell of the instrument, enjoying the feel of the ivory just below his fingers. He'd never played for anyone except Mary.

He froze, unsure what to do. Displeasing God wasn't something he wanted, but when Mary slid in beside him on the bench, he was sure she would sing. He wanted to hear her sing almost as badly as she wanted him to play the piano. Temptation won. Levi lowered his fingers onto the keys.

After he played "Amazing Grace" with Mary singing along, they both looked over their shoulders at Adeline, who was dabbing her eyes with a handkerchief.

"Please don't stop," she said. "I had no idea music was a part of either of your lives. I'd always heard it was forbidden."

It is. But Levi played the music in his mind. If Mary recognized the song, she'd sing along. But she mostly just sat next to him, and having her nearby felt almost better than the music.

Natalie sat in her car in the parking lot of Yoder's Stop & Sea. It was a forty-five-minute drive each way for her father, so Natalie wondered what was up. He either had a craving for their fish sandwiches or had suddenly missed her. Or he needed to tell her something she probably didn't want to hear.

Her mother had called but left a voice mail wanting to know about Mary and Levi. Natalie would call her back later and tell her they both seemed very nice and appeared to have Adeline's best interest at heart. Unlike her mother.

She recognized her dad's black Chevy Lumina and breathed a sigh of relief when he stepped out of the car alone. Olive Oil — the name Natalie and her mother had chosen to replace the woman's given name, Olivia — wasn't with him.

Natalie mostly avoided her father these days, but he knew she would have a hard time turning down the sandwiches at this place. And even though the small eatery wasn't anything fancy or expensive, dining out had become a luxury she couldn't afford since she'd moved out.

As they walked toward each other, she wanted to hate him. Partly because he had left them. And partly because he'd lost forty pounds, was in love, and was happy. Natalie and her mother were both gaining weight, bitter in their own ways, and not particularly happy these days. But Natalie was determined to make her own way and find her own happiness. It was up to her mother to do the same and regain a level of self-respect. Her mother was convinced that

Thomas Collins was going straight to hell for what he'd done to his family. And maybe he would, but Natalie wouldn't be the one judging him.

Seeing her father now in the flesh, she was finding it hard to fault him. Maybe because she'd missed him a little. She didn't miss her parents' constant fighting. Perhaps being away from her mother, even for only a couple weeks, had helped put some things in perspective.

"Hey, Nat." Dad had a tendency to shorten everyone's name. Olivia — Liv. Natalie — Nat. Her mother, Cecilia — Cece. He pulled her into a hug and kissed her on the cheek. He held her like he hadn't seen her in years. Natalie figured it had probably been a month.

"How's the apartment?" he asked as they crossed the parking lot toward the entrance. "Mom said you took your furniture finally. That's great."

Natalie swallowed hard. She didn't want to start off their lunch date with a lie. "When did you talk to Mom?"

"She calls most days." He ran a hand through his salt-and-pepper, neatly groomed hair. "Either to yell at me or cry." He looked at Natalie. "Is she drinking?"

Natalie shrugged. She'd played this game

for way too long, each of her parents digging for dirt on the other one.

"I'm just asking because I still worry about her, even if I couldn't be married to her anymore." He opened the door and motioned for Natalie to go in, then they walked to the counter to order. "I love the food here."

Natalie wondered again if he was mostly here for the fish sandwiches they both loved. After they were seated with their food, he said, "Let's talk about you, not your mom."

"No arguments there." Her stomach growled as she took a big bite of her sandwich. There was a sign in the corner featuring the desserts for the day, and one of the offerings was Dr Pepper cake. Maybe she'd splurge since her father was buying.

"Your mom did tell me that you have reconnected with a cousin of mine. Second or third, I guess. Adeline. Percy's wife. I guess the last time we saw Adeline was at Percy's funeral."

Natalie was tempted to tell her father the truth, that her mother wanted her to get in good with Adeline, in hopes that she would leave them her house. But why throw her mother under the bus and stir the pot?

"Yeah, I'm taking a training class for work in Shoals. Mom said it was close to Adeline's house, so I decided to visit her." She placed her napkin in her lap, then smiled. "I visit her every Wednesday, and I was at her house when you texted."

"Wow. That's great that you two struck up a friendship. She's gotta be in her eighties by now."

"I think so." Natalie chewed on her lip. "She has two really nice Amish friends that are painting her house, planning to do yard work, and the girl, Mary, cleans the house for her. And they're doing all of it for free. I met them for the first time today."

"The Amish are giving people." Her father finally took a bite of his sandwich, closing his eyes as he chewed. "As good as I remember." He looked at her. "I haven't been here in a while."

"Adeline's a nice lady. She reminds me of Mimi Jean. But I think she's, like, broke or something. I don't know. Her power was turned off. She said she got it taken care of, but she must really be living on the edge financially."

"Aren't we all." Her father frowned.

Natalie wasn't sure if that was true or not. Olive Oil bought a new car recently.

"Are you going to marry Olivia?"

Her father shrugged as he reached for his water. "Maybe." He took a drink, then set the glass down. "I've missed you, kiddo."

Natalie took a sip of her tea. "Adeline said you're welcome to visit her anytime. She doesn't drive anymore, so I think she's lost touch with any friends she had. She said Mom was welcome, too, but since she's your cousin . . ." Natalie trailed off, not willing to tell her father that her mother rarely changed out of her robe and most of her days began with spiked orange juice.

"Maybe I will pay her a visit."

Natalie narrowed her eyes at him, about to tell him she doubted that, but she stuffed the thought and took a big bite of her sandwich, savoring the flavor.

They talked about the weather and other mundane subjects while they ate. She knew her father usually had a purpose for these rare lunches, so after finishing half of her sandwich she decided to dive in.

"Dad, is something on your mind? Do you have something to tell me?" He'd already said marrying Olive Oil was only a maybe, and Natalie would settle for that as good news for now. The thought of having that woman as her stepmother made her want to gag.

Her father opened his mouth and tipped his head to one side. "Do I have to have an agenda to spend time with my daughter?"

Natalie raised her eyebrows and sent him a thin-lipped smile. "You usually do."

"That's not true."

They were quiet for a while, and Natalie could feel the tension building. His eye twitched, a sure sign he was nervous. Her father definitely had something big to discuss with her.

"Dad, what is it?"

He put down his sandwich and leaned against the back of his chair, locking eyes with her. "Liv and I are moving."

Natalie took a deep breath and blew it out slowly. "Well, that's good, right? You've been saying that you guys need a bigger place."

A muscle in her father's jaw clenched, his eye still twitching. "Natalie, we're moving to Mississippi. I got a great job offer, and Liv and I both think I should take it."

Her mouth fell open.

"I know Mississippi is a long way from Indiana, but we'll fly you to see us as often as we can."

Tears formed in the corners of Natalie's eyes. She'd been mad at him for running out on her and her mother, but logically she thought she would eventually heal from that. How could they mend their relationship if he was so far away?

"Please don't cry," he said. "Your mother

pulls that too. I have to be able to live my life, Natalie."

Fighting tears, she swallowed. Maybe it was the way he told her, but she wasn't hungry anymore. She slowly stood, lifted her purse to her shoulder, and started toward the door.

"Nat, wait!"

She turned around, walked back to the table, and picked up the remaining half of her sandwich, then hurried out of the restaurant. At least she'd have something for dinner tonight.

She slowed her pace in the parking lot. Surely her father would run after her. When he didn't, she got in her car, leaned her head against the steering wheel and cried. Five minutes later, her father still hadn't come to check on her.

"I miss you, Mimi Jean," she said aloud through her tears.

Since she couldn't talk to Mimi Jean, she'd go to the person who reminded her most of her grandmother.

She pulled out of the parking lot, sniffling. Mary and Levi were probably still there, but she didn't care. She wanted to talk to Adeline. Ever since she gave Adeline the essay to read, she'd felt closer to her. At least someone in the world knew what was in

Natalie's heart.

After she turned on Adeline's street, her heart flipped in her chest as a shot of adrenaline rushed through her. There were lights. Lots of flashing lights. An ambulance.

"No, God, no. Please don't let anything have happened to Adeline."

Natalie screeched her car to a halt, jumped out, and ran across the yard.

CHAPTER 11

Mary sat beside Adeline in the hospital waiting room in Bedford, and Natalie was on the other side of her cousin. Levi was unconscious, and they were waiting to find out how serious his injuries were.

"I thought that ladder looked a little unsteady sometimes." Adeline's hands were shaking. Mary trembled all over. Natalie's eyes were puffy and red, like she'd been crying. But she looked that way when she returned to Adeline's house, so Mary wasn't sure if something happened with her father, or if she'd gone back to the house for some other reason. The ambulance driver had called the sheriff's office in Orleans to see if someone could get word to Levi's family.

Mary glanced around the room. A man with a bloody bandage wrapped around his arm was looking at his cell phone. A mother cuddled her toddler on her lap as the baby slept. An elderly couple sat by the wall, and the man had a nasty cough.

"I wish they would tell us something." Mary folded her hands in her lap. Her maroon dress was splattered with the white paint that had spilled on Levi and the area surrounding him when he fell. Adeline and Natalie had paint on them as well.

Mary and Adeline had heard a loud clunk while they were cleaning up the lunch dishes. They rushed outside and found Levi under the ladder and not moving. Somehow, he'd fallen backward and pulled the ladder down with him. Natalie got there a while later, after the ambulance arrived.

"Best to let me do the talking," Adeline whispered to Mary, stiffening when a doctor entered the room.

Mary glanced at the others in the waiting room but turned back to the doctor, a man who looked to be about the age of her father, when he walked toward them. Despite Adeline's suggestion, Mary couldn't stay quiet.

"Is he okay?" She swallowed the knot in her throat.

"Are you Levi's family?" He addressed the question to Mary. She was the only person dressed in Amish clothing.

Adeline cleared her throat. "Yes. I'm his grandmother, and this is his wife." She nodded toward Mary, then turned to Natalie. "And this is his sister."

Mary's eyes widened. She wasn't sure why Adeline would lie, but she was too concerned about Levi to argue.

"Levi hasn't woken up yet. Right now, I can't tell you much. We're running tests and hope to have more information soon."

"Can we go see him?" Mary blinked back tears as Adeline reached for her hand and squeezed.

"Right now, they've taken him to have a CAT scan, but he should be back soon. He's in intensive care, so I'd ask that only one or two of you go in at a time."

Adeline nodded, her hand shaking, but her grip tightening on Mary's hand. "All right," she said softly.

"I'll have someone let you know when you can go back." The doctor turned and walked down the hall.

"I don't know what I'll do if anything happens to that boy," Adeline said. "He was working at my home, for free."

Natalie took hold of Adeline's other hand. "Everything is going to be fine. I just know it."

There was no way for any of them to know if Levi would be okay. "Why did you lie to the doctor?" Mary tucked a few hairs beneath her *kapp.*

Adeline sighed. "I wasn't sure if they'd let us go see Levi since we aren't family." She looked toward the ceiling. "Please forgive my lie, Lord, but I love these kids."

Mary squeezed her hand. They were quiet for a while, then Mary lowered her head to pray.

"Are you praying?" Natalie asked in a whisper as she leaned over Adeline.

"Ya." Mary lowered her head again. Adeline did the same.

"I should pray, too, even though I'm not very good at it."

Natalie hadn't lowered her gaze when Mary looked up at her. "You can't be good or bad at it. Just talk to *Gott* like a friend and ask for healing for Levi."

Natalie nodded. Mary hadn't expected to like her. She wasn't sure why she had that preconceived feeling. Maybe it was the bout of jealousy when she first saw her. After spending a little more time together, Natalie seemed genuine. And it was nice of her to sit with Mary and Adeline at the hospital when she'd only just met Levi and Mary.

The door to the waiting room flew open and a line of Amish folks poured in. Adeline stood and went to the older woman and almost fell into her arms.

"Oh, Helen. He fell off the ladder. We don't know anything yet." Adeline eased out of the woman's arms and dabbed at the corner of one eye. "The doctor said he hasn't woken up yet. They are running some tests."

The eldest man, presumably Levi's father, took off his straw hat and held it to his chest as he listened. The other family members gathered around, closing in on Adeline, the boys removing their hats.

Mary counted. Six boys and three girls, just like Levi said.

"We prayed all the way here." Levi's mother was a heavy woman, and she walked with a slight limp. She had a kind face and warm eyes.

"I think that's all we can do for now." Adeline smiled a little as her eyes drifted to Levi's siblings. "What a fine family you have, Helen."

Mary thought about Lydia. Her situation at home was a mess. But Mary's family was healthy and okay. She reminded herself to be grateful for *Gott*'s grace, and that everything is His will. Things just didn't make sense sometimes.

Her bottom lip trembled as she fought the urge to cry.

There were barely enough seats to accommodate Levi's family, and the elderly couple had relocated to the other side of the room so Levi's parents, brothers, and sisters could all sit together. They all had their heads lowered, and Mary stayed respectfully quiet, even though she wanted to meet them all, to know them.

Everyone looked up when the door opened. The same doctor as before walked toward Mary, and she stood up on weak knees.

He put a hand on her arm, then glanced around at the group. "More family, I'm assuming?"

Levi's parents and brothers and sisters nodded.

"I wanted to let Levi's wife know that we're running behind on a couple tests. It might be a while longer before we have the final results."

"Wife? Levi doesn't have a *fraa*." Helen stood up and searched Mary's face. "At least not that we know of."

Mary wished the floor would open up and swallow her. All eyes were on her. She didn't know what to say, so she stayed quiet. It was Adeline's lie, and eventually Adeline spoke up and told the doctor the truth, and Helen's expression softened.

The room was solemn after the doctor

left. But Mary caught Helen staring at her several times. She even whispered something in Levi's father's ear while keeping an eye on Mary.

It was only a few minutes later when a nurse came out and said two people could go in to see Levi. Helen stood right away and limped to where Mary was sitting, then held out her hand. "I'm Helen, Levi's *mudder.*"

A tear rolled down Mary's face, and she didn't have any words to offer the woman. "Let's go see our boy," Helen said as she put an arm around Mary. "I'm sure he'll be anxious to see his *fraa.*"

Mary shook her head. "I'm so sorry."

The woman squeezed Mary's shoulders. "Don't be. I suspect that out of everyone in that room, you are the one he will open his eyes for."

Mary put an arm around Helen's waist when she felt the woman struggling to walk. "I hope so," she said softly.

Levi blinked a few times, trying to adjust to the bright light around him. He eyed the rainbow of flowers on either side of him. Azaleas, roses, daffodils, begonias, and an abundance of other robust blooms created a bouquet of color that lined the path he walked on toward a stone cottage in the distance.

Butterflies in all colors flitted about with each step he took on the cobblestone path, as he grew closer to a place he'd never seen before but was somehow familiar with. He looked above at the brilliant blue sky without a cloud in sight. Birds tweeted around him, and a pair of cardinals sailed right in front of him. He felt like he should be scared, but he wasn't.

When he reached the wooden door of the cottage, he lifted his hand to knock, but the door gently swung open, revealing a pure white floor. It wasn't tiled or wood. And it looked way too clean to step on, but Levi did.

The cottage was one big room with three windows streaming light that appeared as white as the floor. Only one thing was in the large room. A white piano and a bench. Levi had never seen such a beautiful instrument, grand in every sense of the word.

He froze. Had he died? Was this heaven? Or the other place?

The moment he had the thought, he knew the answer, despite the object that fueled his temptations standing only a few feet from him. Feelings of joy and love wrapped around him like a warm blanket on a cold night as he sat on the piano bench.

He drew in a deep breath and placed his hands on the keys. Then he played, and the music flowed through his veins, soothed his soul, and filled him with a pleasure he'd been craving. There wasn't any guilt. He was as free as the doves flying outside one of the windows.

Here, he was safe from his thoughts. Closing his eyes, he let the music fill his soul like a bear preparing for hibernation, in case this was the last of the soul-quenching food he'd so desperately craved. Maybe he could always carry the feeling with him.

He wasn't sure how long he played, but when he opened his eyes, Mary smiled. Then his eyes drifted to his mother, and she pushed back the hair on his forehead and kissed him there.

"Thank the Lord." His mother wept. "The doctor said you're going to be fine. You have a nasty concussion, but you will probably get to go home tomorrow."

Levi flinched when he shifted his position in the bed, and his head throbbed on one side like there were thousands of marbles rolling around inside. "What happened?"

"You fell off the ladder at Adeline's *haus.*" Mary swiped a tear from her eye. "We were so scared."

Levi reached for her hand. "*Danki* for being here."

Mary blushed, but he wasn't letting go of her hand just because his mother was in the room.

"I need to go let everyone know you are all right." *Mamm* kissed him on the forehead again and smiled. "I'm sure you're in *gut* hands here with your *fraa.*" She glanced at Mary and grinned before she left.

"Maybe *Mamm* is the one who hit her head. She thinks we're married?" Levi tried to smile, but even the small movement made his head hurt.

"Adeline told the hospital staff we were all family, in case your actual family wasn't here when they finally allowed someone to see you." Grinning and still blushing, she said, "Adeline said I was your wife, she was your grandmother, and Natalie was your sister."

Levi laughed, then regretted it. "How did Natalie know?"

Mary explained that Natalie had come back looking upset, but they didn't know what was wrong.

Then Levi's stomach roiled. "Who all is here?"

"Everyone. Your whole family."

He cringed again, but this time because

he suspected they'd all come straight from their work. They each had one outfit for Sundays, some of which had come from Percy's clothes that Adeline had given them. But on most days, Levi's family probably looked like misfits compared to Mary's. Jacob always wore pants that were way too short. Abram wasn't fond of baths. Lloyd and Ben smelled like horses if they'd had a shoeing job. Levi dressed similarly, but he had been at Adeline's to paint, so that excused his clothes. When he'd taken Mary to eat pizza, he'd worn his Sunday clothes.

Levi was about to make excuses for his family, but then he remembered a piano. A white room, a white piano, a cobblestone path, and a one-room cottage.

"I have something to tell you. Something important."

His mother returned, saying everyone wanted to see him, and the doctors had agreed to two at a time. Mary squeezed his hand, but then let go and excused herself, promising to see him soon.

"Bye, *mei fraa,*" he said softly, trying to grin. She smiled, her cheeks bright red, then told his mother goodbye before she left.

"She seems like a lovely *maedel.*" *Mamm* put her hand on his.

She is.

■ ■ ■ ■

Natalie showed up at Adeline's the following Saturday wearing an old pair of overalls she'd used when she dressed as a scarecrow for Halloween one year. Her class was over, and her new work schedule made it inconvenient to see Adeline on Wednesdays, but she wanted to keep up the relationship with her new friend.

She liked Mary and Levi, too, but Levi was out of commission for a couple weeks — not even allowed to drive the buggy. In addition to the concussion — which he was prescribed rest for — he also had a sprained ankle and some bad bruising on his back. Natalie knew a thing or two about painting, and she wanted to be productive and help Adeline like everyone else.

By lunchtime Natalie was covered in paint.

"Have you been to see Levi since he went home from the hospital?" She savored Adeline's chicken salad sandwiches, and Mary brought cakes and pies from the bakery. Natalie wasn't much good in the kitchen, but maybe she'd experiment so she could contribute something next weekend.

"*Nee,* it's too far for the horse to travel forty miles to Orleans." Mary glanced at

Adeline. "I was going to ask you if I could spend the night and go the rest of the way tomorrow, but we have worship service tomorrow."

Natalie took a sip of tea, careful not to spill any on the red furniture. Her mother might think it was hideous, but Natalie loved it. She liked everything about Adeline's parlor. Maybe because there was a lot of laughter, storytelling, and eating.

"Mary." Natalie chuckled. "I have a *car*. I can take you over there later, after I finish painting."

Mary's face lit up. "That would be wonderful. *Danki* so much."

"I know I wouldn't want to be apart from my guy for that long." She blew out an exasperated breath. "Assuming I had a guy."

"And why don't you?" Adeline had laid her head back against the couch, and sometimes she looked like she'd dozed off, but Natalie didn't think she missed anything they said. She'd also noticed that the air-conditioning still wasn't on, even though Adeline told them she'd taken care of it last Saturday.

Natalie thought for a few seconds. "I guess because I've never met anyone who gave me that weird feeling that is presumably love."

Mary chuckled. "That's how I felt when I met Levi." She paused, turning to Adeline. "Levi and I met at Percy's funeral when we were ten. I don't think I ever told you that. He promised to write to me but never did."

Adeline laughed. "Well, it must have been meant to be."

Mary wasn't sure where things stood between her and Levi. They'd only been on one date and shared one kiss, but her stomach swirled with anticipation about seeing him later today. She was also anxious to find out what he wanted to tell her.

For now she was in the parlor enjoying a chicken salad sandwich with Natalie and Adeline. Mary looked forward to Adeline's chicken salad. It was better than her mother's, although she'd never tell *Mamm* that.

Today Mary had helped Adeline organize a closet at the end of the hallway, but they'd gotten sidetracked when Adeline stumbled upon a box of old pictures, mostly of her and Percy. Mary loved hearing Adeline explain where they were and what they were doing in the photos, which were such treasured items to Adeline. Mary wouldn't have a box like that to rummage through when she was older. Her people didn't allow photographs. She hoped her memory was still intact by the time she was Adeline's age.

"We haven't worked on the puzzle today." Mary wiped her mouth with her napkin before she set it on her plate.

Natalie collected their dishes to take to the kitchen. "Adeline and I got a little nervous about the picture when all the tan sections started to look less like sand and more like skin."

Mary stiffened. "Oh."

Natalie left the room, and Mary picked up her empty glass and followed her new friend to the kitchen. In a whisper, Mary asked, "Do you think it's strange that Adeline's electricity isn't on yet? If she paid the bill with her credit card over the phone, shouldn't it have been turned back on by now?"

"Yeah. I think so. Maybe we should ask her to check on it again while we're here." Natalie set the plates in the sink before she motioned for Mary to walk over to the table with the puzzle. "Stand right here. At a distance, the picture starts coming together." She pointed to the section on the left. "That looks like legs."

Mary turned away. "*Ya,* it does."

Natalie put the bread in the pantry, and Mary rinsed out her glass. "I hope I'm not prying, but when you came back to Adeline's last Saturday, it looked like you'd been crying. Is everything all right now?"

Natalie sighed as she leaned against the kitchen counter and put her hands in the pockets of her blue overalls splashed with white paint. It was nice of her to take up where Levi left off.

"My dad and his girlfriend are moving to Mississippi. I've been so mad at him about leaving my mom for this other woman, and I guess I thought we had all the time in the world to somehow get back the relationship we used to have. I figured with time we'd find a way to get through it. I never thought he would move so far away."

Mary leaned against the opposite counter and faced Natalie. She wanted to tell her about Lydia. She was hesitant to tell anyone, but she wished she had a friend her age to talk to about it. Natalie was worldly. Maybe she would see things differently. Mary's mother was in a tizzy trying to hurry and get Samuel and Lydia married, insisting that was the best thing to do since Lydia was pregnant.

Mary looked forward to this new life coming into their family, but she worried for her sister. Her parents were arguing a lot, and her mother was very embarrassed since word had gotten out. Under different circumstances, Mary might have invited Natalie to her house. She'd had *Englisch* friends over for visits before. Usually they didn't become close because those girls were planning to go to college and they just had too many differences. Natalie and Mary had Adeline in common.

"That must be hard for you. Are you close with your mother?" Mary couldn't imagine what a divorce must be like.

Natalie shrugged. "When my mother's perfect life fell apart, she pretty much fell apart too. I feel sorry for her, but I also needed to get away from her. That's why I moved out. I want her to learn to take care of herself. My dad did everything for her. She'd never worked, except to run the household. Plus, her negativity wasn't helping me get on with my life."

Mary nodded. She wanted even more to tell Natalie about her situation at home. Natalie's mother sounded a little like Mary's *mamm.* Pride was frowned upon in their world, but her mother strived for perfection in everything she did. Lydia's mishap had thrown her into a tailspin. Mary had been wondering if she was more like her mother than she wanted to admit, since she had been shouldering a heavy load of embarrassment about Lydia's pregnancy.

They rejoined Adeline in the living room. She was sitting on the couch smiling, her hands folded in her lap and one leg crossed over the other.

Mary wanted to ask her about the electricity as the fan hummed softly, but Adeline looked like she was in another world.

"Adeline, are you all right?" Mary and Natalie walked toward her. Mary had to ask her the question a second time before Adeline looked her way.

"What? Oh yes, dear, I'm fine. I was just listening to Percy play the piano."

Mary glanced at Natalie, who shrugged.

"He'll be done shortly," Adeline said in a whisper. "You girls have a seat."

Mary and Natalie sat down, exchanging confusing glances.

"Isn't it lovely?" Adeline looked like she was in a trance, her eyes twinkling as she kept them focused on the piano.

Mary just nodded.

CHAPTER 12

"I wish Adeline had come with us." Natalie couldn't stop thinking about her odd behavior. She turned on the road Adeline said would take them to Levi's house. Adeline told them she'd never been there, but she knew roughly where it was from Helen. "Do you think she really thinks she's seeing Percy? Maybe she's got the beginnings of Alzheimer's."

"I don't know. She scared Levi and me once when she looked like she was having a heart attack, but she said it was esophageal spasms." Mary paused. "I don't think that could have anything to do with her confusion. I think we are the only people who visit her. I'm going to ask to cut back my hours at the bakery so I can see her more often." Mary threw her hands to the dashboard when Natalie hit the brakes too hard, trying to avoid a big pothole in the road.

"Sorry about that." She maneuvered her

car around other dips in the gravel road. "This must not be a county-maintained road. It's a mess."

They were quiet for a while. Natalie pondered ways she might be able to see Adeline more often, but with her job it would be difficult. She cleared her throat.

"Levi's family seemed nice. I talked to some of them while you were in the hospital room with Levi's mother." She paused and bit her lip for a few seconds. "Did you happen to notice the tall guy with the dark hair?"

Mary turned her way and grinned. "You'll have to be more specific. They were all tall, except for the youngest boy, who I think is Abram. And all of the men had dark hair. Levi is the only one with light-colored hair — him and one of his sisters."

"Yeah, I know. But this guy stood out in the crowd. He was just super good-looking." Natalie hadn't stopped thinking about him all week. She was glad she'd worn decent clothes underneath her overalls, which had paint all over them. She'd done a pretty good job scrubbing the paint off her arms and face, and she'd reapplied a little makeup before they left for Orleans, which was only about twenty minutes away by car.

"I'd never met any of Levi's family before

last Saturday. He's talked about them some, but I can't even remember all their names."

"Maybe the cute one I'm talking about will be there today. I'll point him out to you."

Mary twirled the string on her prayer covering. "Be careful. Falling for an Amish man would surely complicate your life."

"Yeah, I know. I wouldn't let that happen." Natalie wasn't very religious. She prayed, but not as much as Mary and Levi's people did. She hadn't been raised going to church, so the whole religion thing was a bit of a mystery. "I'll just look into his gorgeous brown eyes and pretend things are different." She slowed down when she saw a white house with blue trim on the left, with four buggies out front. "Is that the place?"

"I don't know. Get closer to the mailbox and see if there's a name on it."

Natalie pulled up to the mailbox. "Yep. Shetler. Wow. It's kind of a small house for such a large family. But the yard is really pretty. Look at all the flowers." She'd lived around the Amish her entire life. The women were responsible for the yard and landscaping, and most homesteads were pretty. Not all, but most.

She turned onto the driveway.

Mary tucked a few loose hairs beneath her *kapp.* Her chest was tight, her stomach churning. As much as she wanted to see Levi, they'd come unannounced and uninvited. Mary assumed that a family of twelve probably had to keep to a rigid schedule to keep order.

"Look." Natalie pointed to a hand pump near the house. "Does that mean they don't have indoor plumbing?" Her eyes widened.

"Maybe not. There's an outhouse to the side of the house, more in the backyard really." Mary couldn't imagine that to be the case. "It's probably left from a long time ago. Levi told me his family was very Old Order traditional. They don't use propane or solar panels, and they don't use phones at all. But I can't imagine not having indoor plumbing."

Natalie sighed. "I hope I don't have to go to the bathroom while I'm here, if they don't have a regular bathroom in the house. I've been in a few Amish homes, and they all had indoor plumbing. Some of the houses even had things that aren't allowed, like wallpaper and fancy furnishings."

"It depends on what district you live in.

Some bishops are strict and some are more lenient. Where we live in Montgomery, our bishop overlooks a lot." Mary was thankful for that, but an unwed pregnancy would not be overlooked by Bishop Miller.

They climbed the steps that led to the front door. Natalie knocked as Mary held her breath.

A tall, very nice-looking young man answered the door. Mary didn't think he was as handsome as Levi, but based on Natalie's dropped jaw and loss for words, Mary assumed this must be her guy. She was about to speak when Natalie found her voice.

"I don't know if you remember us, but we —"

"I remember you." Natalie's heartthrob stared at her in much the same way Natalie ogled him.

Mary stifled a grin. Even though it was cute, it could be disastrous to encourage any spark that might be trying to fuse. Mary had seen it plenty of times, outsiders trying to convert to their ways. It rarely worked out.

"We're here to see Levi." Mary broke the silence, which finally got the man's attention turned to her. "I'm Mary, Levi's friend."

He pushed open the screen door, and

Mary smelled something delicious baking.

"And I'm Natalie."

"I know." Smiling, he ushered them into the living room.

Natalie tripped over the threshold and would have fallen if the man hadn't caught her around the waist. He let her go right away, but Mary wondered if the act was intentional.

"I'm sorry. We met so many of you at the hospital. I'm embarrassed to say I don't remember your name." Mary breathed in the enticing fragrance.

"Lucas."

Mary cringed when she realized it wasn't cookies or cakes baking. It smelled more like meat in the oven. "I'm so sorry. I just realized that we're intruding at the supper hour."

Lucas chuckled. "*Ach,* I hope you're hungry. *Mamm* is going to force you to stay and eat with us."

Mary could hear loud voices coming from the next room. She hadn't thought this through. She'd just been anxious to see Levi. "We might not have enough time to get back to Adeline's before dark," she whispered to Natalie. "Then I have to drive my buggy home."

"Just stay at Adeline's tonight."

Mary thought for a few seconds. She would enjoy getting to know Levi's family a little bit, but she would miss worship service or be late, even if she left Adeline's at daybreak. She never missed church, so maybe it would be okay. "*Ya,* okay. And I can at least keep an eye on Adeline tonight."

Natalie followed Lucas to the next room with Mary trailing behind them, taking in the living room. It was small and there were a lot of things everywhere. The stack of shoes by the front door was huge. The rack for hats and capes was three times as long as the one at Mary's house. A load of towels was folded on the couch. Disheveled, but clean.

They turned the corner into the dining room where a long table stretched from wall to wall and was filled with men seated and ready to be served. They were all talking over each other, voices rising and falling as topics of conversation changed. Only their father was quiet at the head of the table. He watched his sons as if he were trying to take in every conversation going on.

"We have company," Lucas said above the ruckus. It took a few seconds, but the room went completely silent. All eyes were on Natalie and Mary when Levi's mother — Helen, Mary remembered — walked into the room.

She smiled and walked to Mary, giving her a quick hug, then she said hello to Natalie. "I didn't hear anyone knock, but I knew it would take something pretty important for all my boys to go silent the way they did." She waved an arm toward the men and the boy, Abram. "Carry on."

Helen motioned for Natalie and Mary to follow her into the kitchen where three young women were scrambling with pots and bowls. "We have company."

After greetings were exchanged, Mary apologized for interrupting the supper hour.

"We don't get a lot of company," Levi's sister, who introduced herself as Hannah, said, smiling. "We're happy to have you here."

"And you must stay for supper." Helen wiped her hands on her apron as sweat poured down both sides of her face. A small battery-operated fan was on the windowsill. It was almost unbearably hot in the small kitchen. Each time one of the girls opened a wood-burning oven to retrieve more food, the room got even warmer.

There were two ovens, and Levi's three sisters and mother worked with amazing precision, as if every move they made was timed perfectly. Mary was in awe. She'd never used a wood-burning stove in her life. And like Levi had mentioned, there wasn't a refrigerator either. Mary picked up her jaw when Helen said her name.

"I know you came to see Levi. He's upstairs. It's going to be a few more minutes until we're ready to eat." She smiled and shook her head. "Those boys expect supper every evening at four o'clock, and they all know it's never ready by then." She laughed. "But they like to gather and tell tales about their day. Never a quiet moment in this *haus*."

"I can stay and help you in the kitchen in case Levi and Mary want to be alone." Mary knew Natalie meant no harm with the statement, but it wouldn't be ignored.

Helen and her daughters all stopped what they were doing and looked at Natalie. Helen wiped her hands on her apron again. "It wouldn't be proper for Levi and Mary to be alone in his bedroom."

Natalie pressed her lips together, and Mary couldn't tell if it was to keep from laughing — *Please don't laugh, Natalie* — or, if it was to keep from talking. She eventually said, "Of course. What was I thinking?"

Holding a wooden spoon, Helen pointed toward the living room. "Up the stairs, third door on the right. Please knock. And tell him I'll bring him a plate up soon."

Mary nodded and then followed Natalie past the dining room, into the living room, and up the stairs.

"Really? You can't be alone with a member of the opposite sex?" Natalie whispered.

"*Ya*, of course we can. We're allowed to date when we turn sixteen, and we don't have chaperones. It would just be inappropriate since it's Levi's bedroom."

"Well, I can sit in the hallway if you two want to smooch." Natalie leaned over her shoulder, grinning.

"There's not going to be any smooching." Levi would never kiss her with Natalie there.

"You never know."

They reached the third door on the right, and Natalie pushed it open before Mary had time to remind her to knock.

Natalie took two steps in, and two steps back out, pulling the door closed again.

"What are you doing?" Mary scowled. "Helen said to knock."

Natalie pushed her lips into a pout, which quickly turned into a thin-lipped smile. "Yep. And I suppose we should have. I've always wondered if Amish guys wore boxers or briefs. Now I know." She raised both shoulders, held them there, then lowered them and slapped her arms to her sides. "I have to go to the bathroom, if there is one. If I walk in Levi's room right now, I might die of embarrassment." She took a few steps farther down the hallway, then turned to face Mary and started walking backward. "It's boxers, in case you were wondering."

Natalie disappeared around the corner. Mary stood outside the door unsure what to do. She was about to knock when Levi opened the door, smiling. And dressed. He glanced both ways down the hall, then eased her into his bedroom, leaving the door open.

"When I saw Natalie, I figured you were with her." He chuckled. "Doesn't that girl know how to knock?"

Mary trembled when he caressed her face with the back of his hand, his fingers barely brushing against her lips. "Are you supposed to be out of bed?"

"*Nee,* I'm not." He cupped her cheeks with his hands and kissed her. "I've missed you."

"I've missed you, too, and I've been curious to know what you wanted to tell me." She'd been anticipating the kiss even more, but she was sure whatever Levi had to say was important too.

He took her hand and sighed. "Well, since I'm not supposed to be out of bed, you know what that means." He tugged her toward the bed, and she broke free of his grasp, giggling.

"Levi!" she said in a loud whisper.

"It's okay. I'm on medication, so I'm not really responsible for my actions." He winked as he walked toward her and pulled her into his arms again. His lips touched hers like a whisper at first, then his mouth covered hers, and Mary's knees went weak with a dreamy intimacy she'd never felt before.

"I knew there would be smooching!"

Mary pushed Levi away and turned to face Natalie, who was pointing a finger at them.

Levi laughed. "Don't you *ever* knock?"

Natalie folded her arms across her chest. "Hey. This time the door was *open.*"

"Your *mudder* asked us to stay for supper." Mary tucked her chin for a few seconds before she looked up at him. "I apologized for coming at the supper hour. And your *mamm* said to tell you she'd bring you a plate soon."

"I can't wait that long. Besides, I've been eating up here for a week. I'd like to share a meal with *mei* family, especially since you two are here."

"It smells great. But you said you're supposed to be in bed." Mary put her hands on her hips.

Levi motioned for her to follow him as he stumbled his way out the door.

"Are you okay? You really are on medication, aren't you?" She put an arm around his waist when he started to swerve on the stairs.

Natalie had rushed down ahead of them and was already on the landing.

"I think she might have a crush on your brother, Lucas." Mary removed her arm from around his waist before they came in view of his family.

"*Ya,* I think it might be mutual. Lucas asked me about her after we left the hospital." He stopped and looked at her with glassy eyes. "I hope Natalie brought you in her car or you're not going to get home before dark."

"I probably won't anyway. My horse and buggy are at Adeline's, so I will probably spend the night there. I rarely miss worship service, so I think it should be all right." Pausing, she said, "What did you want to tell me?"

"Something happened to me when I was in the hospital. I'll tell you when we have more time."

"And I need to tell you about Adeline. I

think something might be wrong with her mind."

Levi stopped, the scar on his nose crinkling as he frowned.

"But on a happier note, Natalie did some painting today. She wanted to help, but she stayed off the ladder and touched up some places around the windows."

"That was nice of her."

"*Ya*. But we don't want anything getting started with her and Lucas."

"I agree, but I guess that's up to them."

Levi felt like he imagined a drunk person would, though he'd never tasted alcohol. The pain medication he was on kept him loopy. He still felt like marbles were rolling around in his head, but his ankle and back were better.

Until they joined the others, he hadn't worried about what Mary would think of his family. He was just happy to see her. But as the voices grew louder in the dining room, he hoped his brothers didn't embarrass him. Or his sisters. The girls probably already had him married off.

There were two extra places set at the table, one between two of his sisters and one between Jacob and Lucas. Natalie quickly took the seat next to Lucas. Even if

Levi's siblings embarrassed him, hopefully his mother's cooking would make up for some of it.

"It's nice you felt up to joining us, *sohn.*" Levi's father smiled at him before turning to Mary. "And we are happy to have friends to share a meal with."

His mother set a third place for Levi. After everyone prayed, *Mamm* filled Abram's plate, and Natalie and Mary took offerings from two platters near them, the roast and a large bowl of carrots. Then the rush was on. Levi glanced at Mary, then Natalie. Mary waited patiently, but Natalie fought for spoons the same way Levi's brothers did.

Eventually everyone had a plateful but Mary. She daintily served herself from bowls she could reach, then asked for others to be passed to her. He loved that about her. She was so patient and had great manners. Levi tended to talk with his mouth full, overeat, and had been known to push his peas onto a fork with his finger, a habit from when he was little. He would be a bundle of nerves dining at Mary's house.

As Levi's brothers refilled their plates, Mary held easy conversation with Levi's sisters. They were talking about an upcoming wedding, and Mary said her sister was getting married soon. Levi thought her sister was several years younger than Mary, but maybe he'd misunderstood.

He couldn't stop looking at her. Lucas seemed easily as fixated with Natalie, watching her, smiling at her. *Trouble brewing.* His folks would never allow one of their children to date an *Englischer,* baptized or not. Officially, Lucas could do what he wanted since he hadn't been baptized yet. But house rules trumped the *Ordnung* in some cases, and Levi's father was a stickler about certain things.

After the meal, Levi and Mary walked outside and sat on the swing. He wasn't surprised when Lucas followed Natalie onto the porch. Levi's mother had declined the girls' offers to help clean up.

Lucas sat next to Natalie on the porch steps, but she seemed distracted by something else. Her face was red and scrunched up like she was holding her breath, and she kept wiggling, shifting her weight, and wringing her hands. All of a sudden, she bolted up and said, "I can't stand it anymore!" Then she took off.

"Where is she going?" Lucas asked about the same time Levi did. They watched her run across the yard, then make a sharp turn around the corner.

Mary's face turned a little red. "I guess

251

she's going to the outhouse."

Lucas and Levi exchanged glances. "Why didn't she just use the bathroom inside?" Levi asked.

Mary burst out laughing. "I guess she didn't find one upstairs."

"There's one between two of the bedrooms upstairs and another one downstairs, but you have to pass through *Mamm*'s sewing area. She should have asked." Levi slurred a little as he talked, and he flinched if the swing moved.

"You need to get back to bed." Mary stood, taking Levi's arm and helping him up.

"*Ya,* I guess I do. The doc said one more week of bed rest, and then I'll be able to do light work around here and go back to Adeline's on Saturdays. He suggested I stay off ladders for a while, but I finished most of the ladder work before I fell. I'll finish touching up the paint and start on the yard."

Natalie raced around the corner, her arms swinging at her sides. It was still a few hours until dark, so it was easy to see that her face was white, and once again, she looked like she was holding her breath. She started shaking her head as she neared them.

"I'm sorry. I really am." She took a deep breath and brought a hand to her chest.

"But I don't see how your family uses that outhouse." Cringing, she crossed her arms over her chest.

Lucas's eyes captured hers as he grinned. "We don't use that outhouse. We use the bathrooms inside."

Levi chuckled. "No one has used that thing in decades. No telling what's down that hole. Maybe snakes or critters."

Natalie's eyes were wide. "Well, someone should have told me!"

Lucas laughed. "Let's go for a walk and give these two a little privacy to say good-bye."

Levi turned to Mary. "I want to kiss you again so bad, but I feel like I might fall over, and someone is surely spying on us from a window somewhere."

"I still want you to tell me what happened at the hospital."

"Ya, ya." Levi told her about his dream, and Mary seemed in awe of the details he could recall, her gaze never leaving his. "It was the most wonderful feeling I've ever had in my life."

"I've heard of near-death experiences." Mary touched his arm. "Do you think that's what happened?"

"I don't know. It was more like a dream. But, Mary, it was real. I know it was. It was a glimpse of heaven. *Gott* wouldn't have shown me that piano if it wasn't okay to play it."

They turned toward the yard when they heard laughter. Lucas and Natalie were facing each other, talking and then laughing.

"It won't be *gut* for either of them to take a fancy to the other." Levi shook his head.

"It might be too late," Mary said softly.

CHAPTER 13

Adeline was curled up in Percy's chair. Mary and Natalie were on the red couch, their socked feet propped up on the coffee table, each of them sipping a cup of tea. Adeline had loaned them each nightgowns.

"Natalie, hon, I'm so glad you decided to sleep over too." For the first time in a while Adeline felt safe. The past two nights she'd woken up outside in the yard in the middle of the night, with no idea how she got there. And there were other incidents before that. Little things, like putting her slippers in the refrigerator, and searching for a pack of cigarettes even though she quit smoking thirty years ago.

"It's like a slumber party." Natalie had her blond hair pulled up in a messy bun on top of her head, and she'd taken off her makeup. Adeline was used to seeing Mary without makeup, but she'd never seen her without a prayer covering and had no idea ne girl's dark hair fell well below her waist.

Natalie looked at Mary. "Do your people have slumber parties?"

"*Ya,* but we call them sleepovers."

The girls had already told Adeline about the visit to see Levi, and they'd all laughed about Natalie's trip to the outhouse. Adeline sensed that Natalie might have taken a fancy to one of Levi's brothers.

"Adeline, you've never told us how you and Percy met and fell in love." Mary posed the question with dreamy eyes, the way young people look when they are falling in love.

"Oh my. I don't remember the last time I told this story. Although I recall it often." She paused, smiling. "I remember the first time I saw Percy like it happened yesterday."

Adeline told the girls about the auction, the prize cow, and the details of her first encounter with her husband, including how she'd wanted to be a veterinarian back then. She shared about their courtship two years later and how they were married after only dating for three months.

Mary and Natalie's eyes were wide, their mouths open.

"Our short courtship was rare, even back in those days." Adeline shrugged. "But when you know, you just know." She chuckled.

"And I didn't know that I was five years older than Percy until two months after we'd been married. I asked him how old he was going to be on his birthday." She shook her head. "It didn't matter though. The Lord had blessed our union, and I was sure we'd last until death do us part."

"What happened to you becoming a vet?" Natalie reached for a handful of chips from the bowl on the coffee table. "I've always loved animals. I don't know that I can ever afford to become a veterinarian, but I would love taking care of animals for a living."

Adeline shrugged. "I changed my mind. I was happy being a housewife, and Percy and I wanted lots of children to fill this house. But that wasn't in the Lord's plan. A few years after we were married, I went to college and got my teaching degree. I taught English to thousands of students for twenty-five years. I hope I made a difference in some of their lives."

"Do you still love pets? Levi and I both have a fondness for cats." Mary smiled as she reached for a chip from her stash on a paper towel in her lap.

"Oh yes, I still love the Lord's furry little creatures. I actually had a cat until recently. His name was Smokey. He had beautiful gray fur and a wonderful disposition. If he had a flaw, it was that he loved to catch birds and bring them into the house."

"What happened to him?" Mary asked.

"I don't know. I had him for sixteen years, and a few months ago he just disappeared. He was a wonderful companion."

"I've always wanted a cat," Mary said. "But Lydia is allergic to them."

Adeline recalled Mary's story about Lydia. She didn't want to betray a confidence by inquiring about her in front of Natalie. But she'd been praying for that situation. Maybe the girls would share more with each other, instead of with an old lady who may or may not remember their stories soon.

"I'm going to go to bed. You girls stay up and chat. Those fans you bought do a wonderful job." Adeline eased herself out of Percy's chair.

"Adeline, why isn't the power on?" Natalie raised an eyebrow.

Adeline was sure she called the electric company. She remembered telling them she would pay with her credit card.

She shrugged. "I don't know. But I haven't missed it all that much. I have a propane stove and, thanks to Mary" — she smiled at her lovely Amish friend — "I now have a refrigerator powered with propane. Her father had a small one in his shop. I guess

258

I'm living very similarly to the way you live, Mary." She glanced at Natalie. "But I'm guessing you'd rather have some air-conditioning?"

Natalie giggled. "I think I'm getting used to it too."

"You girls have fun." Adeline kissed them each on the cheek. "Thank you for bringing love back into this house."

Natalie waited until Adeline was gone. "Something isn't right with Adeline."

"She seemed fine tonight. I didn't notice anything odd."

"I did. She kept looking at the piano and smiling." Natalie glanced at the instrument. "You don't think she can really see Percy, do you?"

"*Nee*. I think she cherishes the memories and probably just relives those moments in her mind."

"The electricity should be on by now. I don't understand why it's not." Natalie pulled the band from her hair, gathered it all up, and bundled it on top of her head again. "I called the electric company to see if the problem was on their end or if Adeline was behind on the bill. Since my name isn't on the account, they wouldn't talk to me. I told them she was old and hot, but still . . .

nothing."

"She's old, but I think you're the one who's hot." Mary grinned. "It doesn't seem to bother her, and it's normal for me. I heard you say you were getting used to it."

Grinning, Natalie said, "Well, kinda." She pointed to the piano. "I like that though, the way the glow from the lantern bounces a reflection off the piano." She grimaced. "I thought it might be scary, sitting in the dark, but it's not."

"Luckily, Adeline had lanterns and oil in the garage."

They were quiet for a few moments before Mary asked Natalie about her father, if she was feeling any better about him moving.

"There's nothing I can do about it, so I try not to think about it. I'm staying busy at work, and I'm applying for college scholarships. I'll get to college one way or another, even if I have to take one class at a time and it takes me ten years." She rolled her eyes. "I sure hope it doesn't take that long."

"What kind of schooling will you sign up for?"

"I'm not sure yet."

Natalie wanted to tell Mary about the essay she'd written, the one Adeline had read. But she didn't know Mary very well. She hadn't known Adeline very well either when

she asked her to read it, and she appreciated Adeline taking the time to do so, and
her kind words about it. But it had left Natalie feeling a little exposed.

Mary hung her head for a few moments
before she looked back at Natalie with
glistening eyes and trembling lips.

"What's wrong?"

"My sixteen-year-old *schweschder* is
pregnant." She burst into tears. "And *mei
mudder* is embarrassed and humiliated. It's
brought great shame to our family. But I'm
mostly worried about Lydia. She's only
sixteen, and that's so young."

Natalie could barely understand her
friend. She was crying, gasping for breaths,
and her voice had become tiny and high.
She'd obviously been carrying this burden
for a while.

"I'm guessing she isn't married since she's
so young?"

Mary shook her head. "*Nee.* But *mei mudder* is working hard to get her and Samuel
married quickly. The bishop is involved, and
it's causing such heartache. Lydia and Samuel haven't been baptized, so there is a little
leniency, but it isn't our way for things like
this to happen."

"Things like that happen in all walks of
life, Mary." Natalie pulled her friend into a

hug and stroked her hair the way Natalie's mother used to do with her when she was little. "It will be okay." She held her friend for a while and just kept telling her that everything would be okay. She'd never had a close Amish friend before, even though she'd known plenty of them.

"Levi doesn't know. Please don't tell him." Mary jerked out of the hug, her eyes wide as saucers.

"I won't." Natalie tilted her head to one side. "I'm surprised you haven't told him."

"I will, eventually." She covered her face with her hands. "I probably shouldn't have told you."

"Mary." Natalie touched Mary's arm and left it there until Mary uncovered her face. "I don't think any less of you or your family." She grunted. "Good grief. Look at the mess my family is." Smiling, she said, "Sometimes, we make our own family."

Mary nodded.

They stayed up until two in the morning talking about happier subjects. And they laughed a lot, which they both needed.

Early the following morning, Mary fed her horse some cereal from Adeline's pantry, since that's all she had to give the poor fellow. When she returned to the kitchen,

Adeline was making a pot of coffee.

"Good morning." Mary yawned. She was used to getting up at daybreak, but she wasn't accustomed to staying up until two in the morning.

"And good morning to you." Adeline took three coffee cups from the cabinet. "I'm surprised you're up so early. I woke up to go to the bathroom, and I heard you girls giggling and carrying on." She smiled. "That was nice to hear. I'm glad you two had some time together. Natalie still sleeping?"

Mary nodded as she recalled the relief she'd felt after telling Natalie about Lydia. It seemed to free up her emotions a little and allow her to experience some joy. "*Ya,* we had a *gut* time, but we also talked about some serious issues too."

Adeline laid out a bowl of sugar and took milk from the refrigerator. "I'm sure Natalie talked to you about her parents' divorce. She's had such a hard time with it."

"*Ya,* she did tell me about it." Maybe it would be easier talking about Lydia a second time. "And I told her what's going on with *mei* family too." She waited until Adeline looked up at her, then she took a deep breath. "Lydia is pregnant. As it turns out, she and Samuel were doing more than

263

kissing after all." There was another level of relief to be able to share the news with Adeline.

"Aw, hon. I knew something had been bothering you." She shook her head. "She's so young, and I don't doubt this is hard on your family. I will pray for Lydia, Samuel, and your family." She smiled a little. "But a baby is a blessing, and the good Lord always has a plan."

"Hey, hey." Natalie walked into the room stretching and yawning. "I could have sworn I smelled bacon. Maybe I dreamed it."

"Well, we can certainly get some breakfast going if you girls do the heavy lifting." Adeline pointed to one of the lower cabinets. "My favorite skillet is down there."

Mary gathered everything they'd need to make breakfast, and following the meal, she decided she should probably go home and face the music at her house. She hugged Adeline and Natalie goodbye, yawning the entire time, as was Natalie. But what a wonderful time they'd had chatting and getting to know each other.

By the time she arrived home, her family was back from worship service. Mary had called the night before to let her parents know she'd be staying at Adeline's overnight.

Her father looked above the rims of his reading glasses. "How is Levi doing?"

Mary had told her parents she and Levi were friends. They probably suspected Levi was more than a friend, but Mary had left it at that. "He's much better. He only has one more week of resting, and then he can start on light duty around the farm and at Adeline's house."

"That's wonderful news," *Mamm* said, smiling as she knitted something with yellow yarn. *Daed* echoed her mother's comment.

"Where's Lydia?"

Mamm smiled again. "She's upstairs, probably resting."

Mary hadn't seen things this calm in her house since Lydia announced she was pregnant. Her mother had been aimlessly wandering the house or trying to plan a wedding or thinking up ways to save her family's reputation. And her father had been constantly angry about both Lydia and their mother's actions and attitudes.

But things seemed normal again.

"I'm going to rest too." Mary moved toward the stairs.

"People asked where you were this morning, but we explained that you were visiting a sick friend, and everyone understood."

Leave it to her mother to save face. *"Ya,* okay. *Gut."*

On the way to her room, she paused at Lydia's door. Her sister had been bitter about everything, and she hadn't said much to Mary. But Mary's heart hurt for Lydia. She knocked and opened the door to peek in. Lydia was curled up on the bed, still in her church clothes.

"Please go away." She was lying on her side, her knees pulled to her chest.

Mary sat on the bed. "I'm not going away, and this situation isn't going away. But *Mamm* and *Daed* must have come to terms with everything because they are acting much better than they were a few days ago."

"*Ach,* I'm sure they are." Lydia's shoulder's shook as she started to cry.

Mary scooted closer until she was able to put her hand on her sister's back. "Please talk to me."

"The wedding has been arranged. That's why *Mamm* is so happy. And if *Mamm* is happy, *Daed* is happy."

"When will it be?"

"In two weeks."

Mary rubbed Lydia's back. "I know this wasn't your plan. Or Samuel's. But sometimes our plan isn't *Gott*'s plan."

Lydia swiped at her eyes and stayed in a

fetal position on her side. "This isn't *Gott*'s plan. It can't be. I went against *Gott,* and now I'm being punished."

"Our *Gott* is loving and forgiving, and for whatever reason, this is His will, and you must accept it. We don't always understand *Gott*'s will, but it is for the best."

Lydia rolled onto her back, but kept her legs bent at the knees. She held Mary's gaze, and instead of a young woman about to be a mother, Mary saw a scared child.

"You are going to be okay, Lydia." She placed a gentle hand on her sister's tummy. "You are going to be a *mudder,* and you will be a good one. We must welcome this new life and see him or her as a gift. Looking backward isn't going to do you any good. You and Samuel made a mistake, but now you make the best of it."

Mary didn't know if it was a one-time error in judgment or if they had committed the act more than that. She didn't want to know.

"*Gott* has forgiven you. Just try to embrace the joy about being a *mudder.*"

Lydia put her hand on Mary's. "I want to be a *gut mudder.*" There was a long pause, then Lydia's eyes watered up even more. "But I don't want to marry Samuel, and they can't make me."

Oh dear. "Why not, *mei maedel*? Don't you think that's the best thing to do? I know you're young to be a *fraa,* but it's best for you and the *boppli.*"

Lydia squeezed her eyes closed before she opened them and said, "I don't know if I love Samuel. And every time I look at him, I am reminded about our sin." She put her hands on her stomach, sniffling. "Will I feel that way when I look at our *boppli*?"

Mary wanted to tread lightly, to help her sister, not make things worse, but Lydia was in this spot as a consequence of her actions. "*Nee, mei maedel,* a *boppli* is a gift from *Gott,* no matter how it happened, and you will love this child no matter what." She paused and took a deep breath. "Why were you intimate with Samuel if you didn't know if you loved him?"

"It only happened one time. I thought I loved him. I thought maybe I would know for sure if . . ."

Mary's chest tightened. "Did Samuel push you into having intimate relations with him?"

Lydia scowled. "*Nee.* He would never do that."

Mary didn't think Samuel would coerce Lydia, but she was glad to hear her say it. And her defensiveness led Mary to believe that maybe there was more love than Lydia realized.

"I haven't been baptized. I know that doesn't excuse my sin. But I can choose not to be Amish if they try to make me marry Samuel."

Mary rubbed her temples as tension built. "You can't do that, Lydia."

"*Ya,* I can."

After running a hand through Lydia's loose strands of hair, Mary said, "You can't do that because I would miss you too much." Mary choked back tears. "I love you."

Lydia sat up and threw her arms around Mary and held on tight. "I love you too. But they can't make me marry Samuel. He smells like garlic all the time."

Mary eased away and hung her head. Lydia sounded like the sixteen-year-old child she was. She looked back at her sister. "I'm not sure that's a *gut* enough reason. Maybe you can just tell him not to eat so much garlic."

Lydia locked eyes with Mary. "I already did."

Mary was at a loss for words. She wanted Lydia to be happy, but she could already foresee her mother's wrath if Lydia refused to marry Samuel, and that caused Mary to shiver.

More than anything, Mary feared her sister running away from home.

CHAPTER 14

Levi had looked forward to Saturday all week long. He finished painting and touching up the trim around the windows, little spots Natalie had missed, although he appreciated her doing the work. When his back began to ache a couple hours after lunch, he went inside.

The ladies were in the parlor. Mary was usually barefoot, but Natalie had kicked off her shoes as well, and both women had their feet stretched out on either side of the coffee table. Adeline was in Percy's chair, also barefoot.

"*Wie bischt.* You ladies just lounging around?"

"Hey, we've been working too." Natalie lifted her hands, which were covered with smudges of dirt. "I cleaned the fireplace." She nodded at Mary and Adeline. "And those two went through some things in the extra bedroom and boxed up what Adeline didn't need."

Levi chuckled as he held up both palms. "*Ya, ya.* Okay. I'm done for today, though."

"Maybe you'd want to play the piano?" Adeline crossed one leg over the other as she tipped her head to one side.

Levi remembered how happy Adeline had been when he played and Mary sang along. Adeline said she'd always thought playing an instrument was forbidden, and neither Levi or Mary had commented. What would Natalie think? She'd grown up around Amish folks, so she likely knew a lot of the rules.

"*Ya,* okay." Levi sat on the bench and began to play a melody in his head that he didn't recall playing before, and as his fingers followed the sounds in his mind, he closed his eyes and waited for Mary to join him. When she didn't, he looked over his shoulder. Mary smiled with a gentleness and calm Levi wished he could bottle up and take with him everywhere. Natalie's mouth hung open, her eyes round as saucers. Adeline dabbed at her eyes with a tissue.

Levi stopped. "Did I do something wrong, or play something you didn't like?" He glanced at each of them again.

"Dude." Natalie shook her head. "That

was amazing. I didn't think your people could own instruments, and yet" — she pointed to him — "you play better than concerts I've attended, people I've seen on TV, and . . . just wow. Who taught you to play like that?"

Pride consumed Levi in a way he'd never felt before. The piano was the only thing he'd ever excelled at. "No one taught me. I just know how."

"He's a prodigy," Adeline said as she dabbed at her eyes again. Then she looked upward. "Forgive me, Percy" — her gaze went back to Levi — "but he plays even better than you did."

Levi wasn't sure what a prodigy was, but the pride continued to swell inside him. He could do something the average person couldn't. He'd seen a piano in what he believed was a glimpse at heaven. How could something so beautiful be forbidden? He began to play again. This time he played something a little faster and upbeat. Even though the women's tears appeared to be happy ones, he didn't like to see anyone cry.

They all clapped when he was done, and Levi thought he might explode with gratification. He even took a bow.

Then his mother's words came crashing down around him like it was raining stones.

Sohn, there are a lot of voices that call to us. And sometimes it is difficult to discern who the voice is. But I guarantee you, if you think that piano is calling to you, that isn't the voice of our Lord. It's the other voice. Keep that in mind as temptation calls to you.

Levi considered her words, his upbringing, and the *Ordnung. Maybe the* Ordnung is *wrong.* He heard his mother's voice in his mind again, and his stomach twisted and churned. The joy that had seeped into his veins felt like poison now.

Natalie cleared her throat, interrupting his unwanted thoughts.

"I gotta go." She lifted herself from the couch and hugged Levi. "You're an amazing piano man." Then she hugged Mary and Adeline.

Shortly after Natalie left, Adeline excused herself to take a nap, which she usually did around midafternoon. Levi walked to the couch and sat beside Mary. All day he'd hoped they would have time to be alone so he could kiss her. Now, his heart flipped in his chest, and his mind was a flurry of confusion.

"What's wrong?" Mary touched his hand, and he closed his eyes, hoping some of her gentle calmness would rub off on him. He looked at her when she squeezed his hand.

"I can't stop thinking about that dream or vision I had. I can see it in my mind: the cottage, the flowers, the butterflies, the white room, and the piano."

"It's a lovely image." Mary paused. "Why are you so bothered by it now?"

Levi thought for a few moments. "I'm not sure. At first, I took it as a sign from *Gott* that there was nothing wrong with playing the piano, like He was giving me permission."

"You don't feel that way now?" Mary tipped her head slightly to one side.

"I don't know. Something was different today." He shook his head. "It felt wrong, and I'm confused because even though it didn't feel right today, that vision floats back into my mind. And *mei mamm* said if I feel called to do something, I need to be able to discern who the calling is coming from." He paused. "*Gott* . . . or the other voice."

"I've had those same thoughts sometimes when I'm singing or listening to a song that *mei* parents wouldn't approve of, songs *Gott* might not approve of either. I wonder, too, if it's temptation, or if it really is okay to enjoy music, and our parents, bishop, and the *Ordnung* are wrong." She took in a breath and blew it out slowly. "And it's hard when no one seems to know why these rules about music and instruments exist."

"Maybe I'm being tested and failing."

They sat quietly, still holding hands.

Mary tapped a finger to her chin. "Maybe you need to talk to your bishop."

Levi cringed. "Our bishop is strict. I'd be ashamed to tell him."

Mary nudged him with her shoulder. "Shame is the devil's work."

Levi huffed. "Maybe playing the piano is too." An idea came to him. "What about your bishop? You said he's lenient. Maybe it would be easier for me to talk to him. Maybe I wouldn't feel like he's judging me as much as Bishop Troyer. And I could meet your family."

Mary had met all of his family, and it didn't seem like their chaos and lack of modern conveniences had scared her off. Maybe she was ready for him to meet her family too.

Mary searched her mind for reasons Levi shouldn't meet her family, recalling the way things had been the past week. Lydia moped around like she'd lost her best friend, but no one was yelling or screaming or crying. But Levi would be able to tell that something was wrong with Lydia. And what if there was an unexpected explosion of emotion? Lydia was unpredictable. Would she remain sullen and quiet? Or would she intentionally try to embarrass their mother in front of Levi?

"That's probably not a *gut* idea. I mean, you should probably go to the bishop in your district." She bit her bottom lip and avoided his eyes. Levi's family was warm, gracious, loud, playful, and all the things her family was not.

Mary loved her parents and Lydia, but her mother was uptight, too formal. Too perfect. No one was perfect, but her mother did her best to show that their family was in order. Lydia's actions had sent her into a tailspin, and even though things had calmed down, Mary wasn't sure the spinning was over. *Mamm*'s reputation — and that of her family — had been damaged.

Levi stood up, pulling his hand from Mary's. "I gotta go."

She stood up and followed him. "What's wrong?"

He was out the door and in the yard by the time Mary caught up to him and grabbed his shirt. "Wait!"

Turning around, he folded his arms across his chest. "I have a lot to think about. I just need to go."

"Did I say something wrong? I just feel

like your bishop would be the best one to talk to, that's all." Her heart pounded.

"I just want to think about things." Levi dropped his arms to his sides. "Tell Adeline I'll be back next Saturday. I think I can finish the yard that day."

Mary tucked her chin for a few seconds, letting Levi's words sink in. "What does that mean? You won't be coming on Saturdays anymore, even to visit?"

"I'm needed at home. Helping Adeline was important to *mei mamm.* But we all work on the farm on Saturdays too. I care about Adeline a lot, so I will find time to visit her, maybe when I make trips to town or cart *mei mudder* somewhere."

Mary bit her bottom lip to try to stop the trembling. "What about me?"

Levi took a step closer. He gently took her face in his hands and kissed her, causing her knees to weaken like the last time. But just like Levi's feelings about the piano feeling different for him, this kiss felt different to Mary. Almost like goodbye. He eased away and kissed her on the forehead, then sighed as he looked past her.

When he finally looked at her again, he held her gaze for a while. "I'll see you next Saturday."

Mary's hurt was morphing into anger. He

said he would be finished with the yard work next Saturday, and it sounded like he would be finished with her as well. She raised her chin and forced a smile.

"Fine. See you then." She turned and walked back to the house so Levi couldn't see the tears spilling down her cheeks. Maybe he wasn't who she thought he was. How long had he known he would finish at Adeline's house next Saturday? Maybe the flirting, the kiss, their conversations . . . maybe he'd never planned to take it any further.

Whatever it was, Mary sure wasn't coming to Adeline's next Saturday. As much as she'd miss seeing her and Natalie, saying goodbye to Levi would be too painful.

Levi loved his family, and now he feared he'd been wrong about Mary's acceptance of them. Was she embarrassed of him and the people he loved most in the world? Was it the disarray in the house? His *mamm* and *schweschdere* worked hard to take care of their family. They were poor by Mary's standards. It sounded like she lived a life of forbidden luxury. He had come up with a good reason to meet her family, and maybe help himself out in the process, and she'd shot down the idea right away.

Levi clicked his tongue to set his horse in motion — a horse and buggy he shared with four other people. Mary had her own horse and buggy.

He thought he had found the right person for him, and his heart ached in a way it hadn't before. But too much was at stake right now, and temptation hung in the air around him like a dense fog he couldn't navigate his way out of. The Lord must be mad at him. He had conflicting ideas about playing the piano and confusing thoughts about Mary.

Levi recalled his run-in with the bishop when he was twelve. But Levi was a grown man now. Or, at eighteen he was expected to be a grown man, even though he wanted to cry right now.

He pulled up to the Troyers' house about fifteen minutes later, unsure how the elderly man would feel about an unannounced visitor. The front door was open, probably to let in the breeze, and Levi could see through the screen door as he knocked. Bishop Troyer rose to his feet from a recliner in the corner. He pushed open the screen door, and Levi resisted the urge to run back to his buggy.

Bishop Troyer stepped onto the porch. Levi was tall, but the bishop towered over him, and the man's bushy eyebrows slanted inward, making him always look angry. His gray beard reached almost to his waist. Just the sight of him caused Levi's insides to twitch and made him feel twelve again.

"*Wie bischt,* Levi. What can I do for you?" The bishop motioned for Levi to have a seat in one of the rocking chairs. The elderly man groaned a little as he sat. He had to be in his eighties by now.

Levi was glad to sit down and give his shaking legs a rest. "I-I, um . . . I need to talk to you about something."

The hint of a smile played on the bishop's face. "*Ya,* I assumed so."

"I-I, um . . ." *This is a mistake.*

"Whatever it is, we will work through it together." Bishop Troyer stroked his beard, its length a reminder that the man had years of wisdom.

"I was in an accident not long ago. I fell off a ladder, and I was unconscious for a while." Levi bent at the waist and rested his arms on his legs.

"*Ya,* I know. Your *mudder* told me at worship service. I've been praying for you, and it looks like you are doing well."

Levi nodded, but didn't look at the man. He needed to just spit it out, so he took a deep breath. "I don't understand why we can't play instruments, or why we aren't allowed to sing songs that aren't approved by you and the elders." He looked up and straightened as a frown took over the older man's face. Bishop Troyer's wrinkles connected like the roadmap of a long life, and when he frowned, he looked even older.

"Where is this coming from?"

Levi took off his hat and placed it in his lap as sweat pooled at his temples. "No one can give me a reason why we aren't allowed to play instruments. All I ever hear is that it's just not allowed. I understand the reasoning behind most things in the *Ordnung,* and I follow our rules, but it doesn't make sense to me about music."

Bishop Troyer sighed. "Which instrument have you been playing? Guitar? Harmonica? Something else?"

Levi stared at the older man as his heart hammered in his chest.

"Do you think you are the first person to come to me with this question? I've lived a long life as the bishop in this district. There isn't much I haven't heard." Bishop Troyer paused, coughing. "There are several reasons we don't play instruments or approve of most music. It invokes unnecessary emotions, for one thing."

Levi shook his head, then told the bishop

about his vision of the cottage and piano. He also told him about the piano at Adeline's house. "I think *Gott* gave me a glimpse of heaven."

"Perhaps he did. I've heard of this happening before. The *Englisch* refer to it as a near-death experience." Bishop Troyer leaned to his right and took a handkerchief from his pocket, then dabbed at the sweat on his forehead.

"I think it was more like a dream or a vision, although it felt real to me, like *Gott* was telling me it is okay to play the piano." He kept his eyes fused with the bishop's, challenging him. "And most of the time, playing the piano makes me happy, peaceful even. How can that be wrong?"

"You just said *most* of the time." Bishop Troyer wiped his forehead again.

Levi thought about how he felt earlier today. He wasn't sure how to explain it.

"Levi, you are old enough to understand why we keep things uniform. What if you had a fancy buggy that was bigger and better than anyone else's? I see this with young men who decorate their buggies, put radios inside, and hang ornamental items on the outside." He scowled a little. "More so in other districts than here."

Levi had never done any of those things.

He was too fearful of the bishop's wrath — and his father's — but he'd seen a few boys decorate their buggies during their *rumschpringe.* He nodded.

"These boys who do this are competing, and competition brings forth an emotion that we try to avoid." He raised an eyebrow.

"Pride." Levi recalled the way he felt today when everyone cried and clapped.

The bishop nodded. "Are you a *gut* piano player?"

"Apparently, I'm a great piano player." Levi regretted the comment the moment it came out.

"And proud of it." Bishop Troyer grimaced. "You can do something most people can't, which makes you appear better than them in that regard. And as such, it fills you with pride."

Levi was quiet as he thought about what the bishop said.

"The *Ordnung* teaches us not to be prideful. Not only is pride involved, but why would we want to manipulate our feelings through music? It has a way of making us feel happy or sad even though nothing in our lives has changed since we started listening."

Levi shook his head. "Bishop Troyer, I understand what you're saying." Again, he recalled how proud he'd been when he played for Adeline, Mary, and Natalie earlier. "I know being prideful is wrong. But I believe with all my heart that *Gott* gave me a sign in my vision, dream, near-death experience, or whatever it was. It was a beautiful place filled with love. There was nothing bad there. I know it. Maybe we have misinterpreted that part of the *Ordnung*." Levi surprised himself by being so forthcoming with the bishop.

"Or maybe *you* have misinterpreted your vision."

"How?" Levi's heart wasn't beating hard anymore. He wanted answers, and his desire to understand helped him press on.

"What color is the piano at Adeline's *haus*?"

"Black." Levi couldn't imagine why that mattered.

"Yet it was white in heaven, in a place where you felt nothing but pure love. There are many references to the color white in the Bible, and it is associated with purity and all things good." The bishop coughed again, and Levi waited.

"During our time here on earth, we can't feel pure love. It is *Gott*'s gift to us when we get to heaven, a place where there is no pride, competition, or manipulation of our emotions. My interpretation of your vision is that you can have anything you want in heaven because your earthly feelings won't interfere with your desires. I think *Gott* was trying to tell you that there will come a time when you can play piano all you want. But not here on earth, thus the black piano at your friend's *haus*. Black is the darkest color in the Bible. It absorbs light but doesn't give any back. We are all imperfect sinners who are unable to control our emotions on our own. We don't need devices that add to that challenge."

Levi hung his head, his thoughts steadily becoming more organized. "I understand. I'm just not sure I can give up the piano forever."

Bishop Troyer shrugged. "Some people cannot desist from whatever temptation is thrown at them, and they leave our community to live a life that allows such things. But could you, in good conscience, seek the rite of baptism while continuing to play the piano?"

This wasn't what Levi wanted to hear. He wanted the man to say that Levi's situation was an exception. He didn't respond to the question, and when the bishop stood up, Levi knew their visit was coming to an end.

"*Danki* for seeing me without notice." Levi

put his hat on. "I'm still unsure."

"You are here because you feel shame for what you've done. The Lord doesn't make us feel that way. We bring out that sin on our own." He looped his thumbs beneath his suspenders. "You want me to see things your way so any feelings of shame will subside. I can't do that."

The bishop extended his hand to Levi. "Go in peace, and I will pray that you make the right choice."

Levi thanked him again and left. He had no idea what to do. And if he didn't feel miserable enough, thoughts of Mary assaulted him.

This wasn't his best day.

CHAPTER 15

Natalie slipped into a pair of blue jeans. She'd rather wear shorts since it was blazing hot outside and in Adeline's house. But out of respect for Levi and Mary, she covered herself as best she could. The Amish didn't like to be around people who wore shorts and tank tops, Natalie's normal summer attire. She had just pulled a plain blue T-shirt over her head when she heard a knock at the door.

After peering through the peephole at her mother, she sighed and opened the door.

Sniffling, her mother crossed over the threshold and into Natalie's sparsely furnished apartment. A rocking chair from a friend at work, an end table from the same friend, a bookshelf she purchased at a garage sale, and her blowup mattress and TV in the bedroom. All was visible from the front door.

"I don't understand why you won't take

some furniture from home. I've offered it to you more than once." Her mother glanced around the room. "I'd buy you some if I had any money."

"I'm saving for some furniture, Mom. What's wrong? Why are you crying?" Natalie picked up her cell phone from the kitchen counter. She was anxious to give Adeline a new puzzle to work on since they decided the other one might be too risqué for their Amish friends. The new one she bought came in a box enclosed in plastic with a beautiful beach scene, since Adeline said she liked the beach.

"Your father said he talked to you." Still sniffling, she sat in the rocking chair. "I cannot believe he and that woman are moving to Mississippi."

"I'm not thrilled about it." Natalie waved her hand. "But I'm not heartbroken about it anymore either. He hasn't been a part of our lives for a while."

Natalie considered that a partial version of the truth. It still stung that her father was leaving, but even worse, he hadn't contacted her since she ran out of the restaurant. Her mother wanted someone to commiserate with, and Natalie didn't want to be that person. Things were going well at work. She had new friends who enjoyed activities that didn't include drinking and partying. Before she met Adeline, Mary, and Levi, Natalie had allowed herself to partake in activities that didn't make her feel very good about herself. She was working to become the person she wanted to be, and drinking and partying didn't have a place in that vision.

"He's an awful man." Her mother crossed one leg over the other, kicking her foot into action as she folded her arms across her chest.

"Mom, I gotta go. It's Saturday, and you know I go to Adeline's on Saturday. Mary and Levi are probably already there." She looked at the time on her cell phone again.

"I'm glad you have become friends with Adeline and the two Amish kids. But don't forget my original reason for encouraging you to spend time with Adeline."

Natalie raised her eyebrows. "*Encouraging* me? You practically forced me to do it. You told me you were about to have a nervous breakdown because you were so worried about money. Dad gave you the house so you could sell it and get something smaller. That would give you some money." She paused. "And you could get a job."

Her mother reached into the purse on her lap and pulled out a tissue and blew her nose. "You know, Natalie, sometimes I wonder if you even love me."

"Mom, please don't say that. You know I love you. But I want you to take the initiative to make a better life for yourself."

They were both quiet. Natalie resigned herself to the fact that she wasn't leaving any time soon.

Levi was always the first to arrive on Saturdays, but by eleven o'clock neither Mary or Natalie had shown up, and usually they were both here between nine and ten. Adeline was usually sleeping when Levi got here, so he walked in the house to ask if she knew where the girls were.

"Good morning, Levi." Adeline was dressed in a blue pants suit. The shirt had little white flowers on it. She'd curled her hair or something, too, and her lips were bright red.

"You look nice today." Levi missed the pastries Mary always brought, but he'd also missed Mary all week. Maybe he had been too abrupt with her, but he didn't want to be with someone who was embarrassed to introduce him to her family. Even if he had fallen for her. He would just have to get over her. *When? How long will it take?* He'd never gotten close enough to anyone to allow his heart to be broken. Mary was all he'd thought about for the last week, along with his conversation with the bishop.

Adeline smiled as she pulled a familiar tub from the refrigerator. It would likely be tuna salad or chicken salad. Levi looked forward to it since it wasn't something his mother ever made. They mostly ate stews or soups since his mother and sisters had to cook large quantities. When he'd asked about tuna salad or chicken salad, his mother asked him if he had any idea how many eggs would have to be boiled and peeled to make enough salad to feed them all. He supposed she was right.

"Well, aren't you the charmer." Adeline winked at him.

"Where are the girls?" Levi helped himself to a chocolate chip cookie from a platter on the counter.

"They're store bought," Adeline was quick to say. "Not homemade like your mother's and what Mary brings from the bakery." She pulled a loaf of bread from the pantry. "As for the girls, I don't know where Natalie is. Mary isn't coming. She showed up unexpectedly yesterday. She'd hired a driver so she could run some errands that were too far for her horse to travel, so she stopped by to let me know she wouldn't be here today."

"Did she say why?" Levi lost his appetite as he wondered if it was because of the way he'd treated her last Saturday.

"No. But there is so much going on with her family. I suspect it has something to do with Lydia, but I didn't want to pry."

Levi leaned against the kitchen counter and crossed his ankles, trying to remember if Mary had mentioned anything about problems with her sister. He couldn't think of anything. "What's wrong with Lydia? Is she sick?"

Adeline squeezed her eyes closed and pinched her lips together before she looked at him. "Oops. I thought Mary had probably told you."

"Adeline, please tell me." Levi took off his hat and ran a hand through his sweaty hair. "What's wrong with Mary's *schweschder*?"

Adeline sighed. "I don't know if you'd call it sick, but I feel like it's Mary's place to tell you."

Levi scratched his forehead. *Something is wrong, but she isn't sick.* It seemed like a stretch since Lydia was only sixteen and not married, but it was all he could think of. "Is she with child?"

Adeline nodded. "Since she's not married, it has really turned Mary's home life upside down. She's been very upset about it."

Levi dropped his hat, picked it up, then paced the small kitchen. "I wonder why she didn't tell me. I guess we aren't as close as I thought."

"Hon, maybe she was afraid you would judge her family or think badly of Lydia."

"I wouldn't do that!" Levi practically shouted. He apologized for the outburst when Adeline cut her eyes in his direction.

"I don't really know Mary's family. Her father and Percy were friends and thought a lot of each other. But from what I've gathered from Mary, her mother works hard to maintain a nice home, and she gets a bit unraveled if things stray from what is expected." She spread chicken salad on the bread and clicked her tongue a couple times. "Having your sixteen-year-old unwed daughter get pregnant is straying from the norm. Especially for your people."

"I need to talk to Mary." Levi rubbed his forehead. *I've been a jerk.* All this time, he thought Mary was embarrassed of him. But it sounded like she was ashamed of her own family.

"Well, you take a sandwich to go." Adeline took some plastic wrap from the cabinet. "I'm sure Natalie will be along soon." She eyed the container of chicken salad. "And if not, more for me." Smiling, she said, "Scoot.

Go see your girl. That yard work will still be here next Saturday, and I won't lose a night's sleep if you abandon the project altogether. You kids have been too good to me as it is."

Levi took the sandwich, but then set it on the counter. "I can't go. My horse hasn't rested long enough to make the twenty-mile trip there, and it would be too hard on the ol' girl to travel home, or even back here in that short of a time."

"Call a driver, hon."

"I don't have a phone."

Adeline sighed. "Hmm. Me either."

The screen door in the living room squeaked open and slammed shut.

"What did I miss?" Natalie walked into the kitchen toting a Styrofoam cup in her hand with a bag tucked under her arm.

"Levi needs to go see Mary, but his horse won't make it there and back." Adeline took out two more slices of bread and quickly added the salad.

"No problem. I'll take you. Mary has told me about her family's place. I'd love to see it." Natalie put the bag she brought on the counter and accepted the plastic-wrapped sandwich from Adeline. Levi picked up his from the counter.

"*Danki,* Natalie. I appreciate it."

When they were in Natalie's car and on the road, Levi asked, "Do you know about her sister, Lydia?" He hoped he wasn't breaking yet another confidence.

Natalie glanced at him. "Yeah. She's pregnant."

"Why didn't Mary tell me?" Levi shook his head, his sandwich sitting in his lap still wrapped.

Natalie finished chewing a mouthful of her sandwich. "She's embarrassed. She really broke down when she told me. And it's not so much that she's embarrassed that her unwed sister isn't married — which isn't good, of course — but she's ashamed of the way her family is handling it. There's been a lot of screaming and yelling and upset feelings in a household that usually runs smooth. She didn't want you to see them like that."

She took a small bite of sandwich, and when she swallowed she went on. "She told me Adeline's place is like an escape for her, so I thought she wouldn't want to talk about her home life during our time together. She loves Adeline's house. And she loves Adeline." She looked at him. "And in case you haven't figured it out, she loves you too."

A rush of adrenaline shot through Levi's veins, sending a burst to his heart as it came alive again. "Did she say that?"

"No. We've shared secrets, but Mary is a little private. Aren't most of the Amish secretive when it comes to dating and stuff like that?"

Levi shrugged as he waited for his heartbeat to slow down. "It depends on the district where you live."

"Eat your sandwich, Levi. Everything is going to be fine."

He prayed Natalie was right.

After Levi and Natalie left, Adeline nibbled on her sandwich while sitting in Percy's chair. A nice breeze blew through the parlor, the birds sang outside, and in the distance a dog barked. It was too quiet, though. It sounded the way it had before Levi, Mary, and Natalie came into her life.

"You blessed me with a family of young people late in life, Lord. I thank you for that."

She put the sandwich on the plate and braced herself for the spasm working its way down her esophagus. Squeezing her eyes closed, a hand to her chest, she waited for it to pass. Even after an increase in her medications, the chest pains associated with the spasms were coming more often. Stronger, and they lasted longer.

Adeline took a deep breath when it was over. She missed visiting with her young friends today. When she took her plate to the kitchen, she saw the bag Natalie had carried in with her. She pulled out a puzzle box with a beautiful beach scene on the front. It had been ages since Adeline felt sand between her toes or dipped her feet in the water.

Her last recollection was with Percy on the southern shore of Lake Michigan. In their younger years, they'd traveled to Key West, Florida. Adeline studied the box, but she didn't see anything about where this beach was. It didn't matter. She would enjoy putting it together and drawing on fond memories.

After dumping the pieces on the table, she moved one of the portable fans from the parlor to the kitchen and adjusted it so it blew in her direction and mixed with the cross breeze flowing through the windows. She didn't understand why the electric company hadn't turned on her power, but she'd learned to live without it and it saved her money. *If the Amish can do it, so can I.*

She sorted the pieces and prayed for safe travel for the children and that everything was okay with Mary. Life's upsets could weigh a person down like lead on their shoulders.

After a while of working on the puzzle, Adeline went back to the parlor, toting the fan with her. She put it back in its usual place, went to her bedroom, and returned with Natalie's essay, then reread it.

Mary sat on her bed upstairs. She couldn't make out what was being said, but loud voices — mostly Lydia's — were floating up through the floorboards.

The reprieve from the problems at hand hadn't lasted long. Mary assumed Lydia had told her parents she didn't want to marry Samuel, which would only complicate her mother's life even more. Mary had mostly played by the rules her entire life. Lydia had bucked up to her parents before, but it had never been as serious as now. Lydia and Samuel's future was forever changed. No matter what happened from here on, there was a baby coming. Her younger sister and her boyfriend had succumbed to sin, but God had granted them the gift of a child. Mary didn't understand *Gott*'s will all the time, and sometimes it was hard to trust Him. Especially when so many problems were surrounding her.

She was deep in thought when she heard a car pull in the driveway. Would her parents and Lydia notice it before the passengers got close enough to hear the yelling through the open windows?

She finally shuffled to the window. *Oh no.* There couldn't have been a worse time for Natalie to show up. Her friend had problems of her own and likely wouldn't judge Mary's family, but she'd have preferred a scheduled visit so her dysfunctional family could behave accordingly. As she had the thought, she wondered again if she was more like her mother than she wanted to be.

Her heart skipped a beat when Levi stepped out of the car. Excitement and panic swirled together as her stomach churned. She hurried to pull her hair up, pin it in place, and get her *kapp* on, then she ran downstairs, hoping to intercept her friends before they saw Mary's family at its worst.

Levi tipped back the rim of his hat as his eyes traveled around the place where Mary and her family lived. The house was huge with a perfectly manicured yard, a large red barn in the distance, and another big building near the barn that must be her father's shop.

"Wow. They're like rich Amish people." Natalie pushed dark sunglasses up on her head, also peering around the massive homestead. "Mary told me about her father's business and a little about their house, but I didn't imagine it to be anything like this."

Levi gazed at the big two-story house that would surely accommodate his entire family of twelve. Why did Mary's family need that much room? He recalled what Bishop Troyer said about everyone being uniform. It definitely didn't apply to houses. They'd passed some other large farms on the way to Mary's, and there were a few places where he lived in Orleans that were spacious and well-kept, but he'd never seen a spread like this one.

His emotions where Mary was concerned were all over the place. Levi could never provide for her the way she was used to. His thinking was wrong according to the *Ordnung,* but the thoughts were there just the same. Any way he tossed it around in his mind, Mary's family was rich and his wasn't. If they were all supposed to live the same way, according to the *Ordnung,* this seemed unbalanced to Levi.

When Mary rushed onto the front porch, down the steps, and ran to Levi, his only thought was that he loved this woman. She stopped two feet in front of him and Natalie, her eyes wild with an emotion Levi couldn't identify. He fought the urge to pull her into his arms.

"Are you okay?" Natalie hugged her friend. "We were worried, so we decided to check on you."

"I-I went to see Adeline yesterday and told her I wouldn't be there today. You didn't have to drive all the way here. I'm fine." She gasped. "*Ach, nee.* Is something wrong with Adeline? Has something happened?"

"No, Adeline is fine." Natalie pointed to Levi. "He's the worrywart. He wanted to come see you. Do you have horses in that barn?" She pointed to the red structure.

Mary nodded. "*Ya,* and pigs and goats and chickens."

Natalie rose up on her toes and pressed her palms together. "Oh boy! That's where I'll be." She glanced back and forth between him and Mary. "I think you two need to talk."

Mary's eyes were glassy, almost terrified looking. Levi glanced over her shoulder and saw her parents and a young girl watching them from the window.

"Let's take a walk." Mary pointed to her left.

Levi didn't argue now that he knew Mary's reasons for not wanting him to meet her family. Once they were on the other side of her father's shop, she said, "Why are you here?"

"Why didn't you tell me about Lydia?"

Mary hung her head, shaking it as she covered her face, then she looked up at him with tears in the corners of her eyes. "*Mei* family isn't like yours."

Levi glanced around the property before he met her gaze. "I see that." He looked back at her. "Adeline slipped and mentioned something about Lydia. She didn't mean to betray a confidence. I kind of guessed anyway."

Mary sniffled as a tear rolled down her cheek.

"You should have told me. Why didn't you?" He edged closer to her.

"Lydia is unmarried, sixteen, and pregnant." Another tear rolled down her cheek. "She and my parents fight constantly. I didn't want you to know that. Or see it."

Levi thought for a few moments about what to say, keeping his eyes on the ground. "I thought you were embarrassed to introduce me to your family." He raised one shoulder and then lowered it slowly as he kicked at the grass with one foot. "I mean, you were at *mei haus.*" He looked up and stared into her eyes. "We don't have all this." He waved an arm around the property. "We're an unorganized mess most of the time. Mary . . ." He took in a deep breath. "We're poor compared to you."

Somewhere during Levi's ramblings, Mary had stopped crying.

"So we were born into different lifestyles. It doesn't matter. Our beliefs are the same. I thought your family was wonderful. They're funny, warm, and kind. I loved what you call an 'unorganized mess.' I didn't see it that way, though. At first, I thought you didn't want me to meet them because you found out about Lydia somehow. And I know shame is a sin . . ." She sniffled a little. "But I was afraid of losing you."

Levi pulled her close, wrapping his arms around her. She hugged him tight. As they eased apart, he gently cupped her cheeks and kissed her. Then he kissed her again, and again.

"Well, it looks like you two got things straightened out." Natalie marched up to them smiling, carrying a white cat with circles of black around his eyes.

Mary blushed, but Levi just grinned.

"This fellow is so friendly." Natalie giggled. "And look. His coloring makes him look like he's wearing sunglasses." She dropped her sunglasses from her head to her nose, then held the cat up next to her. "See? We're twins."

Mary laughed. "He showed up about a week ago. I pet him when I'm outside, but he can't come in the house since Lydia is allergic. *Daed* says he's a *gut* barn cat because he'll keep the mice away. But he's so affectionate. He needs a *gut* home."

"Aw, he's so sweet." Natalie nuzzled the cat before she set him down in the grass. He curled around her leg. "Mr. Cat, I'd take you home with me in a heartbeat if the pet deposit at my apartment complex wasn't outrageous. Plus, you'd be alone all day while I'm at work." Her eyes widened. "Adeline! Let's take him to Adeline. I bet she would love this guy, and they'd keep each other company. And I could still see him at Adeline's."

"I think that's a great idea." Levi looked at Mary, and she nodded.

"It's still early in the day. Should we all go back to her house now?" Natalie looked at Mary. "Levi's buggy is there, and I can bring you back later. Let's surprise her with . . ." She tapped a finger to her chin. "What should we call him, or should we let Adeline name him?"

Levi and Natalie bounced ideas around while Mary went to tell her parents she was leaving for a while. He heard loud voices inside. This wasn't the time to meet her folks and Lydia. But it was a clear example of miscommunication all around. Levi vowed right then to always be honest with Mary, and he'd ask her to do the same.

A few minutes later, they piled into Natalie's car. Mary rode in the front seat with Natalie, and Levi held the cat in his lap in case the car ride made him nervous. But the cat laid down on the seat beside him for the entire ride.

"I'm so excited to see her face when we give her the cat." Natalie pulled to a stop in Adeline's driveway.

Levi carried the new pet, following Mary and Natalie. The door was unlocked like always, but Natalie rapped gently on the trim of the screen door.

"This is her nap time," Mary said. "I think it's okay to just go on in and wait until she wakes up."

Natalie eased the door open and Levi put the cat down once the door was closed.

"I hope he doesn't do his business in here. We didn't think to get a cat box or food or anything." Natalie thrust her hands to her hips. "I saw a shallow box in the kitchen pantry. We could probably rip up some newspapers or magazines to put in it. That would do for now. And we all know Adeline has plenty of tuna." She chuckled. "I'll go see what I can find."

Levi wanted to sneak a kiss once Natalie was out of sight in the kitchen, but just as he leaned close to Mary, Natalie screamed. Levi's whole body went cold as he ran to the kitchen, Mary on his heels.

"Is she dead?" Natalie shrieked the words. "Is she? Levi, is she dead? Mary?"

Mary didn't move, so Levi squatted on the floor next to Adeline, whose eyes were closed. He checked for a pulse.

CHAPTER 16

Mary and Natalie were back in the hospital waiting room, but this time it was Levi sitting between them and not Adeline. Earlier, when the doctor came out and asked if they were family, Mary followed Adeline's lead from the last time they were at the hospital, and she answered yes. It wasn't a lie. The foursome had become a family over the past couple months.

"Do you think the cat's okay?" Natalie whispered even though no one else was in the room.

They were waiting for the doctor to talk to them. So far, all they knew was that Adeline had a tumor — "a mass," the doctor called it at first — in her head. Mary had asked if it was related to her esophageal spasms. He'd said no.

"I think the cat will be fine." Mary leaned her head back against the wall and closed her eyes. They'd been waiting for almost three hours while Adeline had tests done. "I left a can of tuna open for him when they were loading Adeline into the ambulance." She yawned, lifting her head. "And I tore up some paper towels and found the box you were talking about in the pantry."

Levi's head leaned against the wall, too, his hat in his lap. Mary wasn't sure if he was asleep or not. They'd all been fairly quiet. The doctor had given them a name for the type of tumor Adeline had. A glioblastoma multiforme. Natalie used her smartphone to Google it. All she said when she was done was that they needed to pray. Mary had been praying since she saw Adeline on the floor.

"I want some coffee so bad, and I'm not even much of a coffee drinker." Natalie stretched her arms in the air as she yawned.

It was only eight o'clock at night, but it felt much later. They were all exhausted with worry.

"I called *mei* parents to let them know where I am." Mary barely nudged Levi to see if he was awake, and he opened his eyes. "Your parents are going to be worried."

"There are twelve of us, including *mei* parents. I doubt I'll be missed." He grinned, then kissed her gently on the lips.

"Hey, we'll have none of that goin' on."

Natalie raised an eyebrow as she looked over a magazine she'd picked up from a nearby table.

They were all trying to keep things light, but Mary's stomach churned, and impatience was building. She'd crossed her legs repeatedly, shifted her weight, and twirled the string of her *kapp* so much it was now a spiral on the right side. Her stomach growled, but she couldn't eat if she tried.

Natalie put the magazine back on the table and paced the small room, which only made Mary more anxious.

It was another fifteen minutes before the doctor emerged. "I have some news to share with you, if you'd all like to follow me."

Levi rose first. Natalie and Mary followed.

"If he takes us into a small room and there is a box of tissues on the table, then it's bad news." Natalie's voice trembled as she whispered in Mary's ear.

Mary fought the urge to cry when the doctor ushered them into such a room. He asked them to take a seat, and Mary slid into a chair next to Levi, who found her hand under the table and held it tightly.

Natalie remained standing. "It's bad, isn't it?"

The doctor offered her a weak smile. "Please, have a seat."

Natalie stayed where she was until Mary said, "Come sit by me."

Once Natalie was seated, the doctor opened the file folder in front of him. He wasn't very old based on his dark hair and sharp features. No wrinkles, shiny white teeth. Mary wished he were older and wiser, which probably wasn't the way to think.

"Have you noticed Adeline becoming confused or losing time?" He glanced at each of them.

"She told me she put her slippers in the refrigerator once," Levi said.

"Just a few little things." Natalie twisted her hands together atop the table. "Is she going to get well?"

Dr. Parks, as he'd introduced himself earlier, closed the file and sighed. "Adeline's tumor is inoperable. Over time, her cognitive issues will get worse. She'll have more trouble processing information and become even more confused. Glioblastomas can be treated, but even with chemotherapy or radiation the patient usually has only a year, or maybe a little longer, to live."

Mary choked back tears.

"If Adeline were younger, surgical resection might be a possibility, but at her age, we feel certain the surgery would be unsuccessful." He paused, glancing at each of them. "Adeline has refused treatment."

"Well, she can't do that." Natalie cried as she spoke.

The doctor looked at her with sympathetic eyes. "If I were in Adeline's shoes, I'd probably do the same thing. It would be a tough road for her and only extend her life for a year or so."

"*Gott* ultimately controls Adeline's destiny." Mary lifted her chin as her lips trembled. "I've heard of people praying away illnesses."

The doctor offered a slight smile. "And I've seen it happen, so I encourage you to pray, of course, but also to be prepared."

"How much time does she have without any treatment?" Natalie's shoulders shook as she spoke.

"A few weeks."

Levi let go of Mary's hand, lowered his head, and put a hand to his forehead.

They were all quiet for a while.

"Adeline said she lives alone, so it's most likely that she will need to stay in the hospital for the duration of her illness."

"She'll hate that!" Natalie spat. "Not happening."

Dr. Parks stood. "I'm going to let you have some time to let this sink in." He paused. "The caregiving of someone in this condition is difficult because the patient slowly loses control of their faculties, and it's very hard for loved ones to watch." He pushed his chair in. "I'll leave you alone for now."

"Can we see Adeline?" Levi asked. His eyes were glassy and red, and as much as Mary wanted to comfort him, she was barely holding it together herself.

"Of course."

After Dr. Parks left the room, Natalie sobbed and Mary let go of the tears she'd been holding back.

"She can't stay in this place." Natalie shook her head, swiping at her tears. "I could move in with her, but I'd have to quit my job, and I have credit cards and bills." She looked at Mary, then Levi. "What are we going to do?"

"I could talk to *mei daed* and see if maybe he could pay for a live-in nurse, but I don't think Adeline would like that." Mary's thoughts swirled and collided as she tried to think of a solution. But every time her thoughts circled back to the end result, she cried.

"I will talk to *mei* parents too. I know we don't have money to donate to Adeline's care, but I could probably stay with her two or three days a week."

"So could I." Mary felt a rush of hope.

"She'd be happier having us with her."

"I could take the weekends, Friday after work until Sunday night." Natalie could barely talk through her tears.

Mary reached her hands out to each side of her. Levi took hold of one, Natalie the other. "Let us pray."

"Can you pray out loud?" Natalie asked. "I've been praying all day, but I don't know God very well. I imagine your people have a direct hotline."

Mary half laughed through her tears. "Sure."

Adeline forced a smile when her young friends came into the room. She wanted to be strong for these kids she'd come to love. "Now, now. It's all right." She held out her arms, and Mary and Natalie both fell into them. Levi turned away, but his shoulders shook as he faced the wall.

"Are you in pain?" Natalie had her head buried on Adeline's shoulder. Adeline stroked the girl's long blond hair.

"No. I'm not in pain." Adeline's head throbbed, but she wasn't sure it had anything to do with the tumor. She was still processing the fact that she'd be joining Percy soon. But she'd be leaving these children. She wouldn't see them get married or have children of their own.

Adeline coughed, and Natalie and Mary stood up. Levi turned around, his eyes red and watery. "Come here, son." She'd never called him that before, but it came as naturally as breathing. He swiped at his eyes and came to her slowly, then hugged her briefly.

"You three listen to me." Adeline fought to control the tremble in her voice. "God gifted me with each of you. Late in life, he gave me the family I never had. After Percy died, not much joy filled my days until you all came along. What a glorious time we've had. Don't be sad. I'll be with Percy soon, even though I will miss you all very much."

She took a deep breath. "If I could ask you a favor, though. There are some things I will need from my house for my stay here at the hospital." Her bottom lip began to tremble. "And I would like to see the place one last time." She managed to hold back her tears. These kids were upset enough.

Mary sat on the bed and reached for Adeline's hand. "We've made other arrangements for you, Adeline. If you'll allow us, we've arranged our schedules so that one of us can be with you at all times so you can stay in your home. We've already spoken to the social worker here at the hospital."

Adeline lowered her head for a few moments, still resolved not to cry. When she looked up, she managed in a shaky voice to say, "I can't let you do that. You have lives and jobs." She shook her head.

Natalie folded her arms across her chest and huffed. "Just try to stop us."

Mary squeezed Adeline's hand. "It's already decided. And the hospital staff is going to send home everything we need to keep you as comfortable as possible." She smiled. "Before you go home to Percy, we are going to finish that puzzle of the beach scene. Natalie told us the other one wasn't turning out the way we thought. We're going to cook wonderful meals. And Levi can play the piano for you."

Adeline couldn't hold back anymore as the tears spilled down her cheeks. "I love each of you as my own."

Natalie's cheeks were also wet, but she smiled a little. "We have a surprise for you when you get home."

Adeline couldn't imagine. "What kind of surprise?"

"You'll see."

Her young friends smiled at each other. Adeline didn't care what the surprise was. She knew she would love it.

■ ■ ■ ■

Levi had never struggled to control his emotions the way he was today. He would play the piano as often as Adeline wanted. He loved her, and he wasn't going to deny her a dying wish. He would still consider the bishop's words and decide what to do, but he wondered if maybe his musical ability had been a gift and not a punishment. Maybe the Lord had lent him the gift to use for this very purpose, to give Adeline peace and comfort before she went to be with Him.

He wanted to break down and sob as they said their goodbyes, but all three of the women were crying hard, and Levi was determined to stay strong for them, today and until the end.

As they exited the hospital, Levi wondered about Adeline's house. They all stopped in the parking lot. "Should we make arrangements to get her electricity turned on? Won't she need it, being sick and all?" Levi didn't have the financial means, but maybe Mary or her father did.

"I've gotten used to no air conditioner." Natalie blew her nose, then laughed through her tears. "I'm practically Amish now."

Mary raised an eyebrow. "I think you still have a ways to go." She pointed to her own maroon dress, black loafers, and then at her prayer covering.

Not to mention, Natalie seemed confused about her relationship with *Gott.*

"Point taken." Natalie dug in her purse for her keys, and they started walking again. "But Adeline would be more comfortable with air-conditioning, I'm sure."

Levi recalled when his brother, Lloyd, was really sick a few years ago. He'd been in bed for two weeks during August. "Have either of you been in Adeline's basement?"

"I have," Mary said. "There isn't anything stored down there. She told me she had it all brought upstairs when she had the estate sale. Why?"

Natalie unlocked the car and they all got in. Levi climbed in the back seat, and it made him think of the cat. "Adeline won't be released until tomorrow. We need to check on the cat and make sure it has enough food and water."

Natalie nodded as she started the car. "Now, what about the basement?"

"The dirt around the basement keeps it cooler than the air temperature, especially in the summer. When my *bruder* was sick in August one time, *mei daed* set him up in

318

the basement because it was cooler. And one summer when the temperatures stayed in the upper nineties for several days, our whole family slept down there."

"I don't think Adeline will want to sleep in the basement. That sounds depressing." Natalie growled a little. "And I just remembered, even if we do get her electricity turned on, the air conditioner isn't working."

Mary lowered her head from where she sat in the front seat and started to cry again. "I can't believe this is happening."

Then Natalie began to cry, which caused Levi to tear up in the back seat. He did his best to hide it, keeping his head turned toward the window so Natalie wouldn't see from the rearview mirror.

"This reminds me of when my Mimi Jean, my grandma, died." Natalie swerved a little, and Levi asked if she was okay to drive.

"Yeah, I can drive. It's just hard to think about Adeline being gone. It's hard to think about anyone else living in her house." She was quiet for a few moments. "I hope whoever buys it will take good care of it and fill it with the family Adeline always wanted."

Mary sniffled and lifted her head. "Adeline told me she was leaving the house to the church she and Percy used to attend."

Natalie's ears perked up, and she smiled. Her mother was the last person who deserved that house. The only thing Natalie wanted from Adeline was love, and the thought of losing the woman brought on more tears.

It was almost ten by the time Natalie turned the car into Adeline's driveway. They checked on the cat before Levi got in his buggy and headed home. Then Natalie drove Mary to her house before she went home and fell onto her air mattress and cried.

She allowed herself a complete meltdown and was in the throes of it when her phone rang. No one would call this late at night but her mother. She was tempted to let it go to voice mail, but she answered and told her mother about Adeline.

"That's so nice, honey, what you and your Amish friends are doing for Adeline," her mother said, ending with a sigh. "Even though I hate to see you going through this."

Then why don't you offer to help us by staying with Adeline some of the time? Natalie tossed the thought as soon as she had it. Her mother didn't even know Adeline, and it would feel like an invasion if anyone outside their circle tended to her.

"How much time does she have?"

A ball of fire burned in the pit of Natalie's stomach, and she was tempted to throw it at her mother, knowing good and well she just wanted the house. Natalie felt relieved that the church was getting it. If Adeline had left it to Natalie, she'd have felt guilty for the rest of her life, and she'd have to deal with her mother.

Natalie walked to the kitchen. "A few weeks." She poured herself a glass of water and gulped it down while her mother offered sympathies that Natalie was only half hearing.

"Honey, I know you don't want to take anything from home to use in your apartment, but is there anything that Adeline might need?"

Natalie set the glass on the counter. Hard. She wanted to throw it against the wall. Leave it to her mother to step in at the last minute in an effort to ensure any inheritance that might be coming their way. Natalie was on the verge of telling her mother about the house, but she changed her mind when another thought came to her.

There could be nights when she and Mary would be staying at Adeline's together. She knew Mary and Levi wouldn't stay under the same roof together, even if they were in separate rooms. If she and Mary needed to stay overnight, Natalie wouldn't have minded sleeping on Adeline's old air mattress, but the situation would be stressful enough.

"You know that tan couch in your study, the one you said pulled into a bed? Adeline has a horrible couch in her living room with springs poking out everywhere. She has the red furniture in the parlor, but that couch is more like a loveseat. If you wanted to loan us that sleeper sofa, that would be good. If I'm there at the same time as Mary, it would give me a place to sleep."

Mary was going to talk to her father about getting the power turned on, but the only reason would be to run the air-conditioning, which wasn't working, so they decided against it. The ruckus of having workers in the house would be bothersome for Adeline.

"Of course you can have the sleeper sofa. And not on loan. You can have it. There's also an old coffee table in the basement and two end tables."

Natalie swiped at her eyes. She wanted to believe her mother was being kind, and she certainly had her good qualities. Lately those attributes were buried beneath her grief over the divorce and lack of money.

"Thank you, Mom. I'll make arrangements for someone to pick it up and take it to Adeline's." If the church was going to use the house, at least it would already be furnished. Maybe the pastor and his wife would live there. Hopefully they had lots of children. Adeline would like that.

"You just let me know what you need." Her mother ended the call, and Natalie sat on the kitchen floor.

This was the mother she remembered, a woman who did for others and loved her family. For a while, it had seemed like a memory. She would pray for her mother. And she would pray for Adeline. How were they going to handle it when Adeline's mind started to go? How long would it be before she didn't remember any of them? Two weeks? Three? A month?

She pulled her knees up to her chest as she leaned against the kitchen cabinets. Then she closed her eyes, wanting God to guide her, but not knowing what to ask for. She'd heard Mary say that all things were of God's will, but her friend also prayed aloud for a miracle for Adeline when they last prayed together. Natalie wasn't ready to commit to everything being God's will. It scared her. What if His will had nothing to do with a miracle for Adeline?

God, I don't know You very well, but I want to know You better. And right now, I have some specific requests. She thought for a few moments. *I want a miracle, for You to completely heal Adeline. But if that can't happen, I pray that You will keep her from having pain. No pain, God. Please. And when her mind starts to go, I hope she still feels joy in her heart. And please show me, Mary, and Levi the best ways to take care of Adeline, ways to make her last days on this earth happy ones.*

Food didn't sound good, but she made a slice of toast, slathered butter and grape jelly all over it, then refilled her glass of water and carried it to her makeshift bed. After she forced herself to eat it, she reached for a magazine on the nightstand. She never turned a page. It was the cover that sparked an idea. A wonderful idea that she was going to check into tomorrow. A warm sensation swirled around her as sadness mixed with joy and hope.

Natalie glanced up. "Is that You, God?"

She was weary, but she was sure she heard, "Yes, my child," in her mind.

Her idea was approved by God. Of course it was. He'd put it into her mind. Tomorrow she'd put the plan into action.

Chapter 17

Wednesday, Mary read over Adeline's signed release papers with trembling hands, hoping and praying they were doing the right thing. Mary, Natalie, and Levi had adjusted their schedules to take her home from the hospital that afternoon.

Natalie had taken off work today, but it wouldn't be an option for her to miss too much or she wouldn't be able to pay her bills, so weekends were still the best times for her to stay with Adeline.

Mary's family told her to do what she needed to do for Adeline, but that she was expected to be at Lydia's wedding the following day. Despite her sister's resistance, the wedding was still happening. Mary halfway expected her sister to bolt from the ceremony.

Mary packed up the few things Adeline had accumulated during her stay at the hospital. A toothbrush, toothpaste, and a few other toiletries. Lastly, she put a vase filled with flowers from Natalie's father near the other items. Natalie had balked at the gift, but it pleased Adeline, and that's what mattered.

When a nurse came in to explain the medications, the best way to help Adeline bathe when she could no longer do it herself, and all the other duties a caregiver would need to provide, Mary wondered again if they were doing the right thing by taking Adeline home. What if they did something wrong or caused her more harm than good?

The hospital provided a wheelchair and walker for them to take home, saying something about it being covered by Medicare. When a hospital employee came for Adeline, she frowned at the wheelchair and the young man dressed in blue scrubs.

"I don't need this just yet." Adeline raised her chin and pressed her lips together.

"Hospital policy," he said, winking. "And if you behave yourself, I won't pop any wheelies down the hall."

Adeline still scowled as she eased herself into the chair, but then she looked up at the man and said, "I think I'd enjoy the wheelies."

"Hold on to your purse," he said as he

rushed out of the room. When Adeline laughed, Levi, Mary, and Natalie rushed into the hallway, and the orderly did indeed have the wheelchair up on the back two wheels.

Mary smiled, hoping there would be lots of laughter for however long Adeline had left.

Natalie carried the small grocery bag of Adeline's things, Levi held the vase of flowers, and Mary had a large bag of medications and a folder with instructions for Adeline's care.

Adeline dozed off in the front seat of the car on the way to her house, lightly snoring, so everyone stayed quiet. They were all surprised to see a second horse and buggy in front of Adeline's house when they pulled in the driveway. As Mary got out of the car, a man walked onto the porch, closing the door behind him.

Mary gasped and ran to him. "*Daed,* what's wrong? Why are you here? Is everything okay?"

Her father nodded. "*Ya, ya.* All is well at home. Adeline might say she is used to no air-conditioning, but she's not. And she's sick. I went to the electric company and explained the situation, and I paid her bill."

Mary brought a hand to her chest.

"Daed . . ."

Natalie stepped forward carrying the flowers and small bag. She introduced herself to Mary's father, while Levi helped Adeline out of the car. "I tried to find out about her electricity, but they wouldn't tell me anything."

"I'm not sure why. Maybe because I went there in person and told them that Adeline was ill," he told Natalie before he turned to Mary. "The air-conditioning just needed Freon so I found an AC company to come out earlier. The house is cooling nicely."

Mary threw her arms around her father's neck. *"Danki, Daed."* She fought not to burst into tears again.

He kissed her on the cheek. "You're welcome, *mei maedel.*" He cupped her chin in his hand. "Don't get too used to all this luxury." He grinned, then turned to Adeline and Levi when they approached.

"Adeline, you should lock your doors." Mary's father smiled, then hugged Adeline.

She hung on to him for a long time. "Not much to steal these days." She chuckled a little. "What are you doing here anyway?"

Levi walked up and extended his hand before Mary's father could answer. "I'm Levi."

"I suspected as much." Her father smiled,

and Mary recognized approval when she saw it.

Mary thanked her father again before he left and told him she'd get a ride home from Natalie. He encouraged her not to be out late or oversleep in the morning. She nodded, hoping the wedding would take place and actual vows would be exchanged.

Everyone's mood lifted when they walked into a cool living room and Adeline's surprise scurried to meet them. She brought two hands to her chest and drew in a deep breath, smiling. "Come here, my precious little friend." She scooped the cat into her arms, then looked at each of them. "He's mine?"

"Yep." Natalie stepped forward to pet the animal already purring in Adeline's arms. "He was chasing mice in Mary's barn, and we thought he'd be happier here. And since we adore kitties . . ." She gave the animal a final scratch, then nodded to the couch, coffee table, and end tables. Adeline had been so excited about the cat rushing to her, she hadn't noticed the furniture or that it was cool in the house.

"When I told my mom that sometimes Mary and I might be here at the same time, she insisted you have this furniture." Natalie walked over to the couch and sat down.

"It makes into a bed, so one of us can sleep in the bedroom with the twin bed, and one of us can sleep on the couch." Grinning, she said, "And no springs poking out in the back. The old couch is in the basement. I'm the one who left the door open so my friends could bring it in. I hope that's okay."

"Of course." Adeline carried the cat to the couch and sat while Levi folded up the wheelchair and walker. Adeline had asked him to put them in a closet somewhere, that she didn't want to see those things until she needed them.

"How lovely of your mother to do this, Natalie." Adeline nuzzled the cat with her nose, then looked at Mary. "And I believe your father gets credit for the air-conditioning. How nice of him to take care of that." She grinned. "Just as I was getting used to living like the Amish." She scratched the cat behind its ears. "I'm glad my electricity came back on so we can enjoy your father's efforts. I knew I paid that bill."

Mary just smiled.

They had lunch in the parlor, but instead of chicken salad, it was a pizza they'd picked up on the way.

"Thank you, Mary, for the pizza." Adeline took a big bite, and by looking at her, you wouldn't think anything was wrong. Maybe the doctor was incorrect. Or maybe God was already giving them the miracle they were praying for.

"I-I'd like to still come on Saturdays." Levi glanced at Mary before he looked at Adeline, who grinned.

"I'd like that." Adeline picked up her second slice of pizza.

Mary said she'd like to come on Saturdays, too, so they could all have at least one day to be together. She bit her bottom lip, then sighed. "*Mei schweschder* is getting married tomorrow. If you all could pray for her and Samuel, I'd be grateful."

"Aw, hon," Adeline said. "I know this isn't an ideal situation for young Lydia and Samuel, but God will lead them."

Mary wanted to believe that. "Lydia is confused about her feelings for Samuel. Both families are practically forcing them to get married. That wouldn't happen in the *Englisch* world."

Natalie huffed. "Are you kidding me? It does happen. Ever heard of the term 'shotgun wedding'? Believe me, it happens."

Mary took a bite of pizza, her thoughts all over the place. Her heart ached for Lydia. She was worried about providing the proper care Adeline would need. And selfishly, she wanted some time alone with Levi.

After they finished eating, everyone confirmed their plans. Natalie had created a schedule on her computer, and she gave everyone a copy. "Notice on that Saturday in September that I need to be at a work thing, another training class." She rolled her eyes. "Another class on a weekend that I don't get paid for."

They were all silent and probably wondering the same thing as Mary. Would there still be a need for a schedule next month?

"Mary. Levi. Natalie." Adeline looked at each of them. "There will come a time when I won't be able to think clearly. And based on the information I was given at the hospital, there's no telling what I might say or do." She paused, and the familiar knot formed in Mary's throat. "So, I need to tell you how I feel." She blinked, scratched the cat behind the ears, and went on. "Percy and I always wanted a family in this house, and as you know, it wasn't in the Lord's plan." She smiled. "But then at the eleventh hour of my time on earth, He gifted me with a family. I love all of you very much."

A tear trickled down Mary's cheek.

"No, no, no." Natalie slapped a hand on her knee from where she was sitting next to Adeline. "No tears. I have a surprise for everyone." She glanced at Mary, Levi, then

Adeline.

Mary wiped away the tear as she nibbled on her pizza, but she was also getting more anxious to spend time alone with Levi.

Natalie grinned from ear to ear. "I know we're all planning to be here Saturday. Mary and Levi, can you both be here at nine o'clock?"

They nodded. "Where are we going?" Mary asked.

"It's a surprise."

Adeline chuckled. "Another surprise?" She drew in a quick breath and held her mouth open for a few moments. Mary feared one of her spasms was coming on, even though the doctor at the hospital gave her a different medication that should make them subside altogether.

"What is it, Adeline?" Mary leaned forward.

Adeline held up the cat. "We need a name for this fellow. He has such a unique coloring, all white with those black circles around his eyes."

"Natalie said it looks like he's wearing sunglasses." Mary squinted, peered at the cat. "Or is it a she?"

"No. It's a he," Adeline said as she lifted the cat up again.

For the next hour, they bounced around

names and Levi played the piano for Adeline while Mary sang the songs she knew.

She and Levi shared a love of music, but the last time they talked, they had both started to think they'd been gifted the privileges for a season, a season that would end when Adeline left this world. Mary had stopped listening to some of the songs she didn't think her parents would approve of. Even as Levi played now, beautiful as the music was, Mary sensed that something was different for both of them.

When Levi was done and had rejoined the group, Adeline smiled. "I have the perfect name for our new friend."

They waited.

"Let's call him Maxwell. He looks like a spy wearing sunglasses, and Maxwell Smart was a spy."

Mary, Levi, and Natalie waited for more explanation.

"Ah, never mind. That show was way before your time."

They had already decided that Levi would stay with Adeline tonight and the next two days, then they'd all be back together on Saturday. From then, they would adhere to the schedule Natalie drew up, plus all be at Adeline's house on Saturdays.

"I can't wait for our surprise on Saturday."

Mary couldn't imagine what it might be. "But we probably need to go," she said to Natalie, who nodded. Both women hugged Adeline and kissed her on the cheek, promising to see her Saturday.

"Mary, I hope all goes well with Lydia and Samuel tomorrow." Adeline smiled. "They might surprise everyone."

That's what Mary was worried about — that Lydia would surprise everyone by disappearing overnight or refusing to say her vows.

"I'll walk you out," Levi said before turning to Adeline. "Be right back."

Out on the porch, Natalie dug her keys from her purse. "I'll be in the car and let you two say your goodbyes. But remember, you'll see each other Saturday, so let's keep the smooching to a minimum, and I'll try not to watch and lament about how I have no one to cuddle with."

After Natalie was in the car and looking down, presumably at her cell phone, Mary reached into her purse and handed Levi a phone. "*Mei daed* got this for you. I know it's against the rules where you live, but Adeline's home phone doesn't work, and you wouldn't even be able to call 9–1–1 if something happened. So please accept it as a gift, and you can return it after . . ." Mary blinked back tears.

Levi pulled her into his arms and cupped the back of her head, drawing her close. Mary wanted to stay in the comfort of his embrace forever. God had brought together an unlikely family. A grandmother for Natalie, a friend for all of them. Two people from very different Old Order districts who likely wouldn't have met if not for Adeline and Percy. And Adeline had the family she'd always wanted. *Gott* is *gut.*

Levi slid the phone in his pocket and cupped Mary's face in his hands and kissed her. "I've been wanting to do that all day."

Mary smiled. "Me too."

Then he stepped back a little and took the phone from his pocket. "I'm not sure I know how to use this."

Mary gave him a quick lesson, then he kissed her again when Natalie honked the horn.

"Are you clear on Adeline's medications?"

Levi nodded. "*Gott*'s blessings tomorrow that all goes well for Lydia and Samuel."

"*Danki.*"

"I'll see you Saturday."

Mary twirled the string on her *kapp,* giggling. "What do you think Natalie has planned?"

"I have no idea. I hope it's not something

that will get us in trouble or make us go against the *Ordnung.*" Levi flinched. "Any more than we already have."

"I don't think she'd do that, at least not knowingly."

One more quick peck on the lips, and Mary went to the car.

She took a deep breath. She'd just have to get through tomorrow, then she would have Saturday to look forward to.

Levi added water to his horse's bucket. Adeline had an old lean-to next to a storage building. Levi had brought hay that morning and got the horse settled before Natalie picked him up. It wasn't too far out of the way for her to pick up Mary, but it was a haul to Levi's house, even though they'd done it the other night.

When he went back inside, Adeline's head was against the back of Percy's chair, Maxwell was in her lap, and her eyes were closed.

"Adeline!" He hadn't meant to yell so loud.

She jumped enough to send the cat toppling off her lap. "Good grief, Levi. I must have dozed off. I'm not dead yet."

Levi opened his eyes wide. "I-I'm sorry."

Adeline chuckled. "Don't look so worried.

If we can't laugh about this from time to time, then . . ." She shrugged and yawned. "But I do need to go take my nap."

"Do you need help?" Levi took a few steps her way, his hand outstretched.

Adeline gently slapped it away. "You'll know when I need help. Until then, you don't treat me any differently." She gave a taut nod. "Now, go play your piano, Percy, and lull me to sleep."

Levi didn't move as Adeline shuffled toward her bedroom. Was it a slip of the tongue? He sat in Percy's chair and stared at the piano. He'd been praying that the magnetic pull would lessen. And it had a little. Maybe it was because his desire to play was being fulfilled. Or maybe his longing to play the piano for all these years wasn't intended to hurt him, but to prepare him for this leg of his journey. After a while he went into the kitchen and stared out the window, his thoughts scrambled like overdone eggs.

Mary awoke to a flurry of activity Thursday morning. She'd overslept, and their kitchen was probably already filled with women preparing the meal for the wedding today. She dressed in a hurry, then rushed downstairs.

Most weddings in their area had around a hundred attendees. She'd heard that in larger communities there were as many as four hundred sometimes. Today they were only expecting about fifty people for Lydia and Samuel's wedding since it was such short notice.

"There you are." Mary's mother maneuvered around two women pulling bread from the oven. "I was just going to check on you. You never sleep this late. Are you sick?"

"*Nee,* just tired."

Her mother touched her arm. "It's going to be a lot of work for you and your friends to take care of Adeline, even though you are doing it in shifts. After your *schweschder* has moved out and settled, I'll help with Adeline."

Mary didn't say anything, but she wasn't going to let that happen unless there was a situation that she, Levi, or Natalie couldn't handle. It would feel intrusive to have anyone else there during the precious time Adeline had left. But she nodded anyway.

She tried to picture Lydia and Samuel living in the *daadi haus* on his family's property. Samuel's grandparents were deceased, and his parents weren't ready to give up the main house, so it made sense for now, at least until Lydia and Samuel's family out-grew the *daadi haus.* Assuming they had more *kinner.* Samuel was already the sole provider for his family, and now he was adding a wife and a baby to the mix. Thankfully, he would keep his job working for Mary and Lydia's father. Mary had overheard her father telling her mother he gave Samuel a raise.

"Where is Lydia anyway?" Mary scanned the kitchen. *Has she already snuck out?*

"She was here a minute ago. Maybe she's in the bathroom." Her mother waved an arm around the kitchen. "I don't know, but there is a lot to do."

"Let me go check on Lydia, then I'll be back to help."

Mary found her sister in the upstairs bathroom with the door locked. "Just let me in, okay?"

"I'm busy. Do you mind?"

"Then I'll just wait."

The door opened a little, and Mary walked in. Lydia was sitting on the toilet seat wearing her wedding dress, a blue dress that didn't look much different from what they wore daily, but it was made especially for this event.

"Your *kapp* is on crooked." Mary straightened it, then squatted in front of Lydia and put a hand on her leg. "Everything is going to be okay, *mei maedel.*"

"I don't know. I am sixteen years old, marrying a man I'm not sure I love, and I'm going to be a *mudder.*" Lydia looked into Mary's eyes, as if expecting Mary to offer an argument, words of wisdom, or a way to help her hightail it out of there.

Mary was almost nineteen, and she'd never done more than kiss a boy. She wanted to ask how Lydia and Samuel had let this happen, but now wasn't the time.

"You and Samuel will have a special bond with the child you're carrying. Love is confusing, and maybe you will feel differently after you're married and *Gott* has blessed the union."

Lydia shrugged, then stood. "Maybe. But one thing is for sure. I am never letting Samuel touch me again, not even for a kiss."

It was an immature thing to say, and probably not true, but Mary's sympathies shifted in Samuel's direction. "That's not a marriage."

Lydia pressed her lips together and smiled before she said, "Then I just won't get married." She stormed past Mary and ran down the stairs.

Mary sat on the commode and sighed. She prayed and then dragged herself downstairs. For the next hour, the women continued with food preparations, and the men set up the living room in the same way they did for worship service — men on one side, women and children facing them on the other side, and the bishop and deacons in the middle.

Finally, it was time for everyone to take their places. Lydia had made it this far. But would she actually go through with the wedding?

CHAPTER 18

Saturday morning, Adeline chose an outfit she thought would be appropriate for her surprise today. All she knew was that Natalie was driving them somewhere and they would be spending time outdoors.

She pulled on a pair of white cotton knickers that fell just below her knees and then chose a breezy pink blouse she hadn't worn in a while. Adeline didn't think the color was very becoming on her, but Percy had loved it when she wore pink.

Once dressed, she grabbed a large envelope from the desk and walked to the kitchen. The girls were packing an ice chest with sandwiches, drinks, and snacks they'd brought from home.

"Ah, a picnic is part of my surprise." Smiling, she pressed her palms together. "Now are you going to tell me where we are going?"

Mary chuckled. "Natalie just told me, and

I'm sworn to secrecy. What do you have in the envelope?"

"Just something I need to mail. Where's Levi?" Adeline set the envelope on the table, then poured herself a glass of orange juice and selected a glazed donut from the box on the counter.

"Those are left over from the wedding Thursday. Glazed donuts aren't a traditional offering at weddings, but they're Lydia's favorite, so I picked up some at the bakery on my way home Wednesday. Hopefully they still taste fresh."

"Heavenly," Adeline said after she swallowed her first bite.

"Levi is loading the car." Natalie added a few bottles of water to the ice chest, then Mary dumped ice on top of everything and closed it.

Adeline meandered to the window but was stopped when Natalie gently caught her arm. "Oh, no you don't. If you see what Levi is loading in the trunk, you might figure out where we're going, and we want it to be a surprise."

"All right." She sighed before she turned to Mary. "Did Lydia and Samuel go through with their vows?"

"*Ya.*" Mary shook her head. "But it was hard to watch. Lydia's bottom lip trembled, and she could barely look at Samuel. He didn't look much different. It wasn't the joyous occasion it should have been." She waved a dismissive hand in the air, like she was ending the conversation. "Did everything go okay with Levi sleeping across the hallway the past few nights?"

The girls each took a handle of the ice chest and carried it out to the front door.

"Am I allowed to leave the kitchen yet?" Adeline grabbed the envelope and another donut.

"*Ya,* you can."

She heard the trunk close and cozied up to the girls by the front door. "Yes, everything went fine with Levi." She grinned. "But here are a few things you should know about your young man." With the donut in one hand and the envelope tucked under that arm, she held up a finger with her other hand. "First of all, he offered to make supper, and I was tired, so I let him. But only the first night." She frowned, shook her head. "Don't ever let him do that when you're married."

"Married? We haven't said anything about marriage." Mary brought a hand to her chest, blushing various colors of red.

Adeline rolled her eyes. If the girls could do it, so could she. "Well, we all know it's coming, so don't look so shocked." Pausing, she finished a small bite of donut. "He tried to make tuna salad." The recollection caused her to cringe. "He made it on the stove and served it warm. I honestly don't know what was in it, but I pretended to enjoy it. The boy can't cook is what I'm saying. My old hands are too shaky to do much, but I could at least instruct him on how to make a couple of simple meals. And furthermore, he talks in his sleep."

"What did he say?"

Adeline had Mary's full attention. She wondered if the girl knew how much her feelings for Levi showed. Same with Levi. "I couldn't understand all of it, but I know I heard mentions of pizza, hamburgers, and stew at various times of the night. It didn't keep me up, but I seem to have to use the bathroom a lot during the night, and I'd hear him. You'll need earplugs when you get married. Percy didn't talk in his sleep, but he snored like a congested rhino. Earplugs will be your best friend."

Natalie laughed. "My dad used to snore like that."

The comment seemed a combination of sadness and regret.

"But only happy thoughts today." Natalie slapped her hands to her hips. "Ready?"

Adeline nodded as she took in Natalie's appearance. Her white capri pants and yellow T-shirt contrasted against Mary's long maroon dress. And so did her white sandals against Mary's black socks and black loafers.

Adeline looked outside and smiled when she recognized Percy's pants on Levi, and he had on a short-sleeve blue shirt, suspenders, and his straw hat. Adeline felt for the Amish in the summer. It seemed to her they would have made some adjustments to their clothing over the years to allow for summertime apparel that wasn't so hot. They'd sure made adjustments in other areas — mobile phones, solar panels, and working alongside non-Amish folks.

Adeline eased into the back seat with Mary after the group decided Levi would be the best navigator. A few minutes later, Natalie's car was filled with cool air. It reminded Adeline how grateful she was for air-conditioning in the house again. She never wanted to complain, especially since her Amish friends lived without the luxury all the time. She was glad they were able to enjoy the comfort at her home and in the car now.

As she looked out the window and folded her hands in her lap, she remembered the envelope. "Natalie, can you pull into one of those standing mailboxes? I forgot to put this in my mailbox to be picked up."

"Sure." Natalie drove too fast in Adeline's opinion, but maybe Adeline had just driven too slow.

After they pulled over at a post office and were back on the road, Adeline continued to wonder where they were going. When they took Exit 33 toward Princeton, her heart fluttered. She'd know in about ten minutes if she had figured out their destination.

"Do you know where we're going yet?" Natalie couldn't keep the childlike excitement out of her voice, and Adeline felt giddy too.

Even though she was pretty sure she knew where they were going, she only said, "It feels familiar."

Mary looked over and smiled broadly at Adeline. Natalie's bright eyes found Adeline's through the rearview mirror. Even Levi was grinning like a child.

Adeline pressed her hand to the window, and memories flooded her mind as the lake came into view. Things looked different, more modern, more active. By the time they parked in view of the beach, Adeline was on the verge of tears.

"It's not the ocean, but it has a beach. You're always saying you love the beach." Natalie put the car in Park, but the sweet child had no idea what she'd really done.

Levi opened the trunk and took out the walker he'd packed. He unfolded it and brought it to Adeline. She narrowed her eyes at him through dark-colored sunglasses. Then, just in case he couldn't see or feel her frustration, she kicked the contraption. "Put that thing away before I clobber you with it."

He took a step back. "It's a long walk to the beach. I thought you might need it."

"Levi." Adeline took a step forward. "I have a brain tumor, not a broken leg. If and when I am unable to walk, I will let you know."

He tucked his head for a moment, then shrugged. "*Ya,* okay." He put the walker back in the trunk.

Natalie kicked off her flip-flops and ran toward the sand. "Come on!"

Levi stood rigid near Adeline as he motioned for Mary to go on too. She hurried out of her shoes and socks and took off. Adeline slipped out of her own shoes and waited for Levi to do the same, but he just stood there.

Perhaps she'd been too hard on him. She

held out her arm, even though she could walk perfectly fine on her own. He looped his arm with hers and they made their way to where Mary and Natalie stood. The feel of the sand beneath her toes was a reminder of the good life she'd lived.

"How did you know to bring me here?" She couldn't control the shakiness in her voice or the moisture filling her eyes.

"Uh . . ." Natalie stepped out of the line they were standing in and faced Adeline. "You said you like the beach. I thought about going to Dunes National Lakeshore, but I figured the five-hour drive would have been too long."

Adeline closed her eyes and dug her toes into the sand as the breeze floated across the lake like a soothing reminder that Percy was waiting for her. "This is the perfect surprise. Percy and I used to come here all the time." She opened her eyes, cupped Natalie's cheek with a shaky hand, and said, "I never told you that, though, did I?"

Natalie's eyes glistened as she shook her head.

"I haven't been here in twenty years. When Percy got too sick to travel much, we stopped coming." Adeline closed her eyes again. "We'd spread out a red-checkered blanket and have a picnic. We'd watch the children playing, often longing for our own, but always enjoying the laughter that surrounds little ones. Boats of all sizes passed in front of us."

She opened her eyes when Mary linked her arm with Adeline's. Standing at the water's edge with her young friends, their arms linked, led Adeline to talk to God silently.

Tell Percy I'll be ready to relive all the wonderful moments we shared over the years and to make new ones in Your heavenly paradise.

They stood quietly for a while.

Finally, Levi cleared his throat. "Can I go get the food now?"

Natalie slugged him lightly in the arm. "Is that all you ever think about?"

They all laughed as Levi jogged back to the car.

Mary sat on the blue blanket they spread out for lunch, Levi beside her. After they'd eaten, Adeline and Natalie went for a walk down the beach. Adeline stopped every now and then and pointed something out to Natalie. Mary was sure they just wanted to give her and Levi some time alone.

They'd all spent so much time together and seemed to read each other's minds sometimes. Right now, though, she wasn't sure what was on Levi's mind. His legs were outstretched, hands behind him propping him up, and his hat on the blanket beside him. The breeze off the water, combined with the clouds overhead, cooled the temperature from the heat wave they'd been having.

"What are you thinking about?" Mary crossed her ankles in front of her and leaned back on her hands, pointing her face toward the sun.

"Life." Levi sank back on his elbows.

And death? Mary hoped not. She didn't want to think about Adeline dying. She wanted a happy, memorable day. Lydia's wedding had been hard enough to endure, and she needed to fill up the sad places in her mind with something joyful.

"What do you want out of life? How do you see your future?" Levi turned his face toward hers and captured her eyes with the seriousness of the question.

Mary didn't have to think for long. "I want to marry a man I love, to have a large family, to be the best person I can be, to live my life according to the *Ordnung,* and to accept all things as *Gott*'s will."

Levi leaned over and kissed her gently on the lips, then gazed into her eyes. "How large of a family?" He grinned. "Please don't say ten *kinner.*"

Mary's heart fluttered. She wanted to ask him why he wanted to know. "*Nee,* maybe six."

Levi sat up and rubbed his clean-shaven chin. "Would you like to do those things with me?"

Mary bolted upright, eyes wide, insides swirling. "Levi Shetler, is this a proposal?"

Grinning, he shrugged. "Do you want it to be?"

Mary huffed, even though she was still smiling. "Either it is or it isn't."

He kissed her again, longer this time, lingering as he kissed her temple, then her cheek, and her mouth again. "I love you."

Mary had known for a while that she loved Levi, so it was easy to say it back. "I love you too."

"Then, *ya,* I guess this is a proposal." He stood up and pulled Mary to her feet, then he dropped to one knee and held her hand. "I guess I should do it proper. Mary, will you marry me?"

They were interrupted by a loud scream and both turned toward the sound. In the distance, Natalie was pointing at them and jumping up and down. Adeline waved both arms wildly over her head.

Natalie cupped her hands around her mouth and yelled, "Say yes!"

Levi winked at Mary as she pulled him to his feet and drew him close. "Well?"

She stepped back, tipped her head to one side, and tapped a finger to her chin. "Hmm . . ." Levi's jaw dropped, and Mary laughed. "*Ya*, I'll marry you!"

Levi raised his arm high above his head and gave a thumbs-up sign to Natalie and Adeline. Natalie started jumping up and down and screamed again, which caused all kinds of people up and down the beach to look in their direction.

It was hard for Mary to believe she'd had even one ounce of jealousy toward Natalie when she first met her. Natalie was her best friend now, though Mary suspected she hid her pain sometimes. Mary did, too, at times, and she recognized it in others. She was sure Natalie's parents' divorce weighed more heavily on her mind than she let on.

Mary had a taste of those family problems. Her parents would never divorce. It simply wasn't allowed. But as she recalled the look in her sister's eyes the day before, she wondered if Lydia would be able to stay true to her beliefs and make a good life with Samuel.

She turned back to Levi and smiled. There

would be challenges ahead, but they would face them together.

Natalie fell on the couch in the parlor after unloading the ice chest and checking on the propane for the stove and refrigerator. They had plenty. Adeline's original refrigerator was in the garage, but no one had mentioned swapping them out since the electricity was turned on.

Adeline had to be exhausted. Natalie kicked her feet up on the coffee table and recalled the day's events. A great lunch, wonderful company, and Levi and Mary were engaged. Amid those happy thoughts, she wondered if Adeline would be around to see the wedding. The Amish almost always married in the fall after the harvest. It was August.

"I feel better after my bath." Adeline tightened the belt of her pink robe as she walked into the parlor. "I bet Levi was glad to go home. He stayed here three nights."

"I'm sure he didn't mind." Natalie yawned. Levi's schedule wasn't as rigid as hers and Mary's since he worked on his parents' farm. Natalie and Mary had predetermined hours even though Mary worked part time. Mary had left when Levi did, each going in different directions. "It was a good day today. And Levi and Mary are going to get married."

"Yes, and that makes me very happy." Adeline's gray hair was pulled back by a pink headband, just enough to keep it out of her face. She opened a white jar and started dabbing her face with white cream. "This is what you have to look forward to when you get to be my age." She stopped, stared at the container, and put the lid back on. Only one side of her face had tiny dollops of white. She hastily rubbed them in and pulled the band from her head. "Why bother?" She looked at Natalie and chuckled.

Natalie didn't understand how she could be so nonchalant about dying. "Aren't you scared, Adeline?"

"About dying?"

Natalie nodded. "Yeah. The whole thing terrifies me. I mean, I believe in God, and I believe in heaven, but it still scares me."

"I'm not afraid of dying." She held Natalie's gaze. "I'll be going home and Percy will be there. Only two things worry me . . ."

Natalie pulled her legs from the coffee table and tucked them underneath her. "What?"

"First, I worry that you kids have bitten off more than you can chew when it comes to being my caregivers. I am beyond grateful. It would have been horrible to die in that hospital. But please promise me that if I become too much of a burden for the three of you, you will put me somewhere, whether it's a hospital or hospice. I don't have a lot of money, but there is enough to keep me in hospice, along with my Social Security checks. I worry that you won't be strong enough to make that choice."

"You're not going to be a burden to us, but if you need to scratch it off your worry list, then okay, I promise." Natalie was sure they'd never put Adeline anywhere unless they were jeopardizing her health further by not doing so.

"And the second thing is this." She sighed. "I have been reading the information the hospital sent to me. My condition can cause terrible moodiness, along with the confusion, memory loss, and ultimately not being able to walk. It's likely that all of these things will happen. What's going to happen when I can't control my bodily functions? Have you thought about that? Changing my diapers?" She shivered, then wrapped herself in a hug. "I hope I'm too far gone mentally to have to see that. I will likely pass on with very little dignity intact. I just think that maybe none of us thought this through all the way."

Natalie had thought of all those things. "Adeline, I took care of my Mimi Jean when she was really sick. My mom and I did it in shifts. It was different because her mind was intact, but I bathed her, changed her diapers, and took care of whatever she needed while I was there. We love you. We don't want anyone else doing those things. And you will be with us when you pass, so there will be no indignity about it. Please scratch that off your worry list too." She smiled a little. "And by the way, you're leaving all kinds of legacies. That chicken I made tonight — your recipe — it will live on forever because that was the best chicken I've ever had."

Adeline smiled. "My grandmother's recipe." She tapped Natalie's knee. "Now, young lady, I'm off to bed." She stood and pointed a finger at Natalie. "You should do the same. It was a long but wonderful day."

"Yeah, I will soon."

Adeline blew her a kiss, and Natalie blew one back. Then she found her cell phone in her purse. One missed call. She walked into the kitchen where Adeline couldn't hear her conversation. She hadn't told anyone she was having a phone relationship, of sorts. She wasn't sure how Levi would feel knowing Natalie and Lucas talked for hours every night. Levi didn't even know Lucas had a cell phone. Nor did Levi or anyone else see Lucas slip Natalie his phone number after supper the night she and Mary visited.

She looked forward to their nightly talks. It kept her mind off Adeline dying, her father and Olive Oil moving, and her mother's constant nagging.

"Hey, it's me," she said softly when he answered.

Natalie wouldn't be going to bed anytime soon.

CHAPTER 19

Mary's shift to stay with Adeline was Sunday night through Wednesday morning, then Levi came and stayed until Natalie arrived Friday night. They switched things up when their schedules called for it, but Adeline was never alone. Mary's mother had offered to help several times, but Mary declined, underplaying how much worse Adeline had grown in the past two weeks. She wouldn't want anyone else to see her on the bad days.

"How is she today?" Levi walked in the door carrying three books. "She said she wanted some new things to read."

Mary wiped sweat from her forehead with a tissue, even though it was nice and cool in the house. "She was fine Monday and part of Tuesday night." She laid her head against Levi's chest and whispered, "but she didn't know me last night or this morning."

He tucked the books under one arm and wrapped the other around her. "We knew this was coming."

"It's still hard to watch it happening." When she started to cry, he held her tighter. They'd decided to hold off on telling their families about their engagement. Right now, their focus was on Adeline.

"Keep a close eye on her, even when she goes to the bathroom. Just stand outside the door or something. She's walking funny. It's almost like a sideways walk, and she's not very steady on her feet." She paused to dry her eyes with a tissue from her pocket. "She's not eating much either. Do you think we need to call someone? Do you think we're doing everything we can for her? What if we're doing something wrong or making her worse?"

They walked to the couch in the parlor and sat down. "Is she napping?" Levi nodded toward the hallway as he set the books on the coffee table.

"*Ya.* She's been asleep for three hours. I keep checking on her." Mary grabbed his arm. "What if she passes while one of us is here by ourselves?"

"Mary, she will most likely pass when only one of us is here. So far, there haven't been two of us needed at the same time. Mostly because she's been able to get around on her own."

"A part of me wants to be the one here when it happens, holding her hand as she goes to see Percy. But it scares me too. Natalie said she was with her Mimi Jean when she died. She said it was wonderful and horrible at the same time, that her grandma was out of pain and in a better place, but things happen to the body when a person dies."

"When we think that time is coming, let's all try to make plans to be here. I know it will be hard on Natalie financially, but she'll want to be with Adeline. We all will." Levi kissed her hand, and Mary nodded.

"Hello, lovebirds." Adeline walked into the room on shaky legs, doing the weird sideways walk. "Mary, are you crying?" Adeline eased into Percy's chair.

"*Ya,* we were just talking about Lydia. I'm fine." She dabbed at her eyes and silently asked God to forgive the lie.

"I think about Lydia too." Adeline shook her head. "But she was surrounded by those she loved when she went on to the next world."

Mary's heart plunged at the thought of anything happening to her sister. She glanced at Levi, then back at Adeline. "*Ya.* I'm getting ready to leave now, but Levi will be here for the next couple of nights, okay?"

Adeline's hand twitched like it had a mind of its own, but she didn't seem to notice. "That will be just fine."

Levi stood. "I'm going to walk Mary out. But I'll be right back."

Mary kissed Adeline on the cheek before she followed Levi to the porch, to a spot where they could see Adeline through the window. Mary kept her back to the window since she was having such a hard time controlling her emotions today.

"It's like watching her go crazy and die right before our eyes. And you see what just happened in there." Mary covered her eyes with her hands. "It's harder than I thought." She looked back at Levi. "I just remembered that the social worker from the hospital will be here tomorrow, the same lady who came last week when I was here. She left a message on my phone."

Levi nodded before he kissed Mary again. She then headed to her buggy. As he walked back in the house, he wondered if they'd taken on too much.

Adeline was in Percy's chair with the three books in her lap.

"You found the books I brought for you." Levi sat on the couch and took off his hat.

Adeline was wearing her pink robe with

matching pink slippers. "Yes, I did." She turned one over and read the back cover. "I think this is the one for me."

She'd chosen the one about how to plant a garden. Out of the three he brought from home, that was the last one he thought she would choose. It was an old book of his mother's. The other two were Christian love stories his sisters had read.

"In the spring, I'm going to plant a garden." Adeline opened the book with shaky hands. "I'm going to grow tomatoes and herbs."

"*Ya,* that sounds *gut.*" Levi stared at the piano, wondering if it represented good or evil these days. Adeline asked him to play, and he didn't hesitate. He moved quickly to the bench. Even if it was wrong, he justified the music in an effort not to disappoint her. But, just like before, something was different. He heard the melodies in his mind as clear as ever, and emotions filled his soul, but he felt a detachment from the instrument, almost as if God was reclaiming the gift.

After about fifteen minutes, he stopped playing and looked over his shoulder. Adeline had closed the book. Her eyes were glassy, and both hands trembled.

"I'm having hard time . . . pages turn."

Adeline slurred, misplacing the words.

"Do you want me to read it to you?"

"That would be . . . nice."

Levi didn't read a lot, and big words stumped him sometimes, but he went to the kitchen and returned to the parlor with a chair and set it beside her. Easing the book from Adeline's lap, he turned to the first page and started to read, unsure if she was even hearing him. She stared across the room with a blank look on her face. Her hands shook even more, but Levi kept reading.

His sisters and mother were responsible for the garden, so Levi found the book interesting. Then Adeline started to cry.

"What is it?" He put a hand on her arm. "Adeline, what's wrong?"

She turned to him as a tear trickled down her face. "I have to go . . . bathroom."

"*Ya,* okay. Are you hurting?"

She covered her face with her hands. Levi wasn't sure what to do.

Keeping his hand on her arm, he asked her again if she was in pain.

She shook her head and finally uncovered her face, streaked with tears, a wild look in her eyes — a fearful look. "I'm telling my legs to move, but they won't."

Adeline hated the sight of the wheelchair

and walker, and she'd scolded him more than once for trying to help her when she didn't need it. But now she didn't resist when Levi stood and put one arm around her back, the other under her knees. He lifted her into his arms as she cried, then buried her face against his chest and latched on to his shirt.

"I'm sorry," she said in a whisper.

Levi kissed her forehead as he blinked back his own tears. "There is nothing to be sorry for," he said in a voice he'd used to comfort his younger siblings. Then he carried her to the bathroom, determined to handle this in the most dignified way possible. Afterward, he carried Adeline to her bedroom, tucked her in, and sat with her until she fell asleep.

The social worker from the hospice department, who was also a nurse — Janet — came by in the afternoon. Levi filled Janet in as best he could, a knot growing in his throat with each word.

"Levi, you and your friends can change your mind at any time," she said. "There is no shame in admitting you need help. This must be exhausting for all of you, and painful to see Adeline declining."

He shook his head. "*Nee,* we all want her to be at home, and we want to be with her.

But how will we know when" — he swallowed hard — "when it's her time? We all want to be here together."

They were in the parlor sitting on the couch. Levi never sat in Percy's chair anymore. He'd motioned for Janet to sit on the couch as well because he didn't want her sitting there either.

"She'll stop eating, and she'll sleep a lot." Janet waited a few seconds, maybe because Levi was touching the corners of his wet eyes. "Toward the very end, her breathing will become shallow. Adeline has a do-not-resuscitate order on file with the hospital, meaning she doesn't want to be revived if her hearts stops or she stops breathing." She reached into her purse. "Here is a list of who to call and in what order when the time comes. Have arrangements been made?"

Levi opened his mouth to answer, but his lip trembled. He cleared his throat and tried again. "*Ya*. She will be buried next to her husband, Percy. She told us everything was arranged a long time ago, after her husband died."

Janet nodded. "Good, that is one less thing you kids will have to deal with."

Levi wanted to tell her they weren't kids, but since he felt like one at the moment, he didn't argue. Janet looked to be about his mother's age, so to her, he guessed they were kids.

"Do you have any questions?" Janet stood.

Levi had a hundred questions, but most of them sounded stupid in his mind. How would they know when she was really gone? Was there a defining moment when she would take her last breath? Would she be in pain? Should they cover her face? Should they leave her in the bed?

In his world, the body was on display for two days, then there was a simple service with no flowers or fancy headstones. The life was celebrated, not mourned, at least not at the funeral where the bishop would speak about the deceased person. Levi had been to *Englisch* funerals, including Percy's. They sang hymns, played music, displayed lots of flowers, and held a different kind of ceremony. Natalie would know what to do. So, instead of voicing his worries, he just said, "*Nee,* I don't have any questions."

He ushered Janet to the front door before he went back to the parlor. He picked up the kitchen chair and carried it to Adeline's room where he set it close to her side of the bed. Quietly, he sat down and watched her breathe. He'd ask Natalie what a shallow breath looked like. But for now, Adeline snored lightly.

■ ■ ■ ■

Mary was at the bakery Friday morning when Levi called.

"I think you and Natalie should come now."

Mary's chest tightened. "Is she . . ."

"*Nee,* not yet. But a lady came by. She said Janet sent her. She's a hospice worker, and she said it won't be long. Days, maybe hours."

"Okay." Mary had known this day was coming, and she'd tried to prepare herself for it, but she didn't feel ready at all.

"Mary, I haven't been able to get her to eat anything since Wednesday night. And she's mostly sleeping. She opens her eyes every now and then, but she doesn't say anything."

There was a quiver in Levi's voice. Mary recalled how emotional she'd been when she left Adeline's house on Wednesday. Coughing a little, she took a deep breath and hoped she could at least sound strong for Levi. Men didn't normally cry, and Mary had never understood that unspoken rule. They had to feel just as deeply as women.

"I'll call Natalie." Mary put down the

tongs in her left hand, ended the call with Levi, and turned to her coworker. "I have to go."

She called a driver to meet her at her house in an hour, then she went home to pack a few things. She thought they might be at Adeline's for a few days and opted not to take her buggy.

When she walked through the front door, Lydia was sitting alone in the living room. Even though she and Samuel lived in the *daadi haus* on Samuel's parents' property, it was within walking distance for Lydia to visit. And she visited often, staying nearly all day sometimes.

"Where are *Mamm* and *Daed*?" Mary set her purse on the rocking chair in the corner. Lydia was slouched on the couch like she'd been there a while. There was an empty plate on the coffee table and half a glass of milk. A copy of the *Die Botschaft* was on the couch beside her, along with her *kapp*.

"They went to the bank." Lydia chewed a fingernail, something she'd always done when she was upset or nervous.

"What's wrong?" Mary was anxious to get to Adeline's house, but she was also worried about Lydia.

"Nothing."

It was the same answer every time Mary

asked. She hoped Lydia would eventually open up to her, but now wasn't the time to get into a long conversation. "Levi called me at the bakery. It's Adeline . . ." She couldn't finish her sentence.

Lydia stood up and walked to Mary. "I'm sorry about your friend." She wrapped her arms around Mary and rested her chin on her sister's shoulder. Mary wasn't sure if the hug was for her or because Lydia needed it, but she hugged her sister back. They stayed that way for a while until Lydia eventually let go and went back to the couch.

"You're sure you're okay?" Mary asked again.

"*Ya.* I'm fine."

Mary studied her sister's face for a few seconds to see if her expression said otherwise. She couldn't tell, and she needed to go, so she grabbed her purse and ran upstairs.

She'd called Natalie before she left the bakery. Her phone rang in her purse as she pulled a green dress over her head. The one she'd worn to work was splotched with syrup and flour. Every time her phone rang, her chest tightened. Her only calls were from Natalie and Levi, and each time she worried that Adeline had passed while she

371

wasn't there.

"What's wrong?" she asked Levi when she answered.

"I just think you should hurry."

Mary didn't even drag her small red suitcase out from under the bed. She grabbed two dresses, underclothes, and her toothbrush, then she ran down the stairs, stopping only to pick up her toothbrush when she dropped it.

"Tell *Mamm* and *Daed* I don't know how long I'll be at Adeline's. They'll understand."

Lydia nodded. "I will. I'm sorry for your pain."

"Danki." She pushed the screen door open and stepped onto the porch. *Where is the driver? Please hurry.*

CHAPTER 20

Natalie held tightly to Adeline's hand. Levi and Mary sat on the edge of the bed and had hold of Adeline's other hand.

The room was warm, and Natalie wondered if the AC was going out again. She remembered a time when her father said their air conditioner was leaking Freon, and he had to keep calling to get more until the air conditioner eventually sputtered out.

Occasionally, Natalie dipped a soft rag into a bowl of ice water, wrung it out, and pressed it gently against Adeline's face. She was covered with a thin white sheet. Her breathing was shallow, and Natalie recalled Mimi Jean being like this not long before she passed.

"I wish we knew if she was in pain." Mary hadn't stopped crying for the past hour. Natalie's tears had dried up as if there weren't any left, and Levi tapped his foot continuously, his jaw tight and strained. The hospice lady — Maureen — was in the parlor giving them privacy. She'd told them it wouldn't be long, so she decided to stay.

"I don't think she's in pain." Natalie pressed the cool cloth to Adeline's head again. "Maureen gave her the shot of morphine, and I think we'd see it in her expression if she was hurting."

Natalie had stayed up much too late talking to Lucas. They were going to get together in person soon, but right now Natalie just wanted to be with Adeline, Levi, and Mary. If she allowed herself to think about a potential relationship with Lucas . . . Well, it had disaster written all over it. She was saving to go to college and had plans for her life — plans that didn't include converting to the Amish way of life. But something about Lucas had lured her his way the first time she laid eyes on him. Their nightly conversations were only strengthening her attraction as she got to know him better.

Maxwell stretched all four legs from where he lay at the foot of Adeline's bed. Natalie wondered what they would do with him after Adeline was gone.

"Is she still breathing?" Mary and Levi still held Adeline's hand, but Mary placed her other hand on their friend's chest. "I can't tell."

Natalie remembered that she wasn't able to tell when Mimi Jean had passed. She had to ask someone. As a person prepares to leave this world, the breaths become hard to see or hear. She put her free hand on Adeline's chest.

"I think so," she said in a shaky voice. She locked eyes with Mary, then Levi. Natalie wasn't surprised they'd fallen in love. They were a cute couple, both attractive on the inside and outside. Mary was graceful and confident. Levi was less sure of himself, but he was as tenderhearted as Mary. Natalie thought they were a perfect match.

The two fans in the room hummed as rays of sunshine beamed in through the window, revealing tiny particles that danced like fairy dust in the light. She thought Adeline squeezed her hand. Or did she imagine it?

Adeline opened her eyes and smiled, her gaze landing in the corner of the room. Natalie froze. Adeline looked at each one of them with a soft smile, then she focused on the corner of the room again. "Percy," she whispered.

Then she closed her eyes. Natalie knew it was for the last time.

Three days later, Levi's entire family attended Adeline's funeral, which was held at the church she and Percy used to attend. From there, they went to the cemetery, and as Levi stood next to Mary, he recalled the first time he saw her at Percy's funeral. He never could have predicted at ten years old that the girl who caught him playing piano all those years ago would become his wife. *Gott*'s plan had been set in motion a long time ago.

Mary's parents and her sister and new husband also attended Adeline's funeral. Both families had been introduced before the church service earlier. Levi and Mary still hadn't told their families they were planning to get married, but they had to suspect that the two were in a serious relationship. Levi hadn't left Mary's side, and Mary hadn't left Natalie's side.

Natalie's mother was there, but not her father. Natalie had driven to the funeral with Mary and Levi as passengers. Her mother drove separately and cried buckets during the entire service at the church, and she was still crying now.

"Crocodile tears," Natalie had whispered, scowling at her mother in the church.

Levi didn't know what that meant, but as the preacher offered his final words for Adeline, everyone lowered their heads in prayer. Then people began to disperse, some crying as they made their way to their cars. Levi wondered who many of them were. Why did people show up at a person's funeral instead of while they were alive? It wasn't his place to judge, though.

In the distance, three men waited with shovels. In Levi's community, and most likely in Mary's, the men closest to the deceased person lowered a plain coffin into the ground then filled it with dirt themselves. At an *Englisch* funeral, everyone left before the person was lowered into the ground.

His mother sniffled as she limped toward Levi. She touched his arm, rubbing it slightly before she turned to Mary. "It was lovely to see you again, although I'm sorry it was under such sad circumstances." A smile played across his mother's face as she wiped her eyes. "I suspect we will be seeing a lot more of you."

Mary struggled to say something, but eventually just nodded. Then Levi's father, brothers, and sisters approached them. One by one, they offered condolences, each one wearing their Sunday clothes.

Mary's parents and sister and Natalie's mother offered their sympathies, and so did the preacher.

Eventually, everyone was gone except for Levi, Mary, and Natalie.

"We're supposed to go now." Natalie hung her head and cried.

Levi and Mary wrapped their arms around her, and they stayed in their family circle as Adeline was lowered into the ground. Then Levi asked one of the men for a shovel, and he began tossing dirt into Adeline's grave. Mary asked for a shovel, too, then Natalie did.

When the men saw they weren't needed, they put some distance between them and Adeline's family. Levi, Mary, and Natalie gave thanks for the woman who had brought them all together.

Rest in peace, Adeline.

A week later, Natalie met Mary and Levi at an attorney's office. Apparently Adeline left each of them something in her will.

Natalie had finally told her mother that Adeline left her house to the church, but she didn't tell her until after the funeral. She was afraid her mother wouldn't attend if she told her beforehand. It was bad enough that Natalie's father and Olive Oil — who hadn't moved yet — didn't make time to attend, even if just for Natalie's sake.

She would treasure any trinket Adeline

left to her as a remembrance. Levi, Mary, and Natalie had all agreed that the furniture would stay with the house when it was deeded to the church, and Mary had loaned Natalie money for a pet deposit so Maxwell could have a home with her for now.

"Thank you for coming." The attorney sat behind a big desk filled with stacked folders and papers everywhere. Natalie hoped those weren't all dead people files. It was a weird thing to think, but Bob Fletcher — as he'd introduced himself — might as well have been the grim reaper himself. His shoulders slouched as he sat down in the big leather chair behind his desk. His large jowls sagged like water balloons on either side of his face, and unruly gray eyebrows crouched downward above dark eyes that seemed to look through a person instead of at them.

"You three are the heirs to Adeline Collins's estate." Mr. Fletcher looked at each of them as he spoke, seemingly as confused as they were.

"*Nee,* you must be mistaken," Mary said. "Adeline already told us that her house was going to the church. And even though we gave her most of the furniture, we would like it gifted to the church as well."

Mr. Fletcher shook his head, the water balloons jiggling on either side of his face.

"Adeline mailed me a letter detailing her wishes a few weeks ago." Natalie remembered the stop at the post office on the way to the beach.

He pulled a white envelope out of a larger yellow envelope that looked like the one Adeline had mailed that day. He handed it to Natalie, who opened it, took out the letter, and read it aloud.

Dear Natalie, Mary, and Levi,

By the time this letter is read to you, I will be dancing in heaven with my Percy, so please don't shed any more tears. I lived a glorious life, loved the Lord completely, and was gifted with the family I'd always wanted late in life.

Mary and Levi, marriage is a long journey filled with love, joy, and sometimes heartbreak. Work hard to compromise. Recognize and embrace each other's strengths, and don't focus on the flaws. Navigate well and follow the Lord's lead. If you step off the right path, you can usually feel it, and God will gently point you in the right direction if you keep your mind in tune to His. That's all the marriage advice I'm going to offer because the journey is yours.

Percy and I wanted to fill our home

with the laughter of children, but it just wasn't in God's plan for us. But that old house has a personality of its own, and I pray it will nurture you and lots of children, laughing, playing, growing, and learning. Thus, I leave my home to the two of you, along with the contents. Of course, you can't live in it until you're married, but it will be there for you when you are ready. I will regret not seeing you take your vows, but when that day comes, I will be with you in spirit.

You see, the house is meant for you. God was planning all around us. When I sold my belongings, it was out with the old, and in with the new, symbolic of new beginnings. You have filled it with lovely, yet simple Amish furnishings. We went without electricity, yet we did just fine, and you already have a propane refrigerator, stove, and battery-operated fans. There's no phone, and I'd highly suggest you toss those intrusive cell phones, or at least keep the usage to a minimum. And since you both love cats and haven't been able to have one of your own, the house comes with Maxwell, who also brought me much company and love during the short time I had with him.

Mary wept openly. Levi's hand was over his mouth as his eyes grew moist.

Natalie's heart was filled with warmth and joy at the thought of her friends living in Adeline's house, and when that day came, she would hand over Max. She loved the cat, but she felt bad every day that he was in her apartment alone while she was at work. This arrangement would keep all their memories alive, and Natalie would visit often. They'd formed bonding friendships that would go on forever.

Sweet Natalie, I'm so proud of you for wanting to take control of your destiny by furthering your education. And it tickles me pink that you want to be a veterinarian, as I once did. Remember, you are not your parents but your own person. Choose wisely in all you do and maintain a good relationship with the Lord to help guide you in that effort.

Natalie couldn't hold back her own tears now. Her emotional state was caused by a combination of Adeline's words and her talks with Lucas about God. Levi's brother was her friend, but also a spiritual advisor — who just happened to be incredibly handsome.

Natalie, I've left you my money, what's left of it. I didn't have a lot, but it should be enough to pay for your college tuition for at least a couple of years. Work hard and choose your path carefully. You are an independent spirit, but there is some-one special out there for you, so don't shy away when that special someone walks into your life. Follow your dreams, the way you so eloquently expressed yourself in the essay. And you might be the only person in the world who loves my red furniture in the parlor as much as I do, and it's certainly too fancy for Levi and Mary. So, I hope you can think of me and put that furniture to good use.

Natalie's jaw dropped as tears trailed down her cheeks.

So, my sweet friends. Live well and be strong. Walk in the light of the Lord. I love you all very much.

With gratitude and love,

Adeline

Natalie folded the piece of paper, put it back in the envelope, and offered it to the man, but Mary asked if they could keep it, and the lawyer nodded.

Sighing, Mr. Fletcher looked at Natalie. "There is a problem. Adeline doesn't have any money. Not any money to speak of and certainly not enough to sustain you through two years of college. I'm not sure why she thought she did. It may carry you through a semester." He paused, took off his reading glasses, and as his features softened, he didn't look quite so scary.

"Then we will sell the house so Natalie can have enough money to go to school." Mary gave a taut nod of her head. Levi agreed with her.

"No! Are you two crazy? That is your house to live in, and I couldn't bear the thought of someone else living in Adeline's house since she wanted you to have it." Natalie took in a deep breath as her excitement about the possibility of college fled her thoughts. She'd never wanted anything but Adeline's love from the beginning. The money would have been a bonus, but what she'd gained by knowing Adeline far outweighed everything else. "And you know I will be visiting often." She swiped at her eyes. "Besides, I've been applying for scholarships."

Levi whispered something to Mary and she nodded. Natalie was happy for her friends. They wouldn't have the financial burden of buying a house when they were married, and Adeline's dreams would live on through them. Their friendships would live on forever too.

Money was just money.

Later that afternoon, Levi and Mary went to Adeline's house. They walked into the parlor and sat on the red couch, probably for the last time, at least for a while. They stared at the piano. Levi had given a lot of thought to the bishop's words regarding music and instruments. He'd shared the conversation with Mary.

"I'm ready to give it up once and for all." He held Mary's hand as he stared at the piano. "I can't be baptized in good conscience with temptation constantly hanging over me. Besides, with each day my attachment to the piano seems to lessen. I think maybe *Gott* loaned me the talent as a gift to help see Adeline through her final days." He thought about his vision, and it gave him hope that he would play again someday.

"Are you sure? Because I've been having the same thoughts about the music I've been listening to. I want to give it up before baptism."

"I'm sure."

Levi and Mary would be married at the

end of October, two months from now. They'd be baptized in a few weeks.

Natalie was thrilled to get the red furniture, but both Mary and Levi felt terrible that she didn't have enough money to cover her college expenses.

"Do you think the piano is worth much? We need to sell it. We'll be in a new district, but I don't know of any bishop who would allow it in our home." Mary stood and walked to the sleek black instrument and gingerly ran a hand along the side. "It's beautiful, but it's so old it might not bring much money."

Levi walked to her side and stared at the instrument that had tempted him since birth.

"Do you want to play one last time?" Mary touched his arm.

Levi shook his head. "*Nee.* It hasn't felt right the last few times I played for Adeline."

Mary walked around the piano until she found the manufacturer's name. "It says it's a Steinway. Maybe we can get a few hundred dollars for Natalie."

Levi had worried how he would get a house and provide for Mary. But he'd already been offered several construction jobs in the area from folks who had driven by Adeline's house and seen the fresh paint, repaired fences, and landscaped yard. He'd also left some flyers at local businesses.

"Let's talk to a couple piano places and maybe have someone come look at it to see if they want to make an offer. Adeline probably thought you would want the piano, but I think she would agree with our way of thinking." Mary smiled.

"I agree." Levi waited for his chest to tighten since they'd made a decision about the piano. It didn't. He could still hear the melodies in his head, and he had a strong feeling God was leaving him with those memories.

Natalie walked into Adeline's house to meet Mary and Levi a few days after the reading of the will. She hoped that someday she could cross the threshold without crying. After she paused to gather herself, she walked into the kitchen and looked at the puzzle still spread out on the kitchen table, the pieces still not connected. Maybe she, Mary, and Levi would finish it. Adeline would have liked that.

Natalie had made arrangements for the red furniture to be picked up the following day. It smelled like this house, and it would be a constant reminder of Adeline's love. Since it was still here, she moseyed toward the parlor. Levi and Mary's buggies were already outside, so she suspected that's where she'd find them. She gasped when she walked into the room. "Where's the piano?"

Mary ran to her and threw her arms around her. "We've been so excited for you to get here." She eased away, then walked to Levi's side. They were both grinning ear to ear. They'd been secretive about this meeting, not saying much when they asked Natalie to take off work to meet here. She thought it must be important.

"Where's the piano?" she asked again, knowing how much Levi loved it. Adeline was right. Everything had been set up perfectly for them.

"It's not allowed in our life," Levi said. "I only played for Adeline toward the end because I didn't have the heart to deny her. And I think my longing to play was all a buildup to Adeline's final days, to give her comfort. Baptism is a new beginning for us." He smiled at his future wife. She knew they planned to have half a dozen children, and that would take money. She didn't know much about pianos. Her mother said Steinways were expensive, but Percy's piano was really old.

"Well, I'm okay with you selling the piano,

if that's what you're worried about. I've known all along that instruments weren't really allowed for Amish people."

Mary bounced up on her toes before she pushed a white envelope toward Natalie. "*Ya,* we sold it, and we want you to use the money for college."

Natalie shook her head. "No, no, no. Adeline left me the red furniture, and I'm thrilled to have it. Plus, I've applied for scholarships, and the money Adeline had will get me through two semesters, I think. You keep the money."

Levi stepped forward next to Mary. "*Nee,* we wouldn't feel right. The piano was special to Percy but not allowed in our world. Just using the money without purpose wouldn't feel right. Please agree to take it. We want very much for you to have it. Adeline intended to leave us all with something we could use."

Natalie sighed. "I guess a little more money toward school would be helpful, but I . . ." She shook her head. "I don't know."

Mary growled as she bounced up on her toes again. "Take the money!"

Natalie's eyes widened as she grinned. "Good grief, Mary. Settle down." Laughing again, she said, "Okay."

She slid her finger under the flap until the

envelope was open. She pulled out a check, blinking her eyes a few times. The amount couldn't possibly be right. Mary started jumping up and down, clapping her hands like she was a child.

Natalie literally fell on the couch and stared at the cashier's check. "What? I don't understand . . ."

Levi chuckled. "It turned out that Percy made quite the investment back in the seventies. He didn't pay nearly close to what the piano is worth now."

"It's what Adeline would have wanted, Natalie. It's what Levi and I want. We were thrilled to get that much money."

Natalie's eyes were crossing as she continued to eye the amount. "We should at least split it three ways."

"*Nee,* no way." Levi shook his head. Mary did too.

Natalie covered her face with both hands and cried. Levi sat down on one side of her and Mary on the other. They each placed an arm around her.

"It wasn't as hard for me to give up the piano as I thought it would be. Adeline would want it this way. Mary and I have a house to start our lives in when we get married. That's all we need, and each other. To accept that kind of money would feel wrong to us."

Natalie eyed the check again. "Is this for real?"

They both tightened their half hug, answering that it was.

Levi nudged her with his shoulder. "I don't know how much college costs, but I would think this should pay for a good bit of your schooling."

Natalie's mouth fell open. "A good bit? Try all of my tuition and books. I can go full-time. I can quit my job. I can go to vet school." She sobbed. "All things I feared would never happen. That's what eighty-six thousand dollars can do for me!" Natalie would help her mother also. Despite everything, Natalie wouldn't have met Adeline without her mother's urging, even if her mom's intentions were misdirected. A portion of the money might help her mother get on her feet. It was another example of everything coming full circle.

"We know. That's why we asked you to leave work and meet us here." Levi laughed. "We've been so excited to give you the check."

Mary giggled. "He's right."

Natalie thought about what her father had said, about the Amish being giving people.

She'd known Mary and Levi were both generous, but she'd had no idea to what extent.

"We had two piano dealers come look at it. It turned into a bidding war," Mary said. "Something about it having German Kluge keys and keyboard."

"And Renner Blue hammers," Levi added. "Only a few like Percy's were manufactured."

Natalie fought to corral her emotions by taking deep breaths.

"I hope I don't disappoint Adeline." She finally smiled at Mary, then at Levi. "I know pride isn't your thing. But I really want to make the two of you proud of me too."

"You already do." Mary kissed her on the cheek.

Natalie looked forward to a bright future. She couldn't wait to see what was in store for all of them.

EPILOGUE

Mary put her hands on her hips and looked around at her efforts. She'd customized Adeline's house to fit her and Levi, but it still retained the qualities Adeline had held dear as well. She'd left the walls painted in the neutral colors Adeline had chosen, and she had no plans to cover the original wood floors. Wallpaper wasn't allowed, but Mary couldn't bring herself to tear down or paint over the pink and red floral design in the bathroom yet.

Levi didn't like phones in the house, so they had compromised by keeping one cell phone for emergencies only. He was also used to wood-burning stoves in the kitchen, but Mary wasn't giving up her propane-fueled stove and oven. She'd told him if he wanted to eat, those appliances stayed. With his large appetite, he'd conceded on that issue.

She picked up a laundry basket full of

towels that needed folding and dumped them on the bed. They'd asked Natalie if she wanted her furniture back. Levi finally told Mary that Natalie had donated it to Adeline, but Natalie said it wasn't her style. Mary believed her. When she'd visited Natalie's apartment it was in stark contrast to Mary and Levi's home. The outdated red furniture was like a splash of the past mingled with present-day things like a TV and fancy gadgets that looked like they might be from the future.

After she folded the clothes and put everything away, Mary took out Adeline's letter and reread it, like she'd done many times before. Smiling, she put it back in the drawer. There were still tears from time to time, but when grief tried to overwhelm her, she closed her eyes and pictured Percy playing the piano, Adeline sitting in a big red chair nearby.

Levi had more construction jobs than he could count, proving that hard work does pay off, and it turned out he was more talented in that department than his family had given him credit for. He said he still heard piano music in his mind, though he didn't feel a longing to recreate it but to embrace it for the things it represented. Mary understood. Music had brought them together and eventually to Adeline. Now she heard melodies in her mind, floating on a breeze, or when a bird sang, or in children's laughter. Mostly, she heard music when her husband smiled and told her how much he loved her.

Since their marriage three weeks ago, they were settling in nicely.

Natalie stopped by every few days. She'd confessed that she had been seeing Levi's brother, Lucas, and that it was mostly conversations on the phone, but they'd also met for lunch a few times in Shoals. Mary counseled her friend on the dangers associated with the situation, warning her that someone was going to get hurt. But Natalie followed her gut, and Mary had to accept that it was Natalie's journey, not hers. But Mary did wish she'd listen for *Gott*'s will as much as she followed her instincts. Lucas seemed to be good for her in that way, so once again, it was hard to understand *Gott*'s plans.

Lydia and Samuel were expecting their baby in January. As the holidays approached, Lydia's belly had begun showing. It was mostly hidden by her dress but obvious if she turned or sat a certain way. Their mother had recovered from the embarrassment of the entire situation and was now wrapped up in baby preparations, always knitting or sewing something for the new arrival.

Mary still worried about Lydia, who continued to mope around like she'd lost her best friend, her shoulders slumped, lip rolled under. Mary wondered what life was like for her and Samuel when no one was around. In a group gathering, they barely spoke to each other.

She reminded herself that, just like Natalie, it was Lydia's journey, her road to travel. She prayed they would choose wisely in ways the Lord would approve of.

Mary opened the front door when she heard Maxwell scratching to get in. He went straight to his bed in front of the fireplace and stretched out in front of the glowing timbers. Mary walked around him and added another log to the fire.

Supper was in the oven and Levi would be home soon. She was cooking chicken enchiladas from a recipe Natalie found for her on the Internet. It wasn't a meal she would have had at home. Her mother stuck to traditional recipes handed down for generations, just as Levi's mother had done at their home. Mary didn't have disdain for dishes with a Mexican flare, but she wasn't crazy about them either. But recently, Levi told her that he ate chicken enchiladas at a Mexican restaurant during one of his lunch breaks, and that he enjoyed them more than anything he'd ever eaten. This was Mary's gift to him this evening after he came home from a hard day's work. Compromise.

She smiled and thought of Adeline as she basked in the wonderful journey she and Levi were on, anxious to see what *Gott* had planned for them next.

A NOTE FROM THE AUTHOR

Dear Readers,

Thank you for traveling with me on Mary, Levi, Natalie, and Adeline's journey. It was a pleasure getting to know these beloved characters along the way, and I hope that you enjoyed the story as much as I loved writing it.

Details of my life find ways into my books, and *Hearts in Harmony* was no exception. Remember when Adeline tells Mary that Levi can't cook, that he made her a warm tuna meal that was horrible? When I was dating my husband, he cooked a similar meal for me, and I knew right away that I would be doing the cooking when we were married, lol.

Also — and I feel this is important — I suffered for years with esophageal spasms, like Adeline had. My description of the pain associated with the spasms is spot on. It feels like what I imagine a heart attack feels like, and I usually had at least one per day. I was blessed to have a doctor who wouldn't give up on a diagnosis, and I now take medication that controls these very painful spasms. I only have three or four per year now. So, I encourage anyone who suspects they might suffer with this condition to seek help. There are medications that can be life-changing.

And my dear readers, I had hoped to write one book that might change one life. To have the opportunity to continue to write stories that God puts in my mind is a blessing beyond what I could have ever imagined. Always remember, God's plan for us is bigger and grander than any goals we set out for ourselves. DREAM BIG. PRAY OFTEN. And may you all be blessed.

In His name,
Beth

ACKNOWLEDGMENTS

Much thanks to the Amish families in Southern Indiana who educated me about the various ways that the Plain people vary from district to district. It was a pleasure meeting you all, and I appreciate the time you took away from your busy schedules to talk with me.

To Sharon and Sam Hanners, my deepest gratitude for hauling me all over Southern Indiana and for introducing me to your Amish friends. You have done a lot for my family as well — too much to list here — but please know that you are loved and appreciated very much.

Renee' Griggs, our forty years of friendship is truly a blessing. I know how much you miss your mother. Karen was taken from us much too soon. But I believe that our shared vision of our stroll to the cottage where there was only a white piano was real and that your momma is playing for the masses in heaven. She was special, and we will see her again one day.

To my team at HarperCollins Christian Fiction, it's an honor to work with all of you. None of the books would be possible without your input, creativity, and dedication to each and every project. Thank you! Special thanks to Kim and Jodi!

Natasha, you continue to rock and are always there for me both professionally and personally. You are an amazing person, and I'm blessed to have you in my life.

To my dear friend and assistant Janet, you continue to amaze me. You stay apprised in an industry that seems to change daily, and you are always one step ahead of me, ensuring that I stay on task while you work your magic behind the scenes. You continue to be loved and appreciated.

Patrick, I'm a real pain during the revision process. I know this, lol. Thanks for giving me my space during revisions and deadlines, and for loving me unconditionally. Oh, and for picking up pizzas and going without a hot meal during those times. And for not making me hot tuna salad with mystery ingredients. Love you always, dear.

And my most heartfelt thanks to God, who continues to bless me with stories to tell.

DISCUSSION QUESTIONS

1. Mary and Levi come from very different Amish districts, but they are both grounded in their faith. The *Ordnung* is the understood behavior by which the Amish are expected to live. Do you think that Mary and Levi interpret these rules differently? If so, give some examples.
2. Levi, Mary, and Natalie most likely would have never met if each of their parents hadn't known Adeline in some way. Goodness shines from these three young people from the beginning even though they all have very little in common. What are some of the ways you see God working in their lives to bring them all together?
3. Adeline gets the family she's always wanted, and her house is filled with love. Mary, Levi, Natalie, and Adeline become a family. How do Mary, Levi, and Natalie's experiences affect their relationships within their own biological families?

4. Even though Levi and Mary love each other, lack of communication threatens to tear them apart. What are some examples of their failure to be completely honest with each other, which ultimately leads to them almost parting ways?

5. What did you think about Levi's vision when he was in the hospital? Do you believe that God was showing him heaven? And how did you feel about the bishop's interpretation of the event? Do you believe that God speaks to us in our dreams? Has anything like that ever happened to you or someone you know?

6. Levi is a prodigy with a gift that is forbidden by his Amish upbringing. Do you believe that God gifted Levi with his musical abilities solely for the purpose of playing piano for Adeline? It would seem so since Levi's magnetism toward the piano begins to diminish as Adeline is close to passing, and then his longing for the instrument subsides almost altogether. He and Mary begin to hear and see the melodies they love in other ways. Can you name some of the ways God replenishes their love of music?

7. For Mary and Levi to be together, they must agree to compromise as related to their individual upbringings. What are

some of the ways they do this?

8. The bishop explains to Levi that music invokes unnecessary emotions as one of the reasons it is forbidden. He also gives a good example of the pride Levi felt at being better at something than his friends and family. Do you agree with the bishop's reasoning and explanation about why playing an instrument is not allowed?

9. There is a tender scene when Levi has to carry Adeline to the bathroom when she can no longer walk, but he doesn't hesitate, determined to carry out the act in the most dignified way as Adeline cries. Have you ever had to be a caregiver for someone you love?

10. By the time Adeline leaves her house to Mary and Levi, it is already set up as an Amish home without any of the characters realizing it. Did you see God with His hand in this carefully orchestrated plan? What are ways in which this happened to get to the end result?

11. Adeline's love for Percy was evident throughout the entire story. Before she drifts off to heaven, she opens her eyes and says Percy's name, as if she sees him in the room. Has this ever happened to anyone you know before they died, seeing or speaking the name of a loved one who

went home before them?

12. Do you agree that music invokes unnecessary emotions that have the ability to define or change our moods? In that regard, do you agree — or at least understand why this rule might be in place? How has music played a part in your life?

13. Did you have a favorite character, someone whom you related to the most? If so, who — and why?

ABOUT THE AUTHOR

Beth Wiseman is the award-winning and bestselling author of the Daughters of the Promise, Land of Canaan, and Amish Secrets series, as well as novellas that have been included in many bestselling collections such as *An Amish Year* and *An Amish Garden.*

Visit her online at BethWiseman.com
Facebook: AuthorBethWiseman
Twitter: @BethWiseman
Instagram: bethwisemanauthor

The employees of Thorndike Press hope you have enjoyed this Large Print book. All our Thorndike, Wheeler, and Kennebec Large Print titles are designed for easy reading, and all our books are made to last. Other Thorndike Press Large Print books are available at your library, through selected bookstores, or directly from us.

For information about titles, please call:
  (800) 223-1244

or visit our website at:
  gale.com/thorndike

To share your comments, please write:
  Publisher
  Thorndike Press
  10 Water St., Suite 310
  Waterville, ME 04901